THE SUNDAY PHILOSOPHY CLUB

THE SUNDAY
PHILOSOPHY CLUB

Alexander McCall Smith

Alfred A. Knopf Canada

PUBLISHED BY ALFRED A. KNOPF CANADA

Copyright © 2004 Alexander McCall Smith

All rights reserved under International and Pan-American Copyright Conventions. Published in 2004 by Alfred A. Knopf Canada, a division of Random House of Canada Limited, Toronto, and simultaneously in the United States by Pantheon Books, a division of Random House, Inc., New York, and in Great Britain by Time Warner Books. Distributed by Random House of Canada Limited, Toronto.

Knopf Canada and colophon are trademarks.

National Library of Canada Cataloguing in Publication

McCall Smith, Alexander
The Sunday Philosophy Club / Alexander McCall Smith
ISBN 0-676-97689-1
I. Title.
PR6063.C326S86 2004   823'.914   C2004-901900-7

First Edition

Book design by Pamela G. Parker and Peter Andersen

www.randomhouse.ca

Printed and bound in the United States of America

2 4 6 8 9 7 5 3 1

This is for
James and Marcia Childress

THE SUNDAY PHILOSOPHY CLUB

ISABEL DALHOUSIE saw the young man fall from the edge of the upper circle, from the gods. His flight was so sudden and short, and it was for less than a second that she saw him, hair tousled, upside down, his shirt and jacket up around his chest so that his midriff was exposed. And then, striking the edge of the grand circle, he disappeared headfirst towards the stalls below.

Her first thought, curiously, was of Auden's poem on the fall of Icarus. Such events, said Auden, occur against a background of people going about their ordinary business. They do not look up and see the boy falling from the sky. *I was talking to a friend,* she thought. *I was talking to a friend and the boy fell out of the sky.*

She would have remembered the evening, even if this had not happened. She had been dubious about the concert—a performance by the Reykjavik Symphony, of which she had never heard—and would not have gone had not a spare ticket been pressed upon her by a neighbour. Did Reykjavik really have a professional symphony orchestra, she wondered, or were the players amateurs? Of course, even if they were, if they had come as far as Edinburgh to give a late spring concert, then they deserved an audience; they could not be allowed to come all the way from

Iceland and then perform to an empty hall. And so she had gone to the concert and had sat through a first half which comprised a romantic combination of German and Scottish: Mahler, Schubert, and Hamish McCunn.

It was a warm evening—unseasonably so for late March—and the atmosphere in the Usher Hall was close. She had come lightly dressed, as a precaution, and was glad that she had done so as the temperature in the grand circle inevitably climbed too high. During the interval she had made her way downstairs and had enjoyed the relief of the cooler air outside, eschewing the crush of the bar with its cacophony of conversation. She would find people she knew there, of course; it was impossible to go out in Edinburgh and not see anybody, but she was not in the mood for conversation that evening. When the time came to go back in, she toyed for a few moments with the idea of missing the second half, but she always felt inhibited from any act suggesting a lack of concentration or, worse still, of seriousness. So she had returned to her seat, picked up the programme from where she had left it on the armrest next to her, and studied what lay ahead. She took a deep intake of breath. *Stockhausen!*

She had brought with her a set of opera glasses—so necessary even in the moderate heights of the grand circle. With these trained on the stage so far down below, she scrutinised each player one by one, an activity she could never resist in concerts. One did not stare at people through binoculars normally, but here in the concert hall it was permitted, and if the binoculars strayed to the audience once in a while, who was to notice? The strings were unexceptional, but one of the clarinettists, she noticed, had a remarkable face: high cheekbones, deep-set eyes, and a chin that had been cleaved, surely, by an axe. Her gaze dwelt on him, and she thought of the generations of hardy Icelanders, and Danes before them, that had laboured to bring forth this type: men and women who scratched a living from the thin soil of upland farms; fishermen who hunted cod in steel-grey waters; women who struggled to keep their children alive on dried fish and oatmeal; and now, at the end of all this effort, a clarinettist.

She laid aside the opera glasses and sat back in her seat. It was a perfectly competent orchestra, and they had played the McCunn with gusto, but why did people still do Stockhausen? Perhaps it was some sort of statement of cultural sophistication. We may come from Reykjavik, and it may be a small town far from anywhere, but we can at least play Stockhausen as well as the rest of them. She closed her eyes. It was impossible music, really, and it was not something a visiting orchestra should inflict on its hosts. For a short while she considered the idea of orchestral courtesy. Certainly one should avoid giving political offence: German orchestras, of course, used to be careful about playing Wagner abroad, at least in some countries, choosing instead German composers who were somewhat more . . . apologetic. This suited Isabel, who disliked Wagner.

The Stockhausen was the final item on the programme. When at last the conductor had retired and the clapping had died down— not as warm as it might have been, she thought; something to do with Stockhausen—she slipped out of her seat and made her way to the ladies' room. She turned on a tap and scooped water into her mouth—the Usher Hall had nothing so modern as a drinking fountain—and then splashed some on her face. She felt cooler, and now made her way out onto the landing again. It was at this point, though, that Isabel caught sight of her friend Jennifer standing at the bottom of the short flight of stairs that led into the grand circle.

She hesitated. It was still uncomfortably warm inside, but she had not seen Jennifer for over a year, and she could hardly walk past without greeting her.

Isabel made her way through the crowds.

"I'm waiting for David," Jennifer said, gesturing towards the grand circle. "He lost a contact lens, would you believe it, and one of the usherettes has lent him a torch to go and look for it under his seat. He lost one on the train through to Glasgow and now he's done it again."

They chatted as the last of the crowd made its way down the stairs behind them. Jennifer, a handsome woman, in her early forties—like Isabel—was wearing a red suit on which she had pinned a large gold brooch in the shape of a fox's head. Isabel could not help but look at the fox, which had ruby eyes, and seemed to be watching her. *Brother Fox,* she thought. *So like Brother Fox.*

After a few minutes, Jennifer looked anxiously up the stairs.

"We should go and see if he needs help," she said irritably. "It'll be an awful nuisance if he's lost another one."

They took a few steps up the short set of stairs and looked down towards the place where they could make out David's back, hunched behind a seat, the light of the torch glinting between the seating. And it was at that moment, as they stood there, that the young man fell from the layer above—silently, wordlessly, arms flailing as if he were trying to fly, or fend off the ground— and then disappeared from view.

FOR A BRIEF MOMENT they stared at each other in mutual disbelief. And then, from below, there came a scream, a woman's voice, high-pitched; and then a man shouted and a door slammed somewhere.

Isabel reached forward and seized Jennifer's arm. "My God!" she said. "My God!"

From where he had been crouching, Jennifer's husband straightened up. "What was that?" he called to them. "What happened?"

"Somebody fell," said Jennifer. She pointed at the upper circle, at the point where the top layer joined the wall. "From up there. He fell."

They looked at one another again. Now Isabel moved forward to the edge of the circle. There was a brass rail running along the parapet, and she held on to this as she peered over.

Below her, slumped over the edge of a seat, his legs twisted over the arms of the neighbouring seats, one foot, she noticed, without a shoe, but stockinged, was the young man. She could not see his head, which was down below the level of the seat; but she saw an arm sticking up, as if reaching for something, but quite still. Beside him stood two men in evening dress, one of whom had reached forward and was touching him, while the other looked back towards the door.

"Quickly!" one of the men shouted. "Hurry!"

A woman called out something and a third man ran up the aisle to where the young man lay. He bent down and then began to lift the young man off the seat. Now the head came into view, and lolled, as if loosened from the body. Isabel withdrew and looked at Jennifer.

"We'll have to go down there," she said. "We saw what happened. We had better go and tell somebody what we saw."

Jennifer nodded. "We didn't see much," she said. "It was over so quickly. Oh dear."

Isabel saw that her friend was shaking, and she put an arm about her shoulder. "That was ghastly!" she said. "Such a shock."

Jennifer closed her eyes. "He just came down . . . so quickly. Do you think he's still alive? Did you see?"

"I'm afraid he looked rather badly hurt," said Isabel, thinking, It's worse than that.

THEY WENT DOWNSTAIRS. A small crowd of people had gathered round the door into the stalls, and there was a buzz of conversation. As Isabel and Jennifer drew near, a woman turned to them and said: "Somebody fell from the gods. He's in there."

Isabel nodded. "We saw it happen," she said. "We were up there."

"You saw it?" said the woman. "You actually saw it?"

"We saw him coming down," said Jennifer. "We were in the grand circle. He came down past us."

"How dreadful," said the woman. "To see it . . ."

"Yes."

The woman looked at Isabel with that sudden human intimacy that the witnessing of tragedy permitted.

"I don't know if we should be standing here," Isabel muttered, half to Jennifer, half to the other woman. "We'll just get in the way."

The other woman drew back. "One wants to do something," she said lamely.

"I do hope that he's all right," said Jennifer. "Falling all that way. He hit the edge of the circle, you know. It might have broken the fall a bit."

No, thought Isabel, it would have made it worse, perhaps; there would be two sets of injuries, the blow from the edge of the circle and injuries on the ground. She looked behind her; there was activity at the front door and then, against the wall, the flashing blue light of the ambulance outside.

"We must let them get through," said Jennifer, moving away from the knot of people at the door. "The ambulance men will need to get in."

They stood back as two men in loose green fatigues hurried past, carrying a folded stretcher. They were not long in coming out—less than a minute, it seemed—and then they went past, the young man laid out on the stretcher, his arms folded over his chest. Isabel turned away, anxious not to intrude, but she saw his face before she averted her gaze. She saw the halo of tousled dark hair and the fine features, undamaged. To be so beautiful, she thought, and now the end. She closed her eyes. She felt raw inside, empty. This poor young man, loved by somebody somewhere, whose world would end this evening, she thought, when the cruel news was broached. All that love invested in a future that would not materialise, ended in a second, in a fall from the gods.

She turned to Jennifer. "I'm going upstairs quickly," she said, her voice lowered. "Tell them that we saw it. Tell them I'll be back in a moment."

Jennifer nodded, looking about her to see who was in charge. There was confusion now. A woman was sobbing, one of the women who must have been standing in the stalls when he came down, and she was being comforted by a tall man in an evening jacket.

Isabel detached herself and made her way to one of the staircases that led up to the gods. She felt uneasy, and glanced behind her, but there was nobody around. She climbed up the last few stairs, through one of the archways that led to the steeply racked seating. It was quiet, and the lights suspended from the ceiling above were dimmed in their ornate glass bowls. She looked down, to the edge over which the boy had fallen. They had been standing almost immediately below the point at which he had dropped, which enabled her to calculate where he must have been standing before he slipped.

She made her way down to the parapet and edged along the front row of seats. Here was the brass rail over which he must have been leaning before, and there, down on the ground, a programme. She bent down and picked it up; its cover, she noticed, had a slight tear, but that was all. She replaced it where she had found it. Then she bent over and looked down over the edge. He must have been sitting here, at the very end of the row, where the upper circle met the wall. Had he been further in towards the middle, he would have landed in the grand circle; only at the end of the row was there a clear drop down to the stalls.

For a moment she felt a swaying vertigo, and she closed her eyes. But then she opened them again and looked down into the stalls, a good fifty feet below. Beneath her, standing near to where the young man had landed, a man in a blue windcheater looked upwards and into her eyes. They were both surprised, and Isabel leant backwards, as if warned off by his stare.

Isabel left the edge and made her way back up the aisle between the seats. She had no idea what she had expected to find—if anything—and she felt embarrassed to have been seen by that man below. What must he have thought of her? A vulgar onlooker trying to imagine what that poor boy must have seen during his last seconds on this earth, no doubt. But that was not what she had been doing; not at all.

She reached the stairs and began to walk down, holding the

rail as she did so. The steps were stone, and spiral, and one might so easily slip. As he must have done, she thought. He must have looked over, perhaps to see if he could spot somebody down below, a friend maybe, and then he had lost his footing and toppled over. It could easily happen—the parapet was low enough.

She stopped halfway down the stairs. She was alone, but she had heard something. Or had she imagined it? She strained her ears to catch a sound, but there was nothing. She took a breath. He must have been the very last person up there, all alone, when everybody else had gone and the girl at the bar on the landing was closing up. That boy had been there himself and had looked down, and then he had fallen, silently, perhaps seeing herself and Jennifer on the way down, who would then have been his last human contact.

She reached the bottom of the stairs. The man in the blue windcheater was there, just a few yards away, and when she came out, he looked at her sternly.

Isabel walked over to him. "I saw it happen," she said. "I was in the grand circle. My friend and I saw him fall."

The man looked at her. "We'll need to talk to you," he said. "We'll need to take statements."

Isabel nodded. "I saw so little," she said. "It was over so quickly."

He frowned. "Why were you up there just now?" he asked.

Isabel looked down at the ground. "I wanted to see how it could have happened," she said. "And now I do see."

"Oh?"

"He must have looked over," she said. "Then he lost his balance. I'm sure it would not be difficult."

The man pursed his lips. "We'll look into that. No need to speculate."

It was a reproach, but not a severe one, as he saw that she was upset. For she was shaking now. He was familiar with that. Something terrible happened and people began to shake. It was the reminder that frightened them; the reminder of just how close to the edge we are in life, always, at every moment.

CHAPTER TWO

A T NINE O'CLOCK the following morning Isabel's housekeeper, Grace, let herself into the house, picked up the mail from
the floor in the hall, and made her way into the kitchen. Isabel
had come downstairs and was sitting at the table in the kitchen,
the newspaper open before her, a half-finished cup of coffee at
her elbow.

Grace put the letters down on the table and took off her coat.
She was a tall woman, in her very late forties, six years older than
Isabel. She wore a long herringbone coat, of an old-fashioned cut,
and had dark red hair which she wore in a bun at the back.

"I had to wait half an hour for a bus," she said. "Nothing
came. Nothing."

Isabel rose to her feet and went over to the percolator of
freshly made coffee on the stove.

"This will help," she said, pouring Grace a cup. Then, as
Grace took a sip, she pointed to the newspaper on the table.

"There's a terrible thing in *The Scotsman*," she said. "An accident. I saw it last night at the Usher Hall. A young man fell all the
way from the gods."

Grace gasped. "Poor soul," she said. "And . . ."

"He died," said Isabel. "They took him to the Infirmary, but he was declared dead when he arrived."

Grace looked at her employer over her cup. "Did he jump?" she asked.

Isabel shook her head. "Nobody has any reason to believe that." She stopped. She had not thought of it at all. People did not kill themselves that way; if you wanted to jump, then you went to the Forth Bridge, or the Dean Bridge if you preferred the ground to the water. The Dean Bridge: Ruthven Todd had written a poem about that, had he not, and had said that its iron spikes "curiously repel the suicides"; curiously, because the thought of minor pain should surely mean nothing in the face of complete destruction. Ruthven Todd, she thought, all but ignored in spite of his remarkable poetry; one line of his, she had once said, was worth fifty lines of McDiarmid, with all his posturing; but nobody remembered Ruthven Todd anymore.

She had seen McDiarmid once, when she was a schoolgirl, and had been walking with her father down Hanover Street, past Milnes Bar. The poet had come out of the bar in the company of a tall, distinguished-looking man, who had greeted her father. Her father had introduced her to both of them, and the tall man had shaken her hand courteously; McDiarmid had smiled, and nodded, and she had been struck by his eyes, which seemed to emit a piercing blue light. He was wearing a kilt, and carrying a small, battered leather briefcase, which he hugged to his chest, as if using it to protect himself against the cold.

Afterwards her father had said: "The best poet and the wordiest poet in Scotland, both together."

"Which was which?" she had asked. They read Burns at school, and some Ramsay and Henryson, but nothing modern.

"McDiarmid, or Christopher Grieve, to give him his real name, is the wordiest. The best is the tall man, Norman McCaig. But he'll never be fully recognised, because Scots literature these days is all about complaining and moaning and being injured in one's soul." He had paused, and then asked: "Do you understand what I'm talking about?"

And Isabel had said, "No."

GRACE ASKED HER AGAIN: "Do you think he jumped?"

"We did not see him actually fall over the edge," Isabel said, folding the newspaper in such a way as to reveal the crossword. "We saw him on the way down—after he had slipped or whatever. I told the police that. They took a statement from me last night."

"People don't slip that easily," muttered Grace.

"Yes, they do," said Isabel. "They slip. All the time. I once read about somebody slipping on his honeymoon. The couple was visiting some falls in South America and the man slipped."

Grace raised an eyebrow. "There was a woman who fell over the crags," she said. "Right here in Edinburgh. She was on her honeymoon."

"Well, there you are," said Isabel. "Slipped."

"Except some thought she was pushed," countered Grace. "The husband had taken out an insurance policy on her life a few weeks before. He claimed the money, and the insurance company refused to pay out."

"Well, it must happen in some cases. Some people are pushed. Others slip." She paused, imagining the young couple in South America, with the spray from the falls shooting up and the man tumbling into the white, and the young bride running back along the path, and the emptiness. You loved another, and this made you so vulnerable; just an inch or so too close to the edge and your world could change.

She picked up her coffee and began to leave the kitchen. Grace preferred to work unobserved, and she herself liked to do the crossword in the morning room, looking out onto the garden. This had been the ritual for years, from the time that she had moved back into the house until now. The crossword would start the day, and then she would glance at the news itself, trying to avoid the salacious court cases which seemed to take up more and more newspaper columns. There was such an obsession with human weakness and failing; with the tragedies of peoples' lives; with the banal affairs of actors and singers. You had to be aware of human weakness, of course, because it simply *was,* but to revel in it seemed to her to be voyeurism, or even a form of moralistic tale telling. And yet, she thought, do I not read these things myself? I do. I am just as bad as everybody else, drawn to these scandals. She smiled ruefully, noticing the heading: MINISTER'S SHAME ROCKS PARISH. Of course she would read that, as everybody else would, although she knew that behind the story was a personal tragedy, and all the embarrassment that goes with that.

She moved a chair in the morning room so that she would be by the window. It was a clear day, and the sun was on the blossom on the apple trees which lined one edge of her walled garden. The blossom was late this year, and she wondered whether there would be apples again this summer. Every now and then the trees became barren and produced no fruit; then, the following year, they would be laden with a proliferation of small red apples that she would pick and make into chutney and sauce according to a recipe which her mother had given her.

Her mother—her *sainted American mother*—had died when

Isabel was eleven, and the memories were fading. Months and years blurred into one another, and Isabel's mental picture of the face that looked down at her as she was tucked into bed at night was vague now. She could hear the voice, though, echoing somewhere in her mind; that soft southern voice that her father had said reminded him of moss on trees and characters from Tennessee Williams plays.

Seated in the morning room with a cup of coffee, her second, on the glass-topped side table, she found herself stuck over the crossword puzzle at an inexplicably early stage. One across had been a gift, almost an insult—*They have slots in the gaming industry* (3-5-7). One-armed bandits. And then, *He's a German in control* (7). Manager, of course. But after a few of this standard, she came across *Excited by the score?* (7) and *Vulnerable we opined desultorily* (4, 4), both of which remained unsolved, and ruined the rest of the puzzle. She felt frustrated, and cross with herself. The clues would resolve themselves in due course, and come to her later in the day, but for the time being she had been defeated.

She knew, of course, what was wrong. The events of the previous night had upset her, perhaps more than she realised. She had had trouble in getting to sleep, and had awoken in the small hours of the morning, got out of bed, and gone downstairs to fetch a glass of milk. She had tried to read, but had found it difficult to concentrate, and had switched off the light and lain awake in bed, thinking about the boy and that handsome, composed face. Would she have felt differently if it had been somebody older? Would there have been the same poignancy had the lolling head been grey, the face lined with age rather than youthful?

A night of interrupted sleep, and a shock like that—it was small wonder that she could not manage these obvious clues. She tossed the newspaper down and rose to her feet. She wanted to talk to somebody, to discuss what had happened last night. There was no point in discussing it further with Grace, who would only engage in unlikely speculation and would wander off into long stories about disasters which she had heard about from friends. If urban myths had to start somewhere, Isabel thought that they might begin with Grace. She would walk to Bruntsfield, she decided, and speak to her niece, Cat. Cat owned a delicatessen on a busy corner in the popular shopping area, and provided that there were not too many customers, she would usually take time off to drink a cup of coffee with her aunt.

Cat was sympathetic, and if Isabel ever needed to set things in perspective, her niece would be her first port of call. And it was the same for Cat. When she had difficulties with boyfriends—and such difficulties seemed to be a constant feature of her life—that was the subject of exchanges between the two of them.

"Of course, you know what I'm going to tell you," Isabel had said to her six months before, just before the arrival of Toby.

"And you know what I'll say back to you."

"Yes," said Isabel. "I suppose I do. And I know that I shouldn't say this, because we shouldn't tell others what to do. But—"

"But you think I should go back to Jamie?"

"Precisely," said Isabel, thinking of Jamie, with that lovely grin of his and his fine tenor voice.

"Yes, Isabel, but you know, don't you? You know that I don't love him. I just don't."

There was no answer to that, and the conversation had ended in silence.

SHE FETCHED HER COAT, calling out to Grace that she was going out and would not be back for lunch. She was not sure whether Grace heard—there was the whine of a vacuum cleaner from somewhere within the house—and she called out again. This time the vacuum cleaner was switched off and there was a response.

"Don't make lunch," Isabel called. "I'm not very hungry."

Cat was busy when Isabel arrived at the delicatessen. There were several customers in the shop, two busying themselves with the choice of a bottle of wine, pointing at labels and discussing the merits of Brunello over Chianti, while Cat was allowing another to sample a sliver of cheese from a large block of pecorino on a marble slab. She caught Isabel's eye and smiled, mouthing a greeting. Isabel pointed to one of the tables at which Cat served her customers coffee; she would wait there until the customers had left.

There were continental newspapers and magazines neatly stacked beside the table and she picked up a two-day-old copy of *Corriere della Sera*. She read Italian, as did Cat, and skipping the pages devoted to Italian politics—which she found impenetrable—she turned to the arts pages. There was a lengthy reevaluation of Calvino and a short article on the forthcoming season at La Scala. She decided that neither interested her: she knew none of the singers referred to in the headline to the La Scala article, and Calvino, in her view, needed no reassessment. That left a piece on an Albanian filmmaker who had become established in Rome and who was attempting to make films about his native country. It turned out to be a thoughtful read: there had been no cameras in Hoxha's Albania, apparently—only those owned by the security police for the purpose of photographing suspects. It was not until he was thirty, the director revealed, that he had managed to get his hands on any photographic apparatus. *I was trembling,* he said. *I thought I might drop it.*

Isabel finished the article and put down the newspaper. Poor

man. All those years which had been wasted. Whole lifetimes
had been spent in oppression and the denial of opportunities.
Even if people knew, or suspected, that it would come to an end,
many must have imagined that it would be too late for them.
Would it help to know that one's children might have what one
was not allowed to taste for oneself? She looked at Cat. Cat, who
was twenty-four, had never really known what it was like when
half the world—or so it seemed—had been unable to talk to the
other half. She had been a young girl when the Berlin Wall came
down, and Stalin, and Hitler, and all the other tyrants were distant historical figures to her, almost as remote as the Borgias.
Who were her bogeymen? she wondered. Who, if anyone, would
really terrify her generation? A few days earlier she had heard
somebody on the radio say that children should be taught that
there are no evil people and that evil was just that which people
did. The observation had arrested her: she was standing in the
kitchen when she heard it, and she stopped exactly where she
stood, and watched the leaves of a tree move against the sky outside. There are no evil people. Had he actually said that? There
were always people who were prepared to say that sort of thing,
just to show that they were not old-fashioned. Well, she suspected that one would not hear such a comment from this man
from Albania, who had lived with evil about him like the four
walls of a prison.

She found herself gazing at the label of a bottle of olive oil
which Cat had placed in a prominent position on a shelf near the
table. It was painted in that nineteenth-century rural style which
the Italians use to demonstrate the integrity of agricultural products. This was not from a factory, the illustration proclaimed; this
was from a real farm, where women like those shown on the bottle pressed the oil from their own olives, where there were large,

sweet-smelling white oxen and, in the background, a mousta-chioed farmer with a hoe. These were decent people, who believed in evil, and in the Virgin, and in a whole bevy of saints. But of course they did not exist anymore, and the olive oil probably came from North Africa and was rebottled by cynical Neapolitan businessmen who only paid lip service to the Virgin, when their mothers were within earshot.

"You're thinking," said Cat, lowering herself into the other chair. "I can always tell when you're thinking profound thoughts. You look dreamy."

Isabel smiled. "I was thinking about Italy, and evil, and topics of that nature."

Cat wiped her hands on a cloth. "I was thinking of cheese," she said. "That woman sampled eight Italian cheeses and then bought a small block of farmhouse cheddar."

"Simple tastes," said Isabel. "You mustn't blame her."

"I've decided that I'm not too keen on the public," said Cat. "I'd like to have a private shop. People would have to apply for membership before they could come in. I'd have to approve them. Rather like the members of your philosophy club or what-ever it is."

"The Sunday Philosophy Club is not exactly very active," she said to Cat. "But we'll have a meeting one of these days."

"It's such a good idea," said Cat. "I'd come, but Sunday's a bad day for me. I can never get myself organised to do anything. You know how it is. You know, don't you?"

Isabel did know. This, presumably, was what afflicted the members of the club.

Cat looked at her. "Is everything all right? You look a bit low. I can always tell, you know."

Isabel was silent for a moment. She looked down at the pattern on the tablecloth, and then looked back up at her niece. "No. I suppose I'm not feeling all that cheerful. Something happened last night. I saw something terrible."

Cat frowned, and reached across the table to place a hand on Isabel's arm. "What happened?"

"Have you seen the paper this morning?"

"Yes."

"Did you see that item about the young man at the Usher Hall?"

"Yes," said Cat. "I did."

"I was there," said Isabel simply. "I saw him fall from the gods, right past my eyes."

Cat gave her arm a gentle squeeze. "I'm sorry," she said. "It must have been terrible." She paused. "I know who it was, by the way. Somebody came in this morning and told me. I knew him, vaguely."

For a moment Isabel said nothing. She had expected no more than to tell Cat about what had happened; she had not imagined that she would know him, that poor, falling boy.

"He lived near here," Cat went on to explain. "In Marchmont. One of those flats right on the edge of the Meadows, I think. He came in here from time to time, but I really saw a bit more of his flatmates."

"Who was he?" Isabel asked.

"Mark somebody or other," Cat replied. "I was told his surname, but I can't remember it. Somebody was in this morning—she knew them better—and she told me that it had happened. I was pretty shocked—like you."

"Them?" asked Isabel. "Was he married or . . ." She paused. People often did not bother to marry, she had to remind herself, and yet it amounted to the same thing in many cases. But how did you put that particular question? Did he have a partner? But partners could be anyone, from the most temporary or recent to the wife or husband of fifty years. Perhaps one should just say: Was there somebody else? Which was sufficiently vague to cover everything.

Cat shook her head. "I don't think so. There were two flat-mates. Three of them shared. A girl and another boy. The girl's from the west, Glasgow or somewhere, and she's the one who comes in here. The other one I'm not sure about. Neil, I think, but I may be mixing him up."

Cat's assistant, a silent young man called Eddie, who always avoided eye contact, now brought them each a cup of hot milky coffee. Isabel thanked him and smiled, but he looked away and retreated to the back of the counter.

"What's wrong with Eddie?" whispered Isabel. "He never looks at me. I'm not all that frightening, am I?"

Cat smiled. "He's a hard worker," she replied. "And he's honest."

"But he never looks at anyone."

"There may be a reason for that," said Cat. "I came across him the other evening, sitting in the back room, his feet on the desk. He had his head in his hands and I didn't realise it at first, but he was in tears."

"Why?" asked Isabel. "Did he tell you?"

Cat hesitated for a moment. "He told me something. Not very much."

Isabel waited, but it was clear that Cat did not want to divulge what Eddie had said to her. She steered the subject back to the event of the previous night. How could he have fallen from the gods when there was that brass rail, was there not, which was intended to stop exactly that? Was it a suicide? Would somebody really jump from there? It would be a selfish way of going, surely, as there could easily be somebody down below who could be injured, or even killed.

"It wasn't suicide," Isabel said firmly. "Definitely not."

"How do you know?" asked Cat. "You said you didn't see him actually go over the edge. How can you be so sure?"

"He came down upside down," said Isabel, remembering the sight of the jacket and shirt pulled down by gravity and the exposed flat midriff. He was like a boy diving off a cliff, into a sea that was not there.

"So? People turn around, presumably, when they fall. Surely that means nothing."

Isabel shook her head. "He would not have had time to do that. You must remember that he was just above us. And people don't dive when they commit suicide. They fall feetfirst."

Cat thought for a moment. That was probably right. Occasionally the newspaper printed pictures of people on the way down from buildings and bridges, and they tended to be falling feetfirst. But it still seemed so unlikely that anybody could fall over that parapet by mistake, unless it was lower than she remembered it. She would take a look next time she was in the Usher Hall.

They sipped at their coffee. Cat broke the silence. "You must feel awful. I remember when I saw an accident in George Street, I felt just awful myself. Just witnessing something like that is so traumatic."

"I didn't come here to sit and moan, you know," said Isabel. "I didn't want to sit here and make you feel miserable too. I'm sorry."

"You don't have to say sorry," said Cat, taking Isabel's hand. "You just sit here as long as you like and then we can go out for lunch a bit later on. I could take the afternoon off and do something with you. How about that?"

Isabel appreciated the offer, but she wanted to sleep that afternoon. And she should not sit at the table too long either, as it was meant for the use of customers.

"Perhaps you could come and have dinner with me tonight," she said. "I'll rustle up something."

Cat opened her mouth to speak, but hesitated. Isabel saw this. She would be going out with one of the boyfriends.

"I'd love to," said Cat at last. "The only problem is that I was going to be meeting Toby. We were going to meet at the pub."

"Of course," said Isabel, quickly. "Some other time."

"Unless Toby could come too?" Cat added. "I'm sure he'd be happy to do that. Why don't I make a starter and bring it along?"

Isabel was about to refuse, as she imagined that the young couple might not really want to have dinner with her, but Cat now insisted, and they agreed that she and Toby would come to the house shortly after eight. As Isabel left and began to walk back to the house, she thought about Toby. He had arrived in Cat's life a few months before, and like the one before him, Andrew, she had her misgivings about him. It was difficult to put one's finger exactly on why it was that she had these reservations, but she was convinced that she was right.

CHAPTER THREE

THAT AFTERNOON SHE SLEPT. When she awoke, shortly before five, she felt considerably better. Grace had gone, but had left a note on the kitchen table. *Somebody phoned. He would not say who he was. I told him you were asleep. He said that he would phone again. I did not like the sound of him.* She was used to notes like that from Grace: messages would be conveyed with a gloss on the character of those involved. *That plumber I never trusted called and said that he would come tomorrow. He would not give a time.* Or: *While you were out, that woman returned that book she borrowed. At last.*

She was usually bemused by Grace's comments, but over the years she had come to see that Grace's insights were useful. Grace was rarely wrong about character, and her judgements were devastating. They were often of the one-word variety: *cheat,* she would say about somebody, or *crook,* or *drunkard.* If her views were positive, they might be slightly longer—*most generous,* or *really kind*—but these plaudits were hard to earn. Isabel had pressed her once as to the basis of her assessments of people, and Grace had become tight-lipped.

"I can just tell," she would say. "People are very easy to read. That's all there is to it."

"But there's often much more to them than you think," Isabel had argued. "Their qualities only come out when you get to know them a bit better."

Grace had shrugged. "There are some people I don't want to get to know better."

The discussion had ended there. Isabel knew that she would be unable to change the other woman's mind. Grace's world was very clear: there was Edinburgh, and the values which Edinburgh endorsed; and then there was the rest. It went without saying that Edinburgh was right, and that the best that could be hoped for was that those who looked at things differently would eventually come round to the right way of thinking. When Grace had first been employed—shortly after the onset of Isabel's father's illness—Isabel had been astonished to find that there was somebody who was still so firmly planted in a world that she had thought had largely disappeared: the world of douce Edinburgh, erected on rigid hierarchies and the deep convictions of Scottish Presbyterianism. Grace had proved her wrong.

It was the world which Isabel's father had come from, but from which he had wanted to free himself. He had been a lawyer, from a line of lawyers. He could have remained within the narrow world of his own father and grandfather, a world bounded by trust deeds and documents of title, but as a student he had been introduced to international law and a world of broader possibilities. He had enrolled for a master's degree in the law of treaties; Harvard, where he went for this, might have offered him an escape, but in the event did not. Moral suasion was brought to bear on him to return to Scotland. He almost stayed in America, but decided at the last moment to return, accompanied by his new wife, whom he had met and married in Boston. Once in Edinburgh, he was sucked back into the family's legal practise, where he was never happy. In an unguarded moment he had remarked to his daughter that he regarded his entire working life as a sentence which he had been obliged to serve out, a conclusion that had privately appalled Isabel. It was for this reason that when her time came to go to university, she had put to one side all thoughts of a career and chosen the subject which really interested her, philosophy.

There had been two children: Isabel, the elder of the two, and a brother. Isabel had gone to school in Edinburgh, but her brother had been sent off to boarding school in England at the age of twelve. Their parents had chosen for him a school noted for intellectual achievement, and unhappiness. What could one expect? The placing of five hundred boys together, cut off from the world, was an invitation to create a community in which every cruelty and vice could flourish, and did. He had become unhappy and rigid in his views, out of self-defence—the character armour which Wilhelm Reich spoke about, Isabel thought, and which led to these stiff, unhappy men who talked so guardedly in their clipped voices. After university, which he left without getting a degree, he took a job in a City of London merchant bank, and led a quiet and correct life doing whatever it was that merchant bankers did. He and Isabel had never been close, and as an adult he contacted Isabel only occasionally. He was almost a stranger to her, she thought; a friendly, if rather detached, stranger whose only real passion that she could detect was a consuming interest in the collecting of colourful old share certificates and bonds: South American railway stock, czarist long-term bonds—a whole colourful world of capitalism. But she had once asked him what lay behind these ornately printed certificates of ownership. Fourteen-hour workdays on plantations? Men working for a pittance until they were too weakened by silicosis, or too poisoned by toxins, to work anymore? (Distant wrongs, she thought: an interesting issue in moral philosophy. Do past wrongs seem less wrong to us simply because they are less vivid?)

SHE WENT INTO THE LARDER and retrieved the ingredients for a risotto she would make for Cat and Toby. The recipe called for porcini mushrooms, and she had a supply of these, tied up in a muslin bag. Isabel took a handful of the dried fungus, savouring the unusual odour, sharp and salty, so difficult to classify. Yeast extract? She would soak them for half an hour and then use the darkened liquid they produced to cook the rice. She knew that Cat liked risotto and that this was one of her favourites, and Toby, she imagined, would eat anything. He had been brought to dinner once before, and it was at this meal that her doubts about him had set in. She would have to be careful, though, or she would end up making Grace-like judgements. *Unfaithful.* She had already done it.

She returned to the kitchen and switched on the radio. It was the end of a news programme, and the world, as usual, was in disarray. Wars and rumours of war. A politician, a minister in the government, was being pressed for a response and refusing to answer. There was no crisis, he said. Things had to be kept in perspective.

But there is a crisis, insisted the interviewer; there just is.

That is a matter of opinion; I don't believe in alarming people unduly.

It was in the middle of the politician's embarrassment that

the doorbell sounded. Isabel put the mushrooms into a bowl and went through to the hall to open the door. Grace had suggested that she install a spy hole in order to identify callers before she opened the door, but she had never done so. If anybody rang very late, she could peer at them through the letter box, but for the most part she would open the door on trust. If we all lived behind barriers, then we would be dreadfully isolated.

The man on the doorstep had his back to her and was looking out over the front garden. When the door opened he turned round, almost guiltily, and smiled at her.

"You're Isabel Dalhousie?"

She nodded. "I am." Her glance ran over him. He was in his mid-thirties, with dark, slightly bushy hair, smartly enough dressed in a dark blazer and charcoal slacks. He had small, round glasses and a dark red tie. There was a pen and an electronic diary of some sort in the top pocket of his shirt. She imagined Grace's voice: *Shifty.*

"I'm a journalist," he said, showing her a card with the name of his newspaper. "My name is Geoffrey McManus."

Isabel nodded politely. She would never read his paper.

"I wondered if I could have a word with you," he said. "I gather you witnessed that unfortunate accident in the Usher Hall last night. Could you talk to me about it?"

Isabel hesitated for a moment, but then she stepped back into the hall and invited him in. McManus moved forward quickly, as if he was concerned that she might suddenly change her mind. "Such an unpleasant business," he said, as he followed her into the living room at the front of the house. "It was a terrible thing to happen."

Isabel gestured for him to sit down and she placed herself on the sofa near the fireplace. She noticed that as he sat down he

cast an eye around the walls, as if assessing the value of the paintings. Isabel squirmed. She did not like to vaunt her wealth, and
felt uncomfortable when it came under scrutiny. Perhaps he did
not know, though. The painting by the door, for example, was a
Peploe, and an early one. And the small oil beside the fireplace
was a Stanley Spencer—a sketch for a part of *When We Dead
Awaken.*

"Nice paintings," he said jauntily. "You like art?"

She looked at him. His tone was familiar. "I do like art. Yes. I
like art."

He looked around the room again. "I interviewed Robin
Philipson once," he said. "I went to his studio."

"You must have found that very interesting."

"No," he said flatly. "I don't like the smell of paint, I'm afraid.
It gives me a headache."

McManus was fiddling with a mechanical pencil, releasing
the lead and then pushing it back in again. "May I ask you what
you do? That is, if you work."

"I edit a journal," said Isabel. "A philosophical journal. The
Review of Applied Ethics."

McManus raised an eyebrow. "We're both in the same trade,
then," he said.

Isabel smiled. She was about to say "hardly" but did not. And
in a sense he was right. Her job was a part-time one, involving the
assessment and editing of scholarly papers, but ultimately it was,
as he suggested, about getting words onto paper.

She returned to the subject of the incident. "What happened in
the Usher Hall," she said. "Is there anything more known about it?"

McManus took a notebook out of the pocket of his jacket and
flipped it open. "Nothing much," he said. "We know who the
young man was and what he did. I've spoken to his flatmates and

I'm trying to get in touch with the parents. I'll probably be able to see them this evening. They're up in Perth."

Isabel stared at him. He was proposing to speak to them this evening, in the middle of their grief. "Why?" she asked. "Why do you have to speak to those poor people?"

McManus fingered the spiral binder of his notebook. "I'm writing a story about it," he said. "I need to cover every angle. Even the parents."

"But they'll be terribly upset," said Isabel. "What do you expect them to say? That they're sorry about it?"

McManus looked at her sharply. "The public has a legitimate interest in these things," he said. "I can see you don't approve, but the public has a right to be informed. Do you have any problem with that?"

Isabel wanted to say that she did, but she decided not to engage with her visitor. Anything she said about intrusive journalism would make no difference to the way in which he saw his job. If he had moral qualms about speaking to the recently bereaved, she was sure that these would be kept very much in the background.

"What do you want to know from me, Mr. McManus?" she asked, glancing at her watch. He would be offered no coffee, she had decided.

"Right," he said. "I would like to know what you saw, please. Just tell me everything."

"I saw very little," said Isabel. "I saw him fall, and then, later on, I saw him being carried out on the stretcher. That's all I saw."

McManus nodded. "Yes, yes. But tell me about it. What did he look like going down? Did you see his face?"

Isabel looked down at her hands, which were folded on her lap. She had seen his face, and she had thought that he must

have seen her. His eyes had been wide, with what was either surprise or terror. She had seen his eyes.

"Why would you want to know if I saw his face?" she asked.

"That might tell us something. You know. Something about
what he was feeling. About what happened."

She stared at him for a moment, struggling with her distaste
for his insensitivity. "I didn't see his face. I'm sorry."

"But you saw his head? Was he turned away from you, or facing you?"

Isabel sighed. "Mr. McManus, it all happened very quickly, in
a second or so. I don't think I saw very much. Just a body falling
from above, and then it was all over."

"But you must have noticed something about him," McManus
insisted. "You must have seen something. Bodies are made up of
faces and arms and legs and all the rest. We see individual bits as
well as the whole."

Isabel wondered whether she could ask him to leave, and
decided that she would do so in a moment. But his line of questioning suddenly changed.

"What happened afterwards?" he asked. "What did you do?"

"I went downstairs," she said. "There was a group of people in
the foyer. Everybody was pretty shocked."

"And then you saw him being carried out?"

"I did."

"And that's when you saw his face?"

"I suppose so. I saw him going out on the stretcher."

"Then what did you do? Did you do anything else?"

"I went home," said Isabel sharply. "I gave my statement to
the police and then I went home."

McManus fiddled with his pencil. "And that was all you did?"

"Yes," said Isabel.

McManus wrote something down in his notebook. "What did he look like on the stretcher?"

Isabel felt her heart thumping within her. There was no need for her to put up with any more of this. He was a guest—of sorts—in her house and if she no longer wished to discuss the matter with him, then she had only to ask him to leave. She took a deep breath. "Mr. McManus," she began, "I really do not think that there's much point in going into these matters. I cannot see what bearing it has on any report which you will publish of the incident. A young man fell to his death. Surely that is enough. Do your readers need to know anything more about how he looked on the way down? What do they expect? That he was laughing as he fell? That he looked cheerful on the stretcher? And his parents—what do they expect of them? That they are devastated? Really, how remarkable!"

McManus laughed. "Don't tell me my job, Isabel."

"Ms. Dalhousie, actually."

"Oh yes, Ms. Dalhousie. Spinster of this parish." He paused. "Surprising, that. You being an attractive woman, sexy if I may say so . . ."

She glared at him, and he looked down at his notebook.

"I have things to do," she said, rising to her feet. "Would you mind?"

McManus closed his notebook, but remained seated.

"You've just given me a little lecture on how the press should behave," he said. "I suppose you're entitled to do that, if you wish. But it's a pity your own moral authority is a little bit shaky."

She looked at him blankly, uncertain how to interpret his remark.

"You see, you lied," McManus went on. "You said that you went home, whereas I happen to know, from my conversations with the police, and with somebody else, that you went upstairs. You were seen looking down from the exact spot where he fell. But you very carefully failed to mention this to me. In fact, you said that you went home. Why would you lie to me, I wonder."

Isabel answered quickly. "I had no reason to tell you that. It had nothing at all to do with the incident."

"Really?" sneered McManus. "But what if I said that I thought you know more about this incident than you're letting on? Don't you think I'd be entitled to reach that conclusion now?"

Isabel moved towards the door and opened it pointedly. "I don't have to put up with this in my own home," she said. "If you wouldn't mind leaving now."

McManus rose to his feet, taking his time. "Sure," he said. "It's your house. And I have no wish to outstay my welcome."

She walked to the hallway and opened the front door. McManus followed, stooping for a moment to inspect a painting on the way.

"You have some beautiful things," he said. "Money?"

CHAPTER FOUR

COOKING IN A TEMPER required caution with the pepper; one might put far too much in and ruin a risotto in sheer pique. She felt dirtied by contact with McManus, as she inevitably did on those occasions when she found herself talking to somebody whose outlook on life was completely amoral. There were a surprising number of such people, she thought, and they were becoming more common; people to whom the idea of a moral sense seemed to be quite alien. What had appalled her most about McManus was the fact that he intended to talk to the parents, whose grief counted less for him than the desire of the public to witness the suffering of others. She shuddered. There was nobody, it seemed, to whom one might appeal; nobody who seemed prepared to say: Leave those poor people in peace.

She stirred the risotto, taking a small spoonful to test it for seasoning. The liquid from the soaked porcini mushrooms had imparted its flavour to the rice, and it was perfect. Soon she could put the dish in the lower oven and leave it there until Cat and Toby sat down with her at the table. In the meantime, there was a salad to prepare and a bottle of wine to open.

She felt calmer by the time the doorbell rang and she admitted her guests. The evening had turned cool, and Cat was wearing a full-length brown coat which Isabel had bought her for a birthday several years ago. She took this off and laid it down on a hall chair, revealing a long red dress underneath. Toby, who was a tall young man a year or two older than Cat, was wearing a dark brown tweed jacket and a roll-top shirt underneath. Isabel glanced at his trousers, which were crushed-strawberry corduroy; exactly what she would expect him to wear. He had never surprised her in that respect. I must try, she thought. I have to try to like him.

Cat had brought a plate of smoked salmon, which she took through to the kitchen with Isabel while Toby waited for them in the downstairs drawing room.

"Are you feeling any better?" Cat asked. "You seemed so miserable this morning."

Isabel took the plate of fish from her niece and removed the protective covering of foil.

"Yes," she said. "I'm feeling much better." She did not mention the journalist's visit, partly because she wanted not to be thought to be dwelling on the subject and partly because she wanted to put it out of her mind.

They laid out the salmon and returned to the drawing room. Toby was standing at the window, his hands clasped behind his back. Isabel offered her guests a drink, which she poured from the cabinet. When she handed his drink to Toby he raised it to her and gave the Gaelic toast.

"*Slaint,*" said Toby.

Isabel raised her glass weakly. *Slaint,* she was sure, would be Toby's only word of Gaelic, and she did not like the peppering of one language with words from others; *pas du tout.* So she muttered, under her breath, "*Brindisi.*"

"*Brin* what?" asked Toby.

"Brindisi," said Isabel. "The Italian toast."

Cat glanced at her. She hoped that Isabel would not be mischievous: she was perfectly capable of winding Toby up.

"Isabel speaks quite good Italian," Cat said.

"Useful," said Toby. "I'm no good at languages. A few words of French, I suppose, left over from school, and a bit of German. But nothing else."

Toby reached for a piece of brown bread and smoked salmon. "I can't resist this stuff," he said. "Cat gets it from somebody over in Argyll. Archie somebody, isn't it, Cat?"

"Archie MacKinnon," said Cat. "He smokes it himself in his garden, in one of those old smoking sheds. He soaks it in rum and then puts it over oak chips. It's the rum that gives it that wonderful flavour."

Toby reached for another of the largest pieces.

Cat quickly picked up the plate and offered it to Isabel. "I go up and see Archie when I go to Campbelltown," she said, placing the plate at Isabel's side. "Archie is a wonderful old man. Eighty-something, but still going out in his boat. He has two dogs, Max and Morris."

"After the boys?" said Isabel.

"Yes," said Cat.

Toby looked at the salmon. "What boys?"

"Max and Morris," said Isabel. "Two German boys. The very first comic-book characters. They got up to all sorts of mischief and were eventually chopped into pieces by a baker and made into biscuits."

She looked at Toby. Max and Morris had fallen into the baker's flour vat and had been put into a mixing machine. The biscuits into which they had been made were eventually eaten by ducks. Such a Germanic idea, she thought; and for a moment she imagined that this might happen to Toby, tumbling into such a machine and being made into biscuits.

"You're smiling," said Cat.

"Not intentionally," said Isabel hurriedly. Did one ever mean to smile?

They talked for half an hour or so before the meal. Toby had been skiing with a group of friends and he talked about his off-piste adventures. There had been an awkward moment when they had caused a halfhearted avalanche, but they had managed to get out of trouble.

"A rather close thing," he said. "You know what an avalanche sounds like?"

"Surf?" suggested Isabel.

Toby shook his head. "Thunder," he said. "Just like thunder. And it gets louder and louder."

Isabel imagined the scene—Toby in a strawberry-coloured ski suit with a tidal wave of snow hurtling down towards him, and the sun on the white peaks of the mountains. And then, just for a moment, she saw the snow overtake him and cover his flailing limbs in a churning of white, and then stillness, and there would be nothing but the tip of a ski pole to mark the spot. No, that was an unworthy thought, every bit as bad as imagining him being made into biscuits, and she put it out of her mind. But why had Cat not gone? She enjoyed skiing, but perhaps Toby had not invited her.

"You didn't want to go, Cat?" she asked. It was a potentially awkward question, but there was something in the self-assuredness of this young man that made her feel mischievous.

Cat sighed. "The shop," she said. "I can't get away. I'd have loved to have gone. But I just couldn't."

"What about Eddie?" said Toby. "Surely he's old enough to look after things for a week or so. Can't you trust him?"

"Of course I can trust him," Cat retorted. "It's just that Eddie is a bit . . . vulnerable."

Toby looked sideways at her. He was sitting beside Cat on the sofa near the window and Isabel thought that she detected an incipient sneer. This was interesting.

"Vulnerable?" Toby said. "Is that what you call it?"

Cat looked down at her glass. Isabel watched Toby. There was a touch of cruelty in the face, she thought; just below the surface, below that well-scrubbed, slightly pink look. And the face was very slightly fleshy, she thought, and in ten years' time his nose would begin to droop and . . . She stopped herself. She did not warm to him, but charity, the demands of which one should never forget, nudged at her gently.

"He's a nice boy," Cat mumbled. "He's had a hard time. And I can rely on him absolutely. He's very nice."

"Of course he is," said Toby. "Bit of a wimp, though, isn't he? Just a bit . . . you know."

Isabel had been watching in discreet fascination, but now she felt that she would have to intervene. She did not want Cat embarrassed in this way, even if the prospect of scales tumbling from Cat's eyes was an attractive one. What did she see in him? Was there anything at all, apart from the fact that he was a perfect specimen of a certain sort of thoughtless masculinity? The language of Cat's generation was far harder than that of her own, and more pithily correct: in their terms, he was a *hunk*. But why, she wondered, should anybody actually want a hunk, when non-hunks were so much more interesting?

Look at John Liamor. He could talk for hours and every bit of it was interesting. People would sit, more or less at his feet, and listen to him. What did it matter that he was thin and had that pale, almost translucent skin that went with a certain form of Celtic colouring? He was beautiful, in her eyes, and interesting, and now another woman, somebody whom she would never meet, somebody far away in California or wherever it was, had him for herself.

Isabel had met him in Cambridge. She was at Newnham, in the last year of her philosophy degree. He was a research fellow, a few years older than her, a dark-haired Irishman, a graduate of University College Dublin, who had been awarded a postdoctoral fellowship at Clare College and was writing a book on Synge. He had rooms at the back of the college, looking out over the Fellows' Garden on the other side of the river, and he invited Isabel to these rooms, where he sat and smoked, and looked at her. She was disconcerted by his gaze, and she wondered whether, in her absence, he talked as condescendingly—and wittily—of her as he did of others.

John Liamor felt that most people in Cambridge were provincial—he came from Cork, originally, which presumably was anything but provincial. He despised the products of expensive English schools—"little Lord Fauntleroys"—and he sneered at the clerics who still peopled the college. "Reverend," the title still borne by many dons in subjects as diverse as mathematics and classics, he changed to "Reversed," which Isabel and others, without knowing quite why they should do so, found funny. The principal of his college, a mild man, an economic historian, who had never been anything but generous and accommodating to his Irish guest, he described as the "chief obscurantist."

John Liamor gathered about him a salon of acolytes. These were students who were as much attracted by his undoubted brilliance as by the whiff of sulphur which surrounded his ideas. It was the seventies, and the frothiness of the previous decade had subsided. What remained to believe in, or indeed to mock? Ambition and personal gain, those heady gods of the following decade, were in the wings, but not centre stage, which made a brooding Irishman with an iconoclastic talent an intriguing option. With John Liamor it was not essential to believe in anything; all that was required was the ability to mock. And that was where his real appeal lay; he could sneer at the sneerers themselves because he was Irish and they, for all their radicalism, were still English and therefore, in his view, irretrievably part of the whole apparatus of oppression.

Isabel did not fit easily into this circle, and people remarked on the unlikely nature of the developing liaison. John Liamor's detractors, in particular—and he was not popular in his college, nor in the philosophy department—found the relationship a strange one. These people resented Liamor's intellectual condescension, and its trappings; he read French philosophy and peppered his remarks with references to Foucault. And, for one or two of them at least, those who *really* disliked him, there was something else: Liamor wasn't English. "Our Irish friend and *his* Scottish friend," one of the detractors remarked. "What an interesting, interesting couple. She's thoughtful; she's reasonable; she's civil; he's a jumped-up Brendan Behan. One expects him to break into song at any moment. You know the sort. *I could have cried with pride at the way he died,* and so on. Lots of anger about what we were meant to have done to them back years ago. That sort of thing."

At times she herself found it surprising that she was so attracted to him. It was almost as if there was nowhere else to go; that they were two people thrown together on a journey, who found themselves sharing the same railway compartment and becoming resigned to each other's company. Others found a more prosaic explanation. "Sex," observed one of Isabel's friends. "It brings all sorts of people together, doesn't it? Simple. They don't have to like each other."

"THE PYRENEES," said Isabel suddenly.

Both Toby and Cat stared at her.

"Yes," Isabel continued airily. "The Pyrenees. Do you know that I have never been to the Pyrenees? Not once."

"I have," said Toby.

"I haven't," said Cat. "But I would like to go."

"We could go together," Isabel pressed on, adding, "and Toby, too, of course, if you wanted to come, Toby. We could all go climbing. Toby would lead the way and we would all be roped to him. We'd be so safe."

Cat laughed. "He'd slip, and then we'd all fall to our deaths . . ." She stopped herself suddenly. The remark had come out without her thinking of it, and now she glanced at Isabel apologetically. The whole point of the evening was to take her aunt's mind off what had happened in the Usher Hall.

"The Andes," Isabel said brightly. "Now, I have been to the Andes. And they're just magnificent. But I could hardly breathe, you know, they are so high."

"I went to the Andes once," Toby chipped in. "At university. Our climbing club went. One of the guys slipped and fell. Five hundred feet, if not more."

There was a silence. Toby looked into his glass, remembering. Cat studied the ceiling.

*   *   *

AFTER HER GUESTS had gone, leaving earlier than anticipated, Isabel stood in the middle of the kitchen and stared at the plates stacked above the dishwasher. The evening had not been a conspicuous success. The conversation had picked up slightly over the dinner table, but Toby had gone on at great length about wine—his father was a successful wine importer and Toby worked in the family firm. Isabel saw the way he sniffed at the wine she had poured him, thinking that she might not notice—but she did. There was nothing wrong with it, surely; an Australian cabernet sauvignon, not a cheap one; but then wine people were suspicious of New World wines. Whatever they said to the contrary, there was an ineradicable snobbery in the wine world, with the French in the lead, and she imagined that Toby thought she knew no better than to serve a supermarket red. In fact, she knew more than most about wine, and there was nothing wrong with what she had served.

"Australian," he had said simply. "South Australian."

"Rather nice," said Cat.

Toby ignored her. "Quite a bit of fruit."

Isabel looked at him politely. "Of course, you'll be used to better."

"Good heavens," said Toby. "You make me sound like a snob. This is perfectly . . . perfectly all right stuff. Nothing wrong with it."

He put down his glass. "We had a superb first-growth claret in the office the other day. You wouldn't believe it. The old man fished it out from somewhere. Covered in dust. It faded pretty quickly, but if you took it before it faded, my God!"

Isabel had listened politely. She felt slightly cheered by his performance as she thought that Cat would be bound to tire of this sort of talk, and of Toby with it. Boredom would set in sooner rather than later, and when that happened it would eclipse whatever else it was that she liked about him. Could Cat really be in love with him? Isabel thought it was unlikely, as she detected a sensitivity to his faults—the eyes cast ever so slightly upwards, for example—whenever he made a remark which embarrassed her. We are not embarrassed by those we love; we may experience passing discomfort, but it is never embarrassment in the true sense. We forgive them their shortcomings, or we may just never notice them. And she had forgiven John Liamor, of course, even when she had found him one night with a student in his rooms at the college, a girl who giggled and wrapped herself in his discarded shirt, while John merely looked out the window and said, "Bad timing, Liamor."

It might be simpler, she reflected, not to allow oneself to be in love with anybody; just to be oneself, immune to hurt from others. There were plenty of people like that who seemed content with their lives—or were they? She wondered how many of these people were solitary by choice, and how many were alone because nobody had ever come into their lives and relieved them of their loneliness. There was a difference between resignation, or acceptance, in the face of loneliness and choosing to be solitary.

The central mystery, of course, was why we needed to be in love at all. The reductionist answer was that it was simply a matter of biology, and that love provided the motivational force that encouraged people to stay together to raise children. Like all the arguments of evolutionary psychology, it looked so simple and so obvious, but if that was all that we were, then why did we fall in love with ideas, and things, and places? Auden had captured this potential in pointing out that as a boy he had fallen in love with a pumping engine, and thought it "every bit as beautiful as you." Displacement, the sociobiologists would say; and there was the old Freudian joke that tennis is a substitute for sex. To which there was only one reply: that sex could equally well become a substitute for tennis.

"Very funny," Cat had said when Isabel had once pointed this out to her. "But surely it's absolutely right. Our emotions all seem geared towards keeping us in one piece, as animals, so to speak. Fear and flight. Fighting over food. Hatred and envy. All very physical and connected with survival."

"But might one not equally say that the emotions have a role in developing our higher capacities?" Isabel had countered. "Our emotions allow us to empathise with others. If I love another, then I know what it is to be that other person. If I feel pity—which is an important emotion, isn't it?—then this helps me to understand the suffering of others. So our emotions make us grow morally. We develop a moral imagination."

"Perhaps," Cat had said, but she had been looking away then, at a jar of pickled onions—this conversation had taken place in the delicatessen—and her attention had clearly wandered. Pickled onions had nothing to do with moral imagination, but were important in their own quiet, vinegary way, Isabel supposed.

AFTER CAT AND TOBY had left, Isabel went outside, into the cool of the night. The large walled garden at the back of the house, hidden from the road, was in darkness. The sky was clear, and there were stars, normally not visible in the city, obscured by all the light thrown up by human habitation. She walked over the lawn towards the small wooden conservatory, under which she discovered a fox had recently made its burrow. She had named him Brother Fox, and had seen him from time to time—a svelte creature running sure-footed along the top of the wall or dashing across the road at night, on impenetrable business of its own. She had welcomed him, and had left a cooked chicken out one night, as an offering. By morning it had disappeared, although she later found a bone in a flower bed, well gnawed, the marrow extracted.

What did she want for Cat? The answer was simple: she wanted happiness, which sounded trite, but was nevertheless true. In Cat's case, that meant that she should find the right man, because men seemed to be so important to her. She did not resent Cat's boyfriends—in principle, at least. Had she done so, the cause of her resentment would have been obvious: jealousy. But it was not that. She acknowledged what was important for her niece, and only hoped that she would find out what she was looking for, what she really wanted. In Isabel's view that was Jamie. And what about myself? she thought. What do I want?

I want John Liamor to walk through the door and say to me: I'm sorry. All these years that we've wasted. I'm sorry.

CHAPTER FIVE

NOTHING MORE ABOUT the incident appeared in what Isabel called the "lower papers" (well, they are, she would defend herself: look at their content); and what she referred to as the "morally serious papers," *The Scotsman* and *The Herald,* were also silent on the subject. For all Isabel knew, McManus might have found out no more, or if he had pieced together a few more scraps of detail, his editor could have deemed it to be too inconsequential to print. There was a limit to what one could make of a simple tragedy, even if it had occurred in unusual circumstances. She assumed that there would be a Fatal Accident Inquiry, which was always held when a death occurred in sudden or unexpected circumstances, and this might be reported when it took place. These were public hearings, before the local judge, the sheriff, and in most cases the proceedings were quick and conclusive. Factory accidents in which somebody was found to have forgotten that a wire was live; a misconnected carbon monoxide extractor; a shotgun that was thought to be unloaded. It did not take too long to unravel the tragedy, and the sheriff would make his determination, as it was called, patiently listing what had gone wrong and what needed to be put right, warning sometimes, but for the most part not passing much comment. And then the court would move on to the next death, and the relatives of the last would make their way out onto the street in sad little knots of regret. The most likely conclusion in this case would be that an accident had occurred. Because it had taken place so publicly, there might be comments on safety, and the sheriff could suggest a higher rail in the gods. But it could be months before any of this happened, and by then, she hoped, she might have forgotten it.

She might have discussed it again with Grace, but her housekeeper, it appeared, had other things on her mind. A friend was experiencing a crisis and Grace was lending moral support. It was a matter of masculine bad behaviour, she explained; her friend's husband was going though a midlife crisis and his wife, Grace's friend, was at her wit's end.

"He's bought an entire new wardrobe," Grace explained, casting her eyes upwards.

"Perhaps he feels like a change of clothing," ventured Isabel. "I've done that myself once or twice."

Grace shook her head. "He's bought teenage clothes," she said. "Tight jeans. Sweaters with large letters on them. That sort of thing. And he's walking around listening to rock music. He goes to clubs."

"Oh," said Isabel. Clubs sounded ominous. "What age is he?"

"Forty-five. A very dangerous age for men, we're told."

Isabel thought for a moment. What might one do in such a case?

Grace supplied her answer. "I laughed at him," she said. "I came straight out and said he looked ridiculous. I told him that he had no business wearing teenage boys' clothing."

Isabel could picture it. "And?"

"He told me to mind my own business," Grace said indignantly. "He said that, just because I was past it, he was not. So I said, past what? And he didn't reply."

"Trying," said Isabel.

"Poor Maggie," Grace went on. "He goes off to these clubs and never takes her, not that she would want to go anyway. She sits at home and worries about what he's getting up to. But there's not much I can do. I did give him a book, though."

"And what was that?"

"It was a dog-eared old book. I found it in a bookshop in the West Port. *One Hundred Things for a Teenage Boy to Do.* He didn't think it funny."

Isabel burst out laughing. Grace was direct, which came, she imagined, from being brought up in a small flat off the Cowgate, a home in which there was no time for much except work, and where people spoke their minds. Isabel was conscious of how far Grace's experience had been from her own; she had enjoyed all the privileges; she had had every chance educationally, while Grace had been obliged to make do with what was available at an indifferent and crowded school. It sometimes seemed to Isabel as if her education had brought her doubt and uncertainty, while Grace had been confirmed in the values of traditional Edinburgh. There was no room for doubt there; which had made Isabel wonder, Who is happier, those who are aware, and doubt, or those who are sure of what they believe in, and have never doubted or questioned it? The answer, she had concluded, was that this had nothing to do with happiness, which came upon you like the weather, determined by your personality.

"My friend Maggie," Grace announced, "thinks that you can't be happy without a man. And this is what makes her so concerned about Bill and his teenage clothes. If he goes off with a younger woman, then there'll be nothing left for her, nothing."

"You should tell her," said Isabel. "You should tell her that you don't need a man."

She made this remark without thinking how Grace might interpret it, and it suddenly occurred to her that Grace might think that this was Isabel suggesting that Grace was a confirmed spinster, who had no chance of finding a man.

"What I meant to say," Isabel began, "was that *one* doesn't need—"

"It doesn't matter," Grace interjected. "I know what you meant."

Isabel glanced at her quickly and then continued, "I'm not one to talk about men, anyway. I wasn't conspicuously successful myself."

But why? she wondered. Why had she been unsuccessful? Wrong man, or wrong time, or both?

Grace looked at her quizzically. "What happened to him, that man of yours? John what's-his-name? That Irishman? You've never really told me."

"He was unfaithful," said Isabel, simply. "All the time when we lived in Cambridge. And then, when we went to Cornell and I was on my fellowship there, he suddenly announced that he was going off to California with another woman, a girl really, and that was it. He just left in the space of one day."

"Just like that?"

"Yes, just like that. America went to his head. He said that it freed him up. I've heard that normally cautious people can go quite mad there, just from feeling free of whatever it was that was holding them back at home. He was like that. He drank more, he had more girlfriends, and he was more impetuous."

Grace digested this. Then she asked, "He's still there, I suppose?"

Isabel shrugged. "I assume so. But I imagine that he's with somebody else by now. I don't know."

"But would you like to find out?"

The answer was that of course she would. Because against all reason, against all personal conviction, she would forgive him if he came back and asked her for forgiveness, which he would never do, of course. And that made her safe from this weakness; the fact that never again would she be bewitched by John Liamor, never again would she be in that particular and profound danger.

SHE WAS ON HER WAY to forgetting the Usher Hall incident two weeks later when she was invited to a party at a gallery to mark the opening of a show. Isabel bought paintings, and this meant that a steady stream of gallery invitations came into the house. For the most part she avoided the openings, which were cramped and noisy affairs, riddled with pretension, but when she knew that there would be strong interest in the paintings on display she might go to the opening—and arrive early, in order to see the work before rival red dots appeared underneath the labels. She had learned to do this after arriving late for the opening of a Cowie retrospective and finding that the few paintings that had been for sale had been bought within the first fifteen minutes. She liked Cowie, who had painted haunting pictures of people who seemed to be cocooned in old-fashioned stillness; quiet rooms in which sad-faced schoolgirls were occupied in drawing or in embroidery; Scottish country roads and paths that seemed to lead into nothing but further silence; folds of cloth in the artist's studio. She had two small Cowie oils and would have been happy to purchase another, but she had been too late and she had learned her lesson.

The show which opened that evening was of work by Elizabeth Blackadder. She had toyed with the idea of buying a large watercolour, but had decided to look at the other paintings before deciding. She did not find anything else that appealed, and when she returned, a red dot had appeared below the watercolour. A young man, somewhere in his late twenties and wearing a chalk-striped suit, was standing in front of it, glass in hand. She glanced at the painting, which seemed even more desirable now that it had been sold, and then she looked at him, trying not to show her annoyance.

"It's wonderful, isn't it?" he said. "I always think of her as a Chinese painter. That delicacy. Those flowers."

"And cats too," Isabel said, rather grumpily. "She paints cats."

"Yes," said the young man. "Cats in gardens. Very comfortable. Not exactly social realism."

"Cats exist," said Isabel. "For cats, her paintings must be social realism." She looked at the painting again. "You've just bought it?" she asked.

The young man nodded. "For my fiancée. As an engagement present."

It was said with pride—pride in the fact of the engagement rather than in the purchase—and Isabel immediately softened.

"She'll love it," she said. "I was thinking of buying it myself, but I'm glad you've got it."

The young man's expression turned to concern. "I'm terribly sorry," he said. "They said that it was available. There was no indication . . ."

Isabel brushed his comment aside. "Of course there wasn't. It's first come, first served. You beat me to it. Exhibitions are meant to be red in tooth and claw."

"There are others," he said, gesturing to the wall behind

them. "I'm sure that you'll find something as good as this. Better, perhaps."

Isabel smiled. "Of course I will. And anyway, my walls are so full I would have had to take something down. I don't need another painting."

He laughed at her comment. Then, noticing her empty glass, he offered to refill it for her, and she accepted. Returning, he introduced himself. He was Paul Hogg, and he lived one block away in Great King Street. He had seen her at one of the gallery shows, he was sure, but Edinburgh was a village, was it not, and one always saw people one had seen somewhere or other before. Did she not think that too?

Isabel did. Of course, that had its drawbacks, did it not? What if one wanted to lead a secret life? Would it not be difficult in Edinburgh? Would one have to go over to Glasgow to lead it there?

Paul thought not. He knew several people, it transpired, who led secret lives, and they seemed to do it successfully.

"But how do you know about their secret lives?" asked Isabel. "Did they tell you themselves?"

Paul thought for a moment. "No," he said. "If they told me, then they would hardly be secret."

"So you found out?" said Isabel. "Rather proves my point."

He had to admit that it did, and they laughed. "Mind you," he said, "I can't imagine what I would do in a secret life, if I had one to lead. What is there to do that people really disapprove of these days? Nobody seems to blink an eyelid over affairs. And convicted murderers write books."

"Indeed they do," said Isabel. "But are these books really any good? Do they really say anything to us? Only the very immature and the very stupid are impressed by the depraved." She was silent for a moment. Then: "I suppose there must be something that people are ashamed of and are prepared to do in secret."

"Boys," said Paul. "I know somebody who goes for boys. Nothing actually illegal. Seventeen-, eighteen-year-olds. But really just boys still."

Isabel looked at the painting, at the flowers and the cats. It was a long way from the world of Elizabeth Blackadder.

"Boys," she said. "I suppose some people find boys . . . how shall I put it? Interesting. One might want to be secretive about that. Not that Catullus was. He wrote poems about that sort of thing. He seemed not in the slightest bit embarrassed. Boys are a recognised genre in classical literature, aren't they?"

"This person I know goes off to Calton Hill, I think," said Paul. "He drives up there in an empty car and drives down again with a boy. In secret, of course."

Isabel raised an eyebrow. "Oh well. People do these things." There were things happening on one side of Edinburgh the other did not know a great deal about. Of course, Edinburgh, it was said, was built on hypocrisy. It was the city of Hume, of course, the home of the Scottish Enlightenment, but then what had happened? Petty Calvinism had flourished in the nineteenth century and the light had gone elsewhere; back to Paris, to Berlin, or off to America, to Harvard and the like, where everything was now possible. And Edinburgh had become synonymous with respectability, and with doing things in the way in which they had always been done. Respectability was such an effort, though, and there were bars and clubs where people might go and behave as they really wanted to behave, but did not dare do so publicly. The story of Jekyll and Hyde was conceived in Edinburgh, of course, and made perfect sense there.

"Mind you," Paul went on, "I have no secret life myself. I'm

terribly conventional. I'm actually a fund manager. Not very exciting. And my fiancée works in Charlotte Square. So we're not
really . . . how might one put it?"

"Bohemian?" said Isabel, laughing.

"That's right," he said. "We're more . . ."

"Elizabeth Blackadder? Flowers and cats?"

They continued their conversation. After fifteen minutes or
so, Paul put his glass down on a windowsill.

"Why don't we go to the Vincent Bar?" he said. "I have to
meet Minty at nine, and I can't be bothered to go back to the flat.
We could have a drink and carry on talking. That's if you'd like to.
You may have other things to do."

Isabel was happy to accept. The gallery had filled up and was
beginning to get hot. The level of conversation had risen, too, and
people were shouting to be heard. If she stayed she would have a
sore throat. She collected her coat, said good-bye to the gallery
owners, and walked out with Paul to the small, unspoilt bar at the
end of the road.

The Vincent Bar was virtually empty and they chose a table
near the front door, for the fresh air.

"I hardly ever go to a pub," said Paul. "And yet I enjoy places
like this."

"I can't remember when I was last in one," said Isabel.
"Maybe in an earlier life." But of course she could remember
those evenings, with John Liamor, and that was painful.

"I was a fund manager in an earlier life, I suspect," said Paul.
"And presumably that's what I'll be in the next."

Isabel laughed. "Surely your job must have its moments," she
said. "Watching markets. Waiting for things to happen. Isn't that
what you do?"

"Oh, I suppose it has its moments," he said. "You have to read a lot. I sit at my desk and go through the financial press and company reports. I'm a sort of spy, really. I collect intelligence."

"And is it a good place to work?" asked Isabel. "Are your colleagues agreeable people?"

Paul did not answer immediately. Lifting his glass, he took a long sip of his beer. When he answered, he looked down at the table as he spoke. "By and large, yes. By and large."

"Which means no," said Isabel.

"No, I wouldn't say that. It's just that . . . well, I lost somebody who worked for me. A few weeks ago. I have—had—two people under me in my department, and he was one of them."

"He went elsewhere?" asked Isabel. "Lured away? I gather that everybody's frantically busy headhunting everybody else. Isn't that the way it works?"

Paul shook his head. "He died," he said. "Or rather, he was killed. In a fall."

It could have been a climbing accident; those happened in the Highlands virtually every week. But it was not, and Isabel knew it.

"I think I know who it was," she said. "Was it at—"

"The Usher Hall," said Paul. "Yes. That was him. Mark Fraser." He paused. "Did you know him?"

"No," said Isabel. "But I saw it happen. I was there, in the grand circle, talking to a friend, and he came falling down, right past us, like a . . . like a . . ."

She stopped, and reached out to touch Paul's arm. He was clutching his glass, staring down at the table, appalled by what she was saying.

CHAPTER SIX

IT ALWAYS HAPPENED when one was in a room with smokers. She remembered reading somewhere that the reason for it was that the surfaces of nonsmokers' clothes were covered with negative ions, while tobacco smoke was full of positive ions. So when there was smoke in the air, it was immediately attracted to the oppositely charged surface, which made one's clothes smell. And that was why, when she lifted up the jacket that she had been wearing the previous evening and which she had left lying across the top of her bedroom chair, she was assailed by the stale, acrid smell of tobacco smoke. There had been smokers in the Vincent Bar, as there always were in bars, and even though she and Paul had sat near the door, it had been enough to leave its mark.

Isabel gave the jacket a good shake before the open window, which always helped, before putting it away in the wardrobe. Then she returned to the window and looked out over the garden, to the trees beside her wall, the tall sycamore and the twin birches which moved so readily in the wind. Paul Hogg. It was a Borders name, and whenever she encountered it she thought of James Hogg, the writer known as the Ettrick Shepherd, the most distinguished of the Hoggs, although there were other, even English, Hoggs.

Quintin Hogg, a lord chancellor (and perhaps slightly porcine in appearance, though, as she reminded herself, one should not be uncharitable to Hoggs), and his son, Douglas Hogg. And so on. All these Hoggs.

They had not stayed long in the bar. The recollection of Mark Fraser's fall had visibly upset Paul, and although he had rapidly changed the subject, a shadow had fallen over their evening. But before they finished their drinks and went their separate ways, he had said something which had made her sit up sharply. *"He would never have fallen. He had a head for heights, you see. He was a climber. I went with him up Buchaille Etive Mhor. He went straight up. An absolute head for heights."*

She had stopped him and asked him what he meant. If he would not have fallen, then had he deliberately jumped? Paul had shaken his head. "I doubt it. People surprise you, but I just cannot see why he would have done that. I spent hours with him earlier that day, hours, and he was not in the least bit down. Quite the opposite, in fact; one of the companies which he had drawn to our attention, and in which we had invested heavily, had come up with a spectacular set of interim results. The chairman had sent him a memo congratulating him on his perspicacity and he was very pleased with this. Smiling. Cat with the cream. Why would he do himself in?"

Paul had shaken his head, and then had changed the subject, leaving her to wonder. And now she was wondering again, as she went downstairs for breakfast. Grace had arrived early and had put on her egg to boil. There were comments on a story in the newspapers; a government minister had been evasive in parliamentary question time and had refused to give the information which the opposition had requested. Grace had put him down as a liar the first time she saw his photograph in the paper, and now here was the proof. She looked at her employer, challenging her to deny the proposition, but Isabel just nodded.

"Shocking," she said. "I can't remember when exactly it was that it became all right to lie in public life. Can you remember?"

Grace could. "President Nixon started it. He lied and lied. And then it came across the Atlantic and our people started to lie too. That's how it started. Now it's standard practise."

Isabel had to agree. People had lost their moral compass, it seemed, and this was just a further example. Grace, of course, would never lie. She was completely honest, in small things and big, and Isabel trusted her implicitly. But then Grace was not a politician, and never could be one. The first lies, Isabel assumed, had to be told at the candidate selection board.

Of course, not all lies were wrong, which was another respect, Isabel thought, in which Kant was mistaken. One of the most ridiculous things that he had ever said was that there was a duty to tell the truth to the murderer looking for his victim. If the murderer came to one's door and asked, *Is he in?* one would be obliged to answer truthfully, even if this would lead to the death of an innocent person. Such nonsense; and she could remember the precise offending passage: *Truthfulness in statements which cannot be avoided is the formal duty of an individual to everyone, however great may be the disadvantage accruing to himself or to another.* It was not surprising that Benjamin Constant should have been offended by this, although Kant responded—unconvincingly— and tried to point out that the murderer might be apprehended before he acted on the knowledge which he had gained from a truthful answer.

The answer, surely, is that lying *in general* is wrong, but that some lies, carefully identified as the exception, will be permissible. There were, therefore, good lies and bad lies, with good lies being uttered for a benevolent reason (to protect the feeling of another, for example). If somebody asked one's opinion of a newly acquired—but tasteless—possession, for instance, and one gave an honest answer, then that could hurt feelings and deprive the other of the joy of ownership. So one lied, and praised it, which was surely the right thing to do. Or was it? Perhaps it was not as simple as that. If one became accustomed to lying in such circumstances, the line between truth and falsehood could become blurred.

Isabel thought that she might visit this issue in detail one day and write a paper on the subject. "In Praise of Hypocrisy" might be a suitable title, and the article might begin: "To call a person a hypocrite is usually to allege a moral failing. But is hypocrisy inevitably bad? Some hypocrites deserve greater consideration . . ."

There were further possibilities. Hypocrisy was not only about telling lies, it was about saying one thing and doing quite the other. People who did that were usually roundly condemned, but again this might not be as simple as some would suggest. Would it be hypocritical for an alcoholic to advise against drinking alcohol, or a glutton to recommend a diet? The recipient of the advice might well level charges of hypocrisy in such a case, but only if the person giving the advice claimed that he did not drink or eat too much himself. If he merely concealed his own vices, then he might still be considered a hypocrite, but his hypocrisy might be no bad thing. It certainly did not harm anybody, and indeed it might even help (provided that it remained undiscovered). This was a topic which would have been ideal for the Sunday Philosophy Club. Perhaps she would try to get people together for precisely such a discussion. Who could resist an invitation to discuss hypocrisy? The members of the club, she suspected.

Her boiled egg placed on the table, she sat down with a copy

of *The Scotsman* and a freshly brewed cup of coffee, while Grace
went off to start the laundry. There was nothing of note in the
paper—she could not bring herself to read an account of the
doings of the Scottish Parliament—and so she quickly passed to
the crossword. Four across: *He conquers all, a nubile tram* (11).
Tamburlaine, of course. It was an old clue and it even appeared as
the final line of one of Auden's poems. WHA, as she thought of
him, liked to do the crossword, and would have *The Times* deliv-
ered to Kirchstetten for that very purpose. There he lived, in his
legendary domestic mess, with manuscripts and books and over-
flowing ashtrays, doing the *Times* crossword each day, with a tat-
tered volume of the big *Oxford* open on a chair beside him. She
would have so loved to have met him, and talked, even just to
thank him for everything that he had written (except the last two
books), but she rather feared that he might have written her off as
one of his legion of bluestocking admirers. Six down: *A homespun
poet, a pig in charge of sheep?* (4). Hogg, naturally. (But a coincidence, nonetheless.)

She finished the crossword in the morning room, allowing
her second cup of coffee to get too cool to drink. She felt uneasy
for some reason, almost queasy, and she wondered whether she
had not perhaps had rather too much to drink the previous
evening. But, going over it, she had not. She had had two small-
ish glasses of wine at the opening, and a further one, if somewhat
larger, in the Vincent Bar. That was hardly enough to unsettle her
stomach or trigger a headache. No, her feeling of unease was not
physical; she was upset. She had imagined that she had recovered from witnessing that awful event, but clearly she had not,
and it was still having its psychological effect. Putting down the
newspaper, she looked up at the ceiling and wondered whether
this was what they called post-traumatic stress disorder. Soldiers

suffered from it in the First World War, although they called it shell shock then, and shot them for cowardice.

She thought of the morning ahead. There was work to be done; at least three journal articles were waiting to be sent out to referees, and she would have to despatch them that morning. Then there was an index to be prepared for a special issue that was due to appear later that year. She did not enjoy indexing and she had been putting the task off. But it would have to be sent to the general editor for approval before the end of the week, which meant that she would have to sit down to it either that day or the following day. She looked at her watch. It was almost nine-thirty. If she worked for three hours she would get through most, if not all, of the index. That would take her to twelve-thirty, or perhaps almost one o'clock. And then she could go and have lunch with Cat, if she was free. The thought cheered her up: a good spell of work followed by a relaxed chat with her niece was exactly what she needed to get over this temporary blue feeling—the perfect cure for post-traumatic stress disorder.

Cat was available, but only at one-thirty, as Eddie had asked to take his lunch break early. They would meet at the bistro opposite the delicatessen; Cat preferred getting out for lunch rather than taking up one of her own few tables. Besides, she knew that Eddie listened to her conversation when he could, and this irritated her.

Isabel made good progress with her index, finishing the task shortly after twelve. She printed out what she had done and put it in an envelope for posting on the way in to Bruntsfield. Finishing the work had lifted her spirits considerably, but it had not taken her mind off her conversation with Paul. That still worried her, and she kept thinking of the two of them, Paul and Mark, climbing together up Buchaille Etive Mhor, roped together perhaps, with Mark turning and looking down at Paul, and the sun on his face. His photograph, published in the newspapers, had shown him to be so good-looking, which seemed to make everything all the sadder, although, of course, it should not. When the beautiful died, it was the same as when the less well blessed died; that was obvious. But why did it seem more tragic that Rupert Brooke, or Byron for that matter, should die, than other young men? Perhaps it was because we love the beautiful more; or because Death's momentary victory is all the greater. Nobody, he says, smiling, is too beautiful not to be taken by me.

The crowd in the bistro had thinned out by one-thirty, when she arrived. There were two tables occupied at the back, one by a group of women with shopping bags stacked at their feet, and another by three students, who were sitting in a huddle over a story that one of them was recounting. Isabel sat down at an empty table and studied the menu while she waited for Cat. The women ate in near silence, tackling long strands of tagliatelle with their forks and spoons, while the students continued their conversation. Isabel could not help but overhear snatches of it, particularly when one of the students, a young man in a red jersey, raised his voice.

". . . and she said to me that if I didn't go with her to Greece, then I couldn't keep the room in the flat, and you know how cheaply I get that. What could I do? You tell me. What would you have done in my position?"

There was a momentary silence. Then one of the others, a girl, said something which Isabel did not catch, and there was laughter.

Isabel glanced up, and then returned to her scrutiny of the menu. The young man lived in a flat which was owned by this anonymous she. She wanted him to go to Greece, and was obviously prepared to use whatever bargaining power she had to see to it that he did. But if she was coercing him in this way, then he would hardly be much of a travelling companion.

"I told her that . . ." Something was said which Isabel missed, and then: "I said that I would come only if she left me alone. I decided to come right out with it. I said that I knew what she had in mind . . ."

"You flatter yourself," said the girl.

"No, he doesn't," said the other young man. "You don't know her. She's a man-eater. Ask Tom. He could tell you."

Isabel wanted to ask, "And did you go? Did you go to Greece?" but could not, of course. This young man was as bad as the girl who had asked him. They were all unpleasant; all sitting there gossiping in this snide way. You should never discuss the sexual offers of others, she thought. *Don't kiss and tell* summed it up nicely. But these students had no sense of that.

She returned to the menu, eager now to shut out their conversation. But fortunately Cat arrived at that moment and she could put the menu aside and give her attention to her niece.

"I'm late," said Cat, breathlessly. "We had a bit of a crisis. Somebody brought in some salmon which was way beyond its sell-by date. They said they had bought it from us, which was probably true. I don't know how it happened. And then they went on about complaining to the hygiene people. You know what that involves. They make the most enormous fuss."

Isabel was sympathetic. She knew that Cat would never deliberately take risks. "Did you sort it out?"

"A free bottle of champagne helped," said Cat. "And an apology."

Cat picked up the menu, glanced at it, and then replaced it

in its stand. She had little appetite at lunch, and would be happy with a minimalist salad. Isabel thought that this might have something to do with working with food all the time.

They exchanged a few scraps of news. Toby was away on a wine-buying trip with his father, but had telephoned the previous evening from Bordeaux. He would be back in a few days' time, and they would be going to Perth for the weekend, where he had friends. Isabel listened politely, but could not feel enthusiastic. What would they do on their weekend in Perth, she wondered, or was that a naïve question? It was hard to put yourself back to your early twenties.

Cat was watching her. "You should give him a chance," she said quietly. "He's a nice person. He really is."

"Of course he is," said Isabel quickly. "Of course he is. I've got nothing against Toby."

Cat smiled. "You're very unconvincing when you're telling lies," she said. "It's quite apparent you don't like him. You can't help showing it."

Isabel felt trapped, and thought: *I'm an unconvincing hypocrite.* There was silence now at the table of students, and she was aware of the fact that they were listening to the conversation. She stared at them, noticing that one of the boys had a small pin in his ear. People who had metal piercing in their heads were asking for trouble, Grace had once said. Isabel had asked why this should be so. Hadn't people always worn earrings, and got away with it? Grace had replied that metal piercings attracted lightning, and that she had read of a heavily pierced man who had been struck dead in an electric storm while those around him, unpierced, had survived.

The students exchanged glances, and Isabel turned away. "This is not the place to discuss it, Cat," she said, her voice lowered.

"Maybe not. But it does upset me. I only want you to try with him. Try to get beyond your initial reaction."

"My initial reaction was not entirely negative," whispered Isabel. "I may not have felt particularly warm towards him, but that's just because he's not really my type. That's all."

"Why isn't he your type?" asked Cat defensively, her voice raised. "What's wrong with him?"

Isabel glanced at the students, who were now smiling. She deserved to be eavesdropped upon, she reflected; *your acts will be returned to you, faithfully, every one.*

"I wouldn't say there's anything wrong with him," she began. "It's just that, are you sure that he's quite . . . quite your intellectual equal? That can matter a lot, you know."

Cat frowned, and Isabel wondered whether she had gone too far. "He's not stupid," Cat said indignantly. "He has a degree from St. Andrews, remember. And he's seen a bit of the world."

St. Andrews! Isabel was just about to say, "Well, there you are: St. Andrews," but thought better of it. St. Andrews had a reputation of attracting well-off young people who came from the upper echelons of society and who wanted to find somewhere congenial to spend a few years while they attended parties. The Americans called such places party schools. In this case, it was an unfair reputation, as many reputations were, but there was at least a modicum of truth in it. Toby would have fitted very well into that social vision of St. Andrews, but it would have been unkind to point that out, and, anyway, now she wanted the conversation to stop. It had not been her intention to become embroiled in an argument about Toby; she did not think it right to interfere, and she must stop herself from drifting into a confrontation with Cat. This would make it more awkward in the future. Besides, he would go off with somebody else before too long and that would be that. Unless—

and here was another appalling thought—unless Toby was interested in Cat for her money.

Isabel tended not to think a great deal about money, a position of privilege, as she well recognised. She and her brother had each inherited from their mother a half share in the Louisiana and Gulf Land Company, and this had left them wealthy by any standards. Isabel was discreet about this, and used her money carefully in respect of herself and generously in respect of others. But the good that she did was done by stealth.

On Cat's twenty-first birthday Isabel's brother had transferred enough to his daughter to allow her to buy a flat and, later, the delicatessen. There was not much left over from that—a wise policy on his part, thought Isabel—but Cat was extremely well off by the standards of her age group, most of whom would be struggling to save the deposit on a flat. Edinburgh was expensive, and thus was out of reach for many.

Toby, of course, came from a well-off background, but his family's money was probably tied up in the business and he was likely not paid much of a salary by his father. Such young men knew exactly how important money was, and they had a talent for sniffing it out. That meant that he might be very interested in the assets which Cat had at her disposal, although Isabel could never make such a suggestion openly. If only she could find some evidence of it, and prove it, as in the denouement of some dreadful drawing-room melodrama, but that would be highly unlikely.

She reached across to reassure Cat as she changed the subject.

"He's perfectly all right," she said. "I'll make an effort, and I'm sure that I'll see his good points. It's my fault for being too . . . too fixed in my views. I'm sorry."

Cat appeared mollified, and Isabel steered the conversation to an account of her meeting with Paul Hogg. She had decided, on her way to the bistro, what she would do about that, and now she explained it to Cat.

"I've tried to forget what I saw," she explained. "It hasn't worked. I still think about it, and then that conversation I had with Paul Hogg last night really disturbed me. Something odd happened that night at the Usher Hall. I don't think that it was an accident. I really don't."

Cat was looked at her dubiously. "I hope you aren't going to get involved," she said. "You've done this before. You've got involved in things that are really none of your business. I really don't think you should do that again."

Cat was aware of the fact that there was no point in upbraiding Isabel: she would never change. There was no reason why she should become involved in the affairs of others, but she seemed to be irresistibly drawn into them. And every time that she did it, it was because she imagined that there was a moral claim on her. This view of the world, with a seemingly endless supply of potential claims, meant that anybody with a problem could arrive on Isabel's doorstep and be taken up, simply because the requirement of moral proximity—or her understanding of moral proximity—had been satisfied.

They had argued about Isabel's inability to say no, which in Cat's view was the root of the problem. "You simply can't get drawn into other people's business like this," she had protested after Isabel had become involved in sorting out the problems of a hotel-owning family that was fighting over what to do with their business. But Isabel, who had regularly been taken for Sunday lunch in the hotel as a child, had considered that this gave her an interest in what happened to it and had become sucked into an unpleasant boardroom battle.

Cat had voiced the same concerns when it came to the unfortunate young man in the Usher Hall. "But this is my business," said Isabel. "I saw the whole thing—or most of it. I was the last person that young man saw. The last person. And don't you think that the last person you see on this earth owes you something?"

"I'm not with you," said Cat. "I don't see what you mean."

Isabel leant back in her chair. "What I mean is this. We can't have moral obligations to every single person in this world. We have moral obligations to those who we come up against, who enter into our moral space, so to speak. That means neighbours, people we deal with, and so on."

Who, then, is our neighbour? she would say to the Sunday Philosophy Club. And the members of the Sunday Philosophy Club would think very carefully about this and come to the conclusion, Isabel suspected, that the only real standard we can find for this is the concept of proximity. Our moral neighbours are those who are close to us, spatially or in some other recognised sense. Distant claims are simply not as powerful as those we can see before us. These close claims are more vivid and therefore more real.

"Reasonable enough," said Cat. "But you didn't come into contact with him in that sense. He just . . . sorry to say this . . . he just passed by."

"He must have seen me," said Isabel. "And I saw him—in a state of extreme vulnerability. I'm sorry to sound the philosopher, but in my view that creates a moral bond between us. We were not moral strangers."

"You sound like the *Review of Applied Ethics*," said Cat dryly.

"I *am* the *Review of Applied Ethics*," Isabel replied.

The remark made them both laugh, and the tension that had been growing dissipated.

"Well," said Cat, "there's obviously nothing that I can do to stop you doing whatever it is you want to do. I may as well help you. What do you need?"

"The address of his flatmates," said Isabel. "That's all."

"You want to speak to them?"

"Yes."

Cat shrugged. "I can't imagine that you'll find out much. They weren't there. How will they know what happened?"

"I want some background," said Isabel. "Information about him."

"All right," said Cat. "I'll find this out for you. It won't be hard."

As she walked home after her lunch with Cat, Isabel thought about their discussion. Cat had been right to ask her about why she involved herself in these matters; it was a question she should have asked herself more often, but did not. Of course, it was simple to work out why we had a moral obligation to others, but that was really not the point. The question which she had to address was what drove her to respond as she did. And one reason for that, if she were honest with herself, might be that she simply found it intellectually exciting to become involved. She wanted to know why things happened. She wanted to know why people did the things they did. She was curious. And what, she wondered, was wrong with that?

Curiosity killed the cat, she suddenly thought, and immediately regretted the thought. Cat was everything to her, really; the child she had never had, her parlous immortality.

CHAPTER SEVEN

ISABEL HAD EXPECTED to spend the evening alone. Her progress with the index had encouraged her to tackle another task which she had been putting off—detailed work on an article which had returned from a reviewer accompanied by a lengthy set of comments and corrections. These had been scribbled in the margins and needed to be collated, a task which was rendered all the more difficult by the reviewer's irritating abbreviations and spidery handwriting. That was the last time he would be used, she had decided—eminent or not.

But Jamie arrived instead, ringing her bell shortly before six. She welcomed him warmly, and immediately invited him to stay for dinner, if he had nothing else planned, of course. She knew that he would accept, and he did, after a momentary hesitation for form's sake. And for the sake of pride: Jamie was Cat's age, twenty-four, and it was a Friday evening. Everybody else would have something planned for that evening, and he would not want Isabel to think that he had no social life.

"Well," he said, "I was thinking of meeting up with somebody, but since you ask . . . Why not?"

Isabel smiled. "It will be potluck, as usual, but I know you're not fussy."

Jamie took off his jacket and left it with his bag in the hall.

"I've brought some music with me," he said. "I thought you might like to accompany me. Later on, that is."

Isabel nodded. She played the piano moderately well and could usually just manage to keep up with Jamie, who was a tenor. He had a trained voice and sang with a well-known chorus, which was another attribute, she thought, which Cat could have taken into consideration. She had no idea whether Toby could sing, but would be surprised if he could. He would also be unlikely to play a musical instrument (except the bagpipes, perhaps, or, at a stretch, percussion), whereas Jamie played the bassoon. Cat had a good ear for music and was a reasonable pianist as well. In that brief period when she and Jamie had been together, she had accompanied him brilliantly, and she had brought him out of him-self as a performer. They sounded so natural together, Isabel had thought. If only Cat would realise! If only she would see what she was giving up. But of course Isabel understood that there was no objectivity when it came to these matters. There were two tests: the best interests test and the personal chemistry test. Jamie was in Cat's best interests—Isabel was convinced of that—but per-sonal chemistry was another matter.

Isabel shot a glance at her guest. Cat must have been suffi-ciently attracted to him in the first place, and she could see why, looking at him now. Cat liked tall men, and Jamie was as tall as Toby, perhaps even slightly taller. He was undoubtedly good-looking: high cheekbones, dark hair that he tended to have cut *en brosse,* and skin with a natural tan. He could have been Por-tuguese—almost—or Italian, perhaps, although he was Scottish on both sides. What more could Cat want? she thought. Really! What else could a girl possibly require than a Scotsman who looked Mediterranean and could sing?

The answer came to her unbidden, like an awkward truth that nudges one at the wrong moment. Jamie was too nice. He had given Cat his whole attention—had fawned on her, perhaps—and she had grown tired of that. We do not like those who are completely available, who make themselves over to us entirely. They crowd us out. They make us feel uneasy.

That was it. If Jamie had maintained some distance, a degree of remoteness, then that would have attracted Cat's interest. That was why she seemed so happy now. She could not possess Toby, who would always seem slightly remote, as if he were excluding her from some part of his plans (which he was, Isabel had convinced herself). It was wrong to think of men as the predators: women had exactly the same inclinations, although often more discreetly revealed. Toby was suitable prey. Jamie, by making it quite apparent that Cat had his complete and unfettered attention, had ceased to interest her. It was a bleak conclusion.

"You were too good to her," she muttered.

Jamie looked at her in puzzlement. "Too good?"

Isabel smiled. "I was thinking aloud," she said. "I was thinking that you were too good to Cat. That's why it didn't work out. You should have been more . . . more evasive. You should have let her down now and then. Looked at other girls."

Jamie said nothing. They had often discussed Cat—and he still nurtured the hope that Isabel would be his way back into Cat's affections, or so Isabel thought. But this new view she was expressing was an unexpected one, no doubt. Why should he have let her down?

Isabel sighed. "Sorry," she said. "I'm sure you don't want to go over all that again."

Jamie raised his hands. "I don't mind. I like talking about her. I want to talk about her."

"Oh, I know," said Isabel. She paused. She wanted to say something to him that she had not said before, and was judging her moment. "You love her still, don't you? You're still in love."

Jamie looked down at the carpet, embarrassed.

"Just like myself," said Isabel quietly. "The two of us. I'm still a bit in love with somebody whom I knew a long time ago, years ago. And there you are, also in love with somebody who doesn't seem to love you. What a pair we are, the two of us. Why do we bother?"

Jamie was silent for a moment. Then he asked her, "What's he called? Your . . . this man of yours."

"John Liamor," she said.

"And what happened to him?"

"He left me," Isabel said. "And now he lives in California. With another woman."

"That must be very hard for you," said Jamie.

"Yes, it is very hard," said Isabel. "But then it's my own fault, isn't it? I should have found somebody else instead of thinking about him all the time. And that's what you should do, I suppose." The advice was halfhearted; but as she gave it she realised it was exactly the right advice to give. If Jamie found somebody else, then Cat might show an interest in him once Toby was disposed of. Disposed of! That sounded so sinister, as if the two of them might arrange an accident. An avalanche, perhaps.

"Could one start an avalanche?" she asked.

Jamie's eyes opened wide. "What an odd thing to ask," he

said. "But of course you could. If the snow is in the right condition, then all you have to do is to shift a bit of it, tread on it, even,
and the whole thing gets going. Sometimes you can start them
just by talking in a loud voice. The vibrations of your voice can
make the snow start to move."

Isabel smiled. She again imagined Toby on a mountainside,
in his crushed-strawberry ski suit, talking loudly about wine. "Do
you know I had the most wonderful bottle of Chablis the other
day. Fabulous. Flinty, sharp . . ." There would be a pause, and the
words "flinty, sharp" would echo across the snowfields, just
enough to start the tidal wave of snow.

She checked herself. That was the third time that she had
imagined him in a disaster and she should stop. It was childish,
uncharitable, and wrong. We have a duty to control our thoughts,
she said to herself. We are responsible for our mental states, as
she well knew from her reading in moral philosophy. The unbidden thought may arrive, and that was a matter of moral indiffer-
ence, but we should not dwell on the harmful fantasy, because it
was bad for our character, and besides, *one might just translate
fantasy into reality*. It was a question of duty to self, in Kantian
terms, and whatever she thought about Toby, he did not deserve
an avalanche or to be reduced to biscuits. Nobody could be said
to deserve that, not even the truly wicked, or a member of that
other Nemesis-tempting class, the totally egotistical.

And who were they, she wondered, these practitioners of
hubris? She had a small mental list of those who might be
warned, for their own protection, of how close they were to
attracting the attentions of Nemesis—a list which was headed by
a local social climber of breathtaking nerve. An avalanche might
reduce his self-satisfaction, but that was unkind; he had his good

side, and such thoughts had to be put aside. They were unworthy of the editor of the *Review of Applied Ethics*.

"Music before dinner," said Isabel briskly. "What have you brought with you? Let me take a look."

THEY MOVED THROUGH to the music room, a small room at the back of the house, furnished with a restored Edwardian music stand and her mother's baby grand piano. Jamie opened his music case and extracted a thin album of music, which he handed to Isabel for examination. She flicked through the pages and smiled. It was exactly the sort of music that he always chose, settings of Burns, arias from Gilbert and Sullivan, and, of course, "O mio babbino caro."

"Just right for your voice," Isabel said. "As usual."

Jamie blushed. "I'm not much good at the newer stuff," he said. "Remember that Britten? I couldn't do it."

Isabel was quick to reassure him. "I like these," she said. "They're much easier to play than Britten."

She paged through the book again and made her choice.

"'Take a pair of sparkling eyes'?"

"Just so," said Jamie.

She began the introduction and Jamie, standing in his singing pose, head tilted slightly forward so as not to restrict the larynx, gave voice to the song. Isabel played with determination—which was the only way to play Gilbert and Sullivan, she thought—and they finished with a flourish that was not exactly in the music but that could have been there if Sullivan had bothered. Then it was Burns, and "John Anderson, My Jo."

John Anderson, she thought. Yes. A reflection on the passage of the years, and of love that survives. *But blessings on your frosty pow, John Anderson, my jo.* There was an ineffable sadness in this line that always made her catch her breath. This was Burns in his gentler mood, addressing a constancy that by all accounts, including his own, eluded him in his own relations with women. What a hypocrite! Or was he? Was there anything wrong with celebrating qualities one lacked oneself? Surely not. People who suffered from *akrasia* (which philosophers knew all about and enjoyed debating at great length) could still profess that it was better to do that which they themselves could not do. You can say that it is bad to overindulge in chocolate, or wine, or any of the other things in which people like to overindulge, and still overindulge yourself. The important thing, surely, is not to conceal your own overindulgence.

"John Anderson" was meant to be sung by a woman, but men could sing it if they wished. And in a way it was even more touching when sung by a man, as it could be about a male friendship too. Not that men liked to talk—still less to sing—about such things, which was something which had always puzzled Isabel. Women were so much more natural in their friendships, and in their acceptance of what their friendships meant to them. Men were so different: they kept their friends at arm's length and never admitted their feelings for them. How *arid* it must be to be a man; how constrained; what a whole world of emotion, and sympathy, they must lack; like living in the desert. And yet how many exceptions there were; how marvellous, for example, it must be to be Jamie, with that remarkable face of his, so full of feeling, like the face of one of those young men in Florentine Renaissance paintings.

"John Anderson," said Isabel, as she played the last chord, and the music faded away. "I was thinking of you and John Anderson. Your friend John Anderson."

"I never had one," said Jamie. "I never had a friend like that."

Isabel looked up from the music, and out the window. It was beginning to get dark, and the branches of the trees were silhouetted against a pale evening sky.

"Nobody? Not even as a boy? I thought boys had passionate friendships. David and Jonathan."

Jamie shrugged. "I had friends. But none I stuck to for years and years. Nobody I could sing that about."

"How sad," said Isabel. "And do you not regret it?"

Jamie thought for a moment. "I suppose I do," he said. "I'd like to have lots of friends."

"You could get lots of friends," said Isabel. "You people—at your age—you can make friends so easily."

"But I don't," said Jamie. "I just want . . ."

"Of course," said Isabel. She lowered the keyboard cover and rose to her feet.

"We shall go through for dinner now," she said. "That's what we shall do. But first . . ."

She turned back to the piano and began to play once more, and Jamie smiled. "Soave sia il vento," may the breeze be gentle, the breeze that takes your vessel on its course; may the waves be calm. An aria more divine than anything else ever written, thought Isabel, and expressing such a kind sentiment too, what one might wish for anybody, and oneself too, although one knew that sometimes it was not like that, that sometimes it was quite different.

AT THE END of their dinner, which they ate in the kitchen, seated at the large pine refectory table which Isabel used for informal dinners—the kitchen being warmer than the rest of the house—Jamie remarked: "There's something you said back there in the music room. You told me about this man, John what's-he-called . . ."

"Liamor. John Liamor."

Jamie tried out the name. "Liamor. Not an easy name, is it, because the tongue has to go up for the *li* and then depress itself for the *ah,* and then the lips have to do some work. *Dalhousie*'s much easier. But anyway, what you said has made me think."

Isabel reached for her coffee cup. "I'm happy to be thought provocative."

"Yes," Jamie went on. "How exactly does one get involved with somebody who doesn't make you happy? He didn't make you happy, did he?"

Isabel looked down at her place mat—a view of the Firth of Forth from the wrong side, from Fife. "No, he did not. He made me very unhappy."

"But did you not see that near the beginning?" asked Jamie. "I don't want to pry, but I'm curious. Didn't you see what it was going to be like?"

Isabel looked up at him. She had had that brief discussion with Grace, but it was not something that she really talked about. And what was there to say, anyway, but to acknowledge that one loved the wrong person and carried on loving the wrong person in the hope that something would change?

"I was rather smitten by him," she said quietly. "I loved him so much. He was the only person I really wanted to see, to be with. And the rest didn't seem to matter so much because of the pain that I knew I'd feel if I gave him up. So I persisted, as people do. They persist."

"And . . ."

"And one day—we were in Cambridge—he asked me to go

with him to Ireland, where he came from. He was going to spend a few weeks with his parents, who lived in Cork. And I agreed to go, and that, I suppose, was when I made the real mistake."

She paused. She had not imagined that she would talk to Jamie about this, as it would be admitting him to something that she would rather have kept from him. But he sat there, and looked at her expectantly, and she decided to continue.

"You don't know Ireland, do you? Well, let me tell you that they have a very clear idea of who they are and who everybody else is, and what the difference is. John had been a great mocker at Cambridge—he laughed at all the middle-class people he saw about him. He called them petty and small-minded. And then, when we arrived at his parents' place in Cork, it was a middle-class bungalow with a Sacred Heart on the kitchen wall. And his mother did her best to freeze me out. That was awful. We had a flaming row after I came right out and asked her whether she disliked me most because I wasn't a Catholic or because I wasn't Irish. I asked her which it was."

Jamie smiled. "And which was it?"

Isabel hesitated. "She said . . . she said, this horrible woman, she said that it was because I was a slut."

She looked up at Jamie, who stared back at her wide-eyed. Then he smiled. "What a . . ." He trailed off.

"Yes, she was, and so I insisted to John that we leave, and we went off to Kerry and ended up in a hotel down there, where he asked me to marry him. He said that if we were married, then we could get a college house when we went back to Cambridge. So I said yes. And then he said that we would get a genuine Irish priest to do that, a 'reversed' as he called them. And I pointed out that he didn't believe, and so why ask for a priest? And then he replied that the priest wouldn't believe either."

She paused. Jamie had picked up his table napkin and was folding it. "I'm sorry," he said simply. "I'm sorry about all that. I shouldn't have asked you, should I?"

"I don't mind," said Isabel. "But it does show how these big decisions are just drifted into in a rather messy way. And that we can be very wrong about everything. Don't be wrong in your life, Jamie. Don't get it all wrong."

CHAPTER EIGHT

THE MESSAGE WAS TAKEN by Grace the following morning, when Isabel was out in the garden. The address she was looking for was 48, Warrender Park Terrace, fourth floor right. The name on the door would be Duffus, which was the name of the girl who had shared with Mark Fraser. She was called Henrietta Duffus, but was known as Hen, and the man, the third of the original three flatmates, was Neil Macfarlane. That was all that Cat had managed to come up with, but it was all that she had asked Cat to find out.

Grace passed on the information to Isabel with a quizzical look, but Isabel decided not to tell her what it was about. Grace had firm views on inquisitiveness and was inevitably discreet in her dealings. She would undoubtedly have considered any en- quiries which Isabel was planning to make to be quite unwar- ranted, and would have made a comment along those lines. So Isabel was silent.

She had decided to visit the flatmates that evening, as there would be no point in calling during the day, when they would be at work. For the rest of that day she worked on the review, read- ing several submissions which had arrived in that morning's post.

This was an important screening process. Like any journal, no matter how academic, the review received contributions that were completely unsuitable and which need not even be sent off to a specialist reader. That morning, though, had brought five serious articles, and these would have to be looked at carefully. She settled down at first to a carefully argued piece on rule utilitarianism in the legislative process, leaving the spicier "Truth Telling in Sexual Relationships: A Challenge to Kant" for later in the morning. That was one for after coffee, she thought; she liked to savour criticism of Kant.

The day passed quickly. The rule utilitarianism article was weighty, but largely unreadable, owing to the author's style. It appeared to be written in English, but it was a variety of English which Isabel felt occurred only in certain corners of academia, where faux weightiness was a virtue. It was, she thought, as if the English had been translated from German; not that the verbs all migrated to the end, it was just that everything sounded so *heavy*, so utterly earnest.

It was tempting to exclude the unintelligible paper on the grounds of grammatical obfuscation, and then to write to the author—in simple terms—and explain to him why this was being done. But she had seen his name and his institution on the title page of the article, and she knew that there would be repercussions if she did this. Harvard!

"Truth Telling in Sexual Relationships" was more clearly written, but said nothing surprising. We should tell the truth, the author argued, but not the whole truth. There were occasions when hypocrisy was necessary in order to protect the feelings of others. (It was as if the author were echoing her own recently articulated thought on the subject.) So we should not tell our lovers that they are inadequate lovers—if that is what they are.

Quite clearly only if that is what they are, thought Isabel. The limits to honesty in that department were particularly severe, and rightly so.

She read the article with some amusement, and thought that it would make a lively read for the review's subscribers, who perhaps needed a bit of *encouragement*. The philosophy of sex was an unusual area of applied ethics, but it had its exponents, who met, she knew, at an annual conference in the United States. The review had occasionally published advance notice of these meetings, but she had wondered whether these bland few sentences gave the full story: *morning session: Sexual Semiotics and Private Space; coffee; Perversion and Autonomy; lunch* (for there were other appetites to consider), and so on into the afternoon. The abstracts of the papers were probably accurate enough, but what, might one wonder, went on *afterwards* at such a conference? These people were not prudes, she suspected, and they were, after all, *applied* ethicists.

Isabel herself was no prude, but she believed very strongly in discretion in sexual matters. In particular, she was doubtful about when it was right, if ever, to publish details of one's own sexual affairs. Would the other person have consented? she wondered; probably not, and in that case one did another a wrong by writing about what was essentially a private matter between two people. There were two classes of persons upon whom a duty of virtually absolute confidentiality rested: doctors and lovers. You should be able to tell your doctor anything, safe in the knowledge that what you said would not go beyond the walls within which it was said, and the same should be true of your lover. And yet this notion was under attack: the state wanted information from doctors (about your genes, about your sexual habits, about your childhood illnesses), and doctors had to resist. And the vulgar curious, of whom there were countless legions, wanted information about your sexual life, and would pay generously to hear it—if you were sufficiently well known. Yet people were entitled to their secrets, to their sense that at least there was some part of their life which they could regard as ultimately, intimately private; because if they were denied this privacy, then the very self was diminished. Let people have their secrets, Isabel thought, although probably unfashionably.

Unfortunately philosophers were notable offenders when it came to self-disclosure. Bertrand Russell had done this, with his revealing diaries, and A. J. Ayer too. Why did these philosophers imagine that the public should be interested in whether or not they slept with somebody, and how often? Were they trying to prove something? Would she have resisted Bertrand Russell? she wondered; and answered her own question immediately. Yes. And A. J. Ayer too.

By six o'clock the backlog of articles had been cleared and covering letters had been written to referees in respect of those which were going to be taken to the next stage. She had decided that six-thirty would be the ideal time to call at number 48, Warrender Park Terrace, as this would give the flatmates time to return from work (whatever that was) and yet would not interfere with their dinner arrangements. Leaving her library, she went through to the kitchen and made herself a cup of coffee before setting off.

It was not a long walk to Warrender Park Terrace, which lay just beyond the triangle of park at the end of Bruntsfield Avenue. She took her time, looking in shopwindows before finally strolling across the grass to the end of the terrace. Although it was a pleasant spring evening, a stiff breeze had arisen and the clouds were scudding energetically across the sky, towards Norway. This was a northern light, the light of a city that belonged as much to the great, steely plains of the North Sea as it did to the soft hills of its hinterland. This was not Glasgow, with its soft, western light, and its proximity to Ireland and to the Gaeldom of the Highlands. This was a townscape raised in the teeth of cold winds from the east; a city of winding cobbled streets and haughty pillars; a city of dark nights and candlelight, and intellect.

She reached Warrender Park Terrace and followed it round its slow curve. It was a handsome street, occupying one side of the road and looking out over the Meadows and the distant pinnacled roofs and spires of the old infirmary. The building, a high tenement in the Victorian manner, rose in six stories of dressed stone, topped with a high-raked slate roof. Some of these roofs were bordered with turrets, like the slated turrets of French châteaux, with ironwork devices at the point. Or the edge of the roofs had stone crenellations, carved thistles, the occasional gargoyle, all of which would have given the original occupants the sense that they were living in some style, and that all that distinguished their dwellings from those of the gentry was mere size. But in spite of these conceits, they were good flats, solidly built, and although originally intended for petit-bourgeois occupation they had become the preserve of students and young professionals. The flat she was visiting must have been typical of numerous such establishments rented by groups of three or four young people. The generous size of the flats made it possible for each tenant to have his or her own room without impinging upon the largish living room and dining room. It would be a comfortable arrangement, which would serve the residents until marriage or cohabitation beckoned. And of course such flats were the breeding ground of lasting friendships—and lasting enmities too, she supposed.

The flats were built around a common stone staircase, to

which access would be gained by an imposing front door. These doors were usually locked, but could be opened from the flats above by the pressing of a button. Isabel looked at the range of bells at the front door and found one labelled "Duffus." She pushed it and waited. After a minute or so a voice sounded through the small speaker of the intercom and asked her what she wanted.

Isabel bent to speak into the tiny microphone on the intercom box. She gave her name and explained that she would like to speak to Miss Duffus. It was in connection with the accident, she added.

There was a brief pause, and then the buzzer sounded. Isabel pushed the door open and began to climb up the stairs, noting that stale, slightly dusty smell which seemed to hang in the air of so many common stairs. It was the smell of stone which has been wet and now has dried, coupled with the slight odour of cooking that would waft out of individual flats. It was a smell that reminded her of childhood, when she had gone every week up such a stairway to her piano lessons at the house of Miss Marilyn McGibbon—Miss McGibbon, who had referred to music which *starred* her; which meant she was stirred. Isabel still thought of *starring* music.

She paused, and stood still for a moment, remembering Miss McGibbon, whom she had liked as a child, but from whom she had picked up, even as a child, a sense of sadness, of something unresolved. Once she had arrived for her lesson and had found her red-eyed, with marks of tears on the powder which she applied to her face, and had stared at her mutely until Miss McGibbon had turned away, mumbling: "I am not myself. I apologise. I am not myself this afternoon."

And Isabel had said: "Has something sad happened?"

Miss McGibbon had started to say yes, but had changed it to

no, and had shaken her head, and they had turned to the scales which Isabel had learned and to Mozart, and nothing more had been said. Later, as a young adult, she had learned quite by chance that Miss McGibbon had lost her friend and companion, one Lalla Gordon, the daughter of a judge of the Court of Session, who had been forced to choose between her family (who disapproved of Miss McGibbon) and her friendship, and who had chosen the former.

THE FLAT WAS ON the fourth floor and by the time that Isabel had reached the landing, the door was already slightly ajar. A young woman was standing just within the hall, and she opened the door as Isabel approached. Isabel smiled at her, taking in at a glance Hen Duffus's appearance: tall, almost willowy, and wide-eyed in that appealing, doelike way which Isabel always associated with girls from the west coast of Scotland, but which presumably had nothing to do with that at all. Her smile was returned as Hen asked her to come in. Yes, Isabel thought as she heard the accent: the west, although not Glasgow, as Cat had said, but somewhere small and couthy, Dunbarton perhaps, Helensburgh at a stretch. But she was definitely not a Henrietta; Hen, yes; that was far more suitable.

"I'm sorry to come unannounced. I hoped I might just find you in. You and . . ."

"Neil. I don't think he's in. But he should be back soon."

Hen closed the door behind them and pointed to a door down the hallway. "We can go through there," she said. "It's the usual mess, I'm afraid."

"No need to apologise," said Isabel. "We all live in a mess. It's more comfortable that way."

"I'd like to be tidy," said Hen. "I try, but I guess you can't be what you aren't."

Isabel smiled, but said nothing. There was a physicality about this woman, an air of . . . well, sexual energy. It was unmistakable, like musicality, or asceticism. She was made for untidy rooms and rumpled beds.

The living room, into which Hen led Isabel, looked out to the north, over the trees that lined the southern edge of the Meadows. The windows, which were generous Victorian, must have flooded the room with light in the day; even now, in the early evening, the room needed no lights. Isabel crossed the room to stand before one of the windows. She looked down. Below them on the cobbled street, a boy dragged a reluctant dog on a lead. The boy bent down and struck the dog on the back, and the animal turned round in self-defence. Then the boy kicked it in the ribs and dragged on the lead again.

Hen joined her at the window and looked down too. "He's a wee brat, that boy. I call him Soapy Soutar. He lives in the ground-floor flat with his mother and a bidie-in. I don't think that dog likes any of them."

Isabel laughed. She appreciated the reference to Soapy Soutar; every Scottish child used to know about Oor Wullie and his friends Soapy Soutar and Fat Boab, but did they now? Where do the images of Scottish childhood come from now? Not, she thought, from the streets of Dundee, those warm, mythical streets which the *Sunday Post* peopled with pawky innocents.

They turned away from the window and Hen looked at Isabel. "Why have you come to see us? You aren't a journalist, are you?"

Isabel shook her head vigorously. "Certainly not. No, I was a witness. I saw it happen."

Hen stared at her. "You were there? You saw Mark fall?"

"I'm afraid I did."

Hen looked behind her for a seat and sat down. She looked down at the floor, and for a moment she said nothing. Then she raised her eyes. "I don't really like to think of it, you know. It's only a few weeks, and I'm already trying to forget about it. But it's not easy, when you lose a flatmate like that."

"Of course. I can understand."

"We had the police round, you know. They came and asked about Mark. Then we had his parents, to come and take his things away. You can imagine what that was like."

"Yes I can."

"And there were other people," Hen went on. "Mark's friends. Somebody from his office. It went on and on."

Isabel sat down on the sofa, next to Hen. "And now me. I'm sorry to intrude. I can imagine what all this is like."

"Why did you come?" asked Hen. It was not said in an unfriendly way, but there was an edge to the question that Isabel picked up. It was exhaustion perhaps; exhaustion in the face of another interrogation.

"I had no real reason," Isabel said quietly. "I suppose it's because I was involved in it and I had nobody to talk to about it— nobody connected with it, if you see what I mean. I saw this thing happen—this horrible thing—and I knew nobody who knew any-thing about him, about Mark." She paused. Hen was watching her with her wide almond eyes. Isabel believed what she was say-ing, but was it the whole truth? And yet she could hardly tell these people that the reason why she was here was sheer curios-ity about what happened; that, and a vague suspicion that there was something more to the incident.

Hen closed her eyes, then nodded. "I understand," she said. "That's fine with me. In a way I'd like to hear about what actually happened. I've imagined it enough."

"You don't mind then?"

"No, I don't mind. If it's going to help you, then that's all right with me." She reached out and touched Isabel's arm. The sympathetic gesture was unexpected, and Isabel felt—unworthily, she thought—that it was out of character. "I'll make some coffee," Hen went on, rising to her feet. "Then we can talk."

Hen left the room, and Isabel leant back into the sofa and looked about her. It was well furnished, unlike many rented flats, which quickly develop a well-used look. There were prints on the wall—the landlord's taste, presumably mixed with that of the tenants: a view of the Falls of Clyde (landlord); *A Bigger Splash,* by Hockney, and *Amateur Philosophers,* by Vettriano (tenants); and *Iona,* by Peploe (landlord). She smiled at the Vettriano—he was deeply disapproved of by the artistic establishment in Edinburgh, but he remained resolutely popular. Why was this? Because his figurative paintings said something about people's lives (at least about the lives of people who danced on the beach in formal clothing); they had a narrative in the same way in which Edward Hopper's paintings did. That was why there were so many poems inspired by Hopper; it was because there was a now-read-on note to everything he painted. Why are the people there? What are they thinking of? What are they going to do now? Hockney, of course, left nothing unanswered. It was very clear what everybody was about in a Hockney picture: swimming, and sex, and narcissism. Had Hockney drawn WHA? She remembered that he had; and he had captured rather well the geological catastrophe that was WHA's face. *I am like a map of Iceland.* Had he said that? She thought not, but he could have. She would write a book one day about quotations which were entirely apocryphal but which could be attributed to people who might have said just that. *I've reigned all afternoon, and now it's snowing.* Queen Victoria.

She had been staring at the Vettriano and now looked away and through the door. There was a mirror in the hall—a long dress mirror of the sort more usually found on the back of wardrobe doors. From where she was sitting she had an unimpeded view of it, and at that precise moment she saw a young man dart out of a door, cross the hall, and disappear into another room. He did not see her, though it seemed as if he was aware of her presence in the flat. And it seemed, too, that he had not intended that she should see him, which she would not have done, save for the strategically placed mirror. And he was quite naked.

After a few minutes Hen returned, carrying two cups. She placed the cups on the table in front of the sofa and sat down next to Isabel again. "Did you ever meet Mark?"

Isabel was on the point of saying yes, for it seemed to her, bizarrely, as if she had, but shook her head instead. "That was the first time I saw him. That night."

"He was a really good guy," said Hen. "He was great. Everyone liked him."

"I'm sure they did," said Isabel.

"I was a bit unsure to begin with, you know, living with two people I hadn't met before. But I took the room here at the same time as they got it. So we all started off together."

"And it worked?"

"Yes, it worked. We had the occasional argument, as one would expect. But never anything serious. It worked very well." Hen picked up her cup and sipped at the coffee. "I miss him."

"And Neil, your flatmate? They were friends?"

"Of course," said Hen. "They sometimes played golf together, although Neil was too good for Mark. Neil is almost a scratch player. He could have been a professional, you know. He's a trainee lawyer with a firm in the West End. Stuffy place, but they all are, aren't they? This is Edinburgh after all."

Isabel picked up her coffee cup and took her first sip. It was instant, but she would try to drink it, out of politeness.

"What happened?" she said quietly. "What do you think happened?"

Hen shrugged. "He fell. That's all that could have happened. One of those freak accidents. He looked over for some reason and fell. What else?"

"Might he have been unhappy?" said Isabel. She made the suggestion cautiously, as it could have been met with an angry response, but it was not.

"You mean suicide?"

"Yes. That."

Hen shook her head. "Definitely not. I would have known. I just would. He wasn't unhappy."

Isabel considered Hen's words. "I would have known." Why would she have known? Because she lived with him; that was the obvious reason. One picked up the moods of those with whom one lived in close proximity.

"So there were no signs of that?"

"No. None." Hen paused. "He just wasn't like that. Suicide is a cop-out. He faced up to things. He was . . . You could count on him. He was reliable. He had a conscience. You know what I mean?"

Isabel watched her as she spoke; the word "conscience" was not one which one heard very much anymore, which was strange, and ultimately worrying. It had to do with the disappearance of guilt from people's lives, which was no bad thing, in one sense, as guilt had caused such a mountain of unnecessary unhappiness.

But there was still a role for guilt in moral action, as a necessary disincentive. Guilt underlined wrong; it made the moral life possible. That apart, there was another aspect to what Hen had said. The words were uttered with conviction, but they could only have been spoken by one who had never been depressed, or gone through a period of self-doubt.

"Sometimes people who are very clear about things on the outside are not so sure inside . . . they can be very unhappy, but never show it. There are . . ." She trailed off. Hen clearly did not appreciate being spoken to in this way. "I'm sorry. I didn't mean to lecture you . . ."

Hen smiled. "That's all right. You're probably right—in general, but not in this case. I really don't think it was suicide."

"I'm sure you're right," said Isabel. "You obviously knew him very well."

For a few moments there was a silence, as Hen sipped at her coffee, apparently deep in thought, and Isabel looked at the Vettriano, wondering what to say next. There seemed little point in continuing the conversation; she was not going to learn much more from Hen, who had probably said as much as she wanted to say and who was, in Isabel's view, not very perceptive anyway.

Hen put her cup down on the table. Isabel moved her gaze from the oddly disturbing picture. The young man whom she had seen in the corridor was now entering the room, fully clothed.

"This is Neil," said Hen.

Isabel rose to shake hands with the young man. The palm of his hand was warm, and slightly moist, and she thought: He's been in the shower. That was why he had been dashing naked across the hall. Perhaps that was not unusual these days; that flatmates, casual friends, should wander about unclothed, in perfect innocence, as children in Eden.

Neil sat down on the chair opposite the sofa while Hen explained why Isabel was there.

"I don't mean to intrude," said Isabel. "I just wanted to talk about it. I hope you don't mind."

"No," said Neil. "I don't mind. If you want to talk about it, that's fine with me."

Isabel glanced at him. His voice was very different from Hen's; from the other side of the country, she thought, but disclosing an expensive education somewhere. He was Hen's age, she thought, or perhaps slightly older, and like her he had a slightly outdoors look to him. Of course, he was the golfer, and what she was seeing was the effect of time spent on blustery Scottish fairways.

"I don't think I should burden you much more," said Isabel. "I've met you. I've talked about what happened. I should let you get on with things."

"Has it helped?" asked Hen, exchanging a glance, Isabel noted, with Neil. The meaning of the glance was quite clear, Isabel thought: she would say to him afterwards, "Why did she have to come? What was the point of all that?" And she would say that because she was nothing to that young woman; she was a woman in her forties, out of it, not real, of no interest.

"I'll take your cup," said Hen suddenly, rising to her feet. "I have to get something going in the kitchen. Excuse me a minute."

"I must go," said Isabel, but she remained on the sofa when Hen had gone out of the room, and she looked at Neil, who was watching her, his hands resting loosely on the arms of the chair.

"Do you think that he jumped?" Isabel asked.

His face was impassive, but there was something disconcerting in his manner, an uneasiness. "Jumped?"

"Committed suicide?"

Neil opened his mouth to say something, but then closed it again. He stared at Isabel.

"I'm sorry to ask you that," she went on. "I can see that you think the answer is no. Well, you're probably right."

"Probably," he said quietly.

"May I ask you another thing?" she said, and then, before her question could be answered, "Hen said that Mark was popular. But might there have been anybody who disliked him?"

The question had been uttered, and now she watched him. She saw his eyes move, to look down at the floor, and then up again. When he answered he did not look at her, but stared out the door, into the hall, as if to look for Hen to answer the question for him.

"I don't think so. No. I don't think so."

Isabel nodded. "So there really was nothing . . . nothing unusual in his life?"

"No. Nothing unusual."

He looked at her now, and she saw in his eyes a look of dislike. He felt—and who could blame him for this?—that it was none of her business to go prying into his friend's life. She had clearly outstayed her welcome, as Hen had made apparent, and now she would have to leave. She rose to her feet, and he followed her example.

"I'd just like to say good-bye to Hen," she said, moving into the hall, followed by Neil. She looked about her quickly. The door out of which he had darted when she had by chance looked into the mirror must be the door immediately to her right.

"She's in the kitchen, isn't she?" she said, turning and pushing open the door.

"That's not it," he called after her. "That's Hen's room."

But Isabel had taken a step forward and saw the large bed-room, with its bedside lamp on and its closed curtain, and the unmade bed.

"Oh," she said. "I'm sorry."

"The kitchen's over here," he said sharply. "That door there." He looked at her sideways. He was nervous, she thought; nervous and hostile.

She withdrew, and walked over to the door which he had indicated. She found Hen, who was embarrassed to be seen sitting on a stool reading a magazine. But she thanked her profusely, and said good-bye, and then left the flat, to the sound of Neil locking the door behind her. She had left them her card, and had said that they could contact her if they ever wanted to, but they had looked at it doubtfully, and she knew that they would not. She had felt awkward and foolish, which, she now thought, was how she deserved to feel. But at least something had become clear.

Hen and Neil were lovers, which was why he had been in her room when she had rung the bell downstairs. Hen had told her that Neil was not yet home, but then she could hardly have explained to her, a complete stranger, that he was in her bed, and at that hour. Of course this vindicated her instinct about Hen, but it had little bearing on her knowledge of how they had lived together, the three of them. It could be, of course, that Mark had felt excluded. Hen implied that she had not known the other two when she first moved into the flat, and this meant that at some point the relationship had become one of more intimate cohabi-tation. This might have changed the dynamics of their communal life, from a community of three friends to one of a couple and a friend. Alternatively, it was possible that Hen and Neil had fallen into each other's arms after Mark's death, for comfort and solace in their shared sorrow, perhaps. She could imagine that this might have been the case, but again it made no difference to her understanding of what might have been going through Mark's head on that evening at the Usher Hall. If she had known him hardly at all before she called on the flat in Warrender Park Terrace, she did not know him any better now. He had been a pleasant young man, popular and not given to self-doubt; no surprise, perhaps, as self-doubt is the territory of the teenager and, much later, of the failing, not of young men in their twenties. If he had been concerned about something, then his concern must have been hidden from those who were closest to him in his daily life.

She walked home slowly. It was a warm evening for the time of year, an evening that had in it just the smallest hint of summer, and there were others making their way home too. Most of them had people to go to, husbands, wives, lovers, parents. Her house awaited her, large and empty, which she knew was the result of choices she had made, but which perhaps were not entirely to be laid at her door. She had not deliberately chosen to fall in love so completely, and so finally, that thereafter no other man would have done. That was something which had happened to her, and the things that happen to us are not always of our making. John Liamor happened, and that meant that she lived with a sentence. She did not ponder it unduly, nor speak to others of it (although she had spoken to Jamie, unwisely perhaps, the previous evening). It was just how things were, and she made the most of it, which was the moral duty which she thought that all of us had, at least if one believed in duties to self, which she did. If x, then y. But y?

CHAPTER NINE

THE FOLLOWING WEEK was uneventful. There was a small amount of work to be done for the review, but with the proofs of the next issue recently sent off to the printers, and with two members of the editorial board out of the country, Isabel was hardly overburdened. She spent much of the time reading, and she also helped Grace in a long-overdue clearing of the attic. But there was still time for thought, and she could not help but return to what she now thought of as *the event.* The feeling of rawness which had followed that evening was certainly fading, but this now seemed to be replaced by a sense of lack of resolution. Her meeting with Hen and Neil had been unsatisfactory, she decided, and now she was left with nothing more that she could do. There was to be a Fatal Accident Inquiry; she had been informed by the procurator fiscal of the date when this would be held and had been told that as the most immediate witness she would be called to give evidence, but the fiscal had implied that it would be an open-and-shut case.

"I don't think that there's much doubt," he said. "We've had evidence that the height of the rail is perfectly adequate and that the only way in which somebody could fall over would be by leaning right over. He must have done that, for whatever reason— perhaps to see if he could see somebody downstairs. So that will be more or less that."

"Then why hold an enquiry?" she had asked, sitting before the fiscal's desk in his sparsely furnished office. He had asked her in for an interview, and she had found him in an office marked *Deaths,* a tall man with a gaunt, unhappy face. On the wall behind him there was a framed photograph. Two young men and two young women sat stiffly in chairs in front of a stone archway: *University of Edinburgh, Law Society Committee,* read the printed inscription below. One of them was the fiscal, recognisable in his lanky awkwardness. Had he hoped for, or expected, more than this job?

The fiscal looked at Isabel and then looked away. He was the deaths officer for Edinburgh. Deaths. Every day. Deaths. Small and big. Deaths. He would do it for a year, and then back to crime in some place like Airdrie or Bathgate. Every day: crime, cruelty, stretching off into retirement. "What's the current expression?" he asked, trying not to show his weariness. "Closure? To give closure?"

So that was it. There had been a totally unexpected tragedy in which nobody was to blame. She had happened to witness it, and she had done what she could to explain it to herself. At the end of the day, it remained unexplained and there was nothing more that she could do, other than to accept the situation.

And so she attempted to concentrate on her reading, which, by coincidence, was apposite to the question in hand. A new work had appeared on the limits for moral obligation—a familiar subject which had been given a twist by a group of philosophers who were prepared to argue that the whole emphasis of morality should shift from what we do to what we do not do. This was a potentially burdensome position, which would be uncomfortable for those who sought a quiet life. It required vigilance and more awareness of the needs of others than Isabel felt that she possessed. It was also the wrong position for one who wanted to forget something. The act of putting something out of one's mind, in this view, could be an act of deliberate and culpable omission.

It was a frustrating and difficult book to read—all 570 pages of it. Isabel felt tempted to put it aside, or to abandon it altogether, but to do this would be to prove the author's point. *Damn him,* she thought. *He's cornered me.*

When at last she finished the book, she shelved it, feeling a frisson of guilty excitement as she chose for it an obscure corner of a high shelf. She did this on a Saturday afternoon, and decided that her persistence with the annoying book should be rewarded with a trip into town, a visit to one or two galleries, and a cup of coffee and a pastry at a coffee bar in Dundas Street.

She travelled into town by bus. As she approached her stop, which was immediately after Queen Street, she saw Toby walking down the hill, carrying a shopping bag. It was the crushed-strawberry corduroy trousers that she noticed first, and she smiled at the thought that this was what the eye should single out, and she was still smiling when she stepped out of the bus. Toby was now twenty or thirty yards ahead of her. He had not seen her watching him from the bus, which was a relief to Isabel, as she did not feel in a mood to talk to him. But now, as she made her way down the hill a safe distance behind him, she found herself wondering what he had been doing. Shopping, obviously, but where was he going? Toby lived in Manor Place, at the other end of the New Town, and so he was not going home.

How mundane, she thought. How mundane my interest in this rather boring young man. What possible reason do I have to think about how he spends his Saturday afternoons? None. But that was an answer which merely fuelled her curiosity. It would be interesting to find out at least something about him; just to know, for example, that he liked to go to Valvona & Crolla to buy pasta. Or that he had a habit of nosing about antique shops (unlikely though that was). Perhaps she would warm to him if she knew more about him. Cat had implied that he had depths of which she was unaware, and she should at least open herself to these. (Moral duty to make an extra effort to overcome her prejudice? No. Five hundred and seventy-odd pages were firmly shelved and that subject was not up for discussion on this outing.)

Toby walked fairly quickly, and in order to keep a constant distance behind him, Isabel had to increase her pace. She saw him cross Heriot Row and continue down Dundas Street. She was now following him, vaguely aware of the ridiculousness of what she was doing, but enjoying herself nonetheless. He will not go into one of the art shops, she had told herself, and he will certainly not be interested in books. What did that leave? Perhaps the travel agency at the corner of Great King Street (a late skiing trip?).

Suddenly Toby stopped, and Isabel, deep in impermissible thought, found herself to have closed the distance between them. She stopped immediately. Toby was looking into a shop-window, peering into the glass front as if trying to make out some detail on a displayed object or the figure on a price tag. Isabel looked to her left. She was standing outside a private house rather than a shop, and so the only window which she had available to stare into was a drawing-room window. She stared, so that if Toby should turn round, he would not see her watching him.

It was an elegant, expensively furnished drawing room, typical of that part of the Georgian New Town. As Isabel looked across the fifteen feet or so of space that separated her from the window, a woman's face appeared and stared back at her in surprise. The woman had been sitting in an armchair and had been hidden from sight; now she looked out and saw another woman looking back in at her.

For a moment their eyes met. Isabel froze in her embarrassment. The woman at the window looked vaguely familiar, but she could not quite place her. For a moment neither did anything more, and then, just as an expression of annoyance began to replace the look of surprise on the householder's face, Isabel dragged her gaze away and looked at her watch. She would put on an act of absentmindedness. Halfway down Dundas Street, she suddenly stopped and tried to remember what it was that she had forgotten. She stood there, staring into space (or a small amount of space) and then she looked at her watch and remembered.

It worked. The woman inside turned away, and Isabel continued down the hill, noticing that Toby had now moved on and was about to cross the street into Northumberland Street. Isabel stopped again, this time with all the legitimacy of a shopwindow before her, and looked into this while Toby completed his crossing.

This was the moment of decision. She could stop this ridiculous pursuit now, while she was still following a route which she could claim, quite truthfully, to have been following already, or she could continue to trace Toby's steps. She hesitated for a moment and then, looking casually up and down for traffic, she sauntered across the street. But even as she did so, it occurred to her that what she was doing was quite ridiculous. She was the editor of the *Review of Applied Ethics,* and she was sidling along an Edinburgh street, in broad daylight, following a young man; she who believed in privacy, who abjured the sheer vulgarity of our nosy, prying age, was behaving like a schoolboy fantasist. Why was it that she allowed herself to get drawn into the business of others, like some sordid *gumshoe* (was that what they called them?).

Northumberland Street was one of the narrower streets in the New Town. Built on a somewhat smaller scale than the streets to the north and the south of it, it had its adherents, who liked what they tended to describe as an "intimacy." Isabel, by contrast, found it too dark—a street without outlook and without that sense of elevation and grandeur which made living in the New Town so exhilarating. Not that she would choose to live there herself, of course; she preferred the quiet of Merchiston and Morningside, and the pleasure of a garden. She looked up at the house on her right, which she knew when John Pinkerton had lived there. John, who had been an advocate and who knew more about the history of Edinburgh's architecture than most, had created a house which was flawlessly Georgian in all respects. He had been such an entertaining man, with his curious voice and his tendency to make a noise like a gobbling turkey when he cleared his throat, but had been so generous too, and had lived up to his family motto, which was simply *Be Kind*. No man had inhabited the city so fully, known all its stones; and he had been so brave on his early deathbed, singing hymns, of all things, perfectly remembered, as he remembered everything. The deathbed: she remembered now that poem that Douglas Young had written for Willie Soutar: *Twenty year beddit, and nou/the mort-claith. / Was his life warth livin? Ay / siccar it was. / He was eident, he was blye / in Scotland's cause.* Just as John had been. Scotland's cause: *Be Kind.*

Toby had slowed down now, and was almost strolling. Isabel was concerned that he might turn round at any point, and in this much smaller street, he could hardly fail to notice her. Of course, that need not be unduly embarrassing; there was no reason why she should not be walking down this particular street on a Saturday afternoon, just as he was doing. The only difference between them, she thought, was that he was clearly going somewhere and she had no idea where she would end up.

At the eastern end of Northumberland Street the road took a sharp turn down to the left and became Nelson Street, a rather more promising street, Isabel had always thought. She had known a painter who lived there, in a top-floor flat with skylights that faced north and which admitted a clear light that suffused all his paintings. She had known him and his wife well, and had often gone for dinner with them before they left to live in France. There he stopped painting, she had heard, and grew vines instead. Then he died suddenly, and his wife married a Frenchman and moved to Lyons, where her new husband was a judge. She heard from her from time to time, but after a few years the letters stopped. The judge, she was told by others, had become involved in a corruption scandal and had been sent to prison in Marseilles. The painter's widow had moved to the south to be able to visit her husband in prison, but had been too ashamed to tell any of her old friends about what had happened. Nelson Street, then, was a street of mixed associations for Isabel.

Swinging his plastic shopping bag as he walked, Toby crossed to the far side of Nelson Street, watched discreetly by a now almost loitering Isabel. He looked up at the tenement building and then briefly glanced at his watch. He was now directly outside a set of five stone steps that led up to the door of one of the ground-floor flats. Isabel saw him pause for a moment, and then he strode up the steps and pushed the button of the large brass bell to the side of the door. She held back now, taking advantage of the cover provided by a van which was parked near the corner of the street. After a moment, the door opened and she saw a young woman, dressed, she thought, in a T-shirt and jeans, come forward from the dark of the hall, momentarily into the light, and there, in Isabel's full view, lean toward Toby, put her arms round his shoulders, and kiss him.

He did not reel back; of course not. He bent forward in her arms, lowered his shopping bag to the floor, and then embraced her, pushing her gently back into the hallway. Isabel stood quite still. She had not expected this. She had expected nothing. But she had not thought that her whimsical decision of five minutes ago would have led to a conclusive affirmation of her earlier intuitions about Toby. Unfaithful.

She stood there for a few minutes more, her gaze fixed on the closed door. Then she turned away and walked back up Northumberland Street, feeling dirtied by what she had seen, and by what she had done. In such a way, and with such a heart, must people creep away from brothels or the locus of an illicit assignation; *mortal, guilty,* as WHA would have it in that grave poem in which he describes the aftermath of the carnal, when sleeping heads might lie, so innocently, upon faithless arms.

CHAPTER TEN

GRACE SAID: "I was standing there at the bus stop, waiting for a bus. They're meant to come every twelve minutes, but that's laughable. Laughable. There was a puddle of water on the road and a car went past, driven by a young man in a baseball cap, back to front, and he splashed this woman who was standing next to me. She was soaked through. Dripping. He saw it, you know. But did he stop to apologise? Of course not. What do you expect?"

"I don't expect anything," said Isabel, warming her hands round her mug of coffee. "It's the decline of civility. Or, should I say, it's the absence of civility."

"Decline, absence, same thing," Grace retorted.

"Not quite," said Isabel. "Decline means less than before. Absence means not there—maybe never was."

"Are you telling me that people used not to apologise for splashing other people?" Grace's indignation showed through. Her employer, she was convinced, was far too liberal on some matters, including young men in baseball caps.

"Some did, I expect," said Isabel soothingly. "Others didn't. There's no way of telling whether there are fewer apologisers these days than before. It's rather like policemen looking younger.

Policemen are the same age as they always were; it's just that to some of us they look younger."

Grace was not to be put off by this answer. "Well, I can tell, all right. Policemen are definitely younger, and manners have gone down the cludgie, right down. You see it every day in the street. You'd have to be blind not to notice. Boys need fathers to teach them how to behave."

The argument, which was taking place in the kitchen, was like all their discussions. Grace defended a proposition and did not move, and they usually ended with a vague concession by Isabel that the matter was very complicated and would have to be thought about, but that Grace was certainly right, up to a point.

Isabel rose to her feet. It was almost ten past nine and the morning crossword called. She picked up the newspaper from the kitchen table, and leaving Grace to continue with the folding of the washing, she made her way to the morning room. Right and wrong. Boys need fathers to teach them the difference between right and wrong. This was true, but like many of Grace's observations it was only half true. What was wrong with mothers for this role? She knew a number of mothers who had brought up sons by themselves, and brought them up well. One of her friends, deserted by her husband six weeks after the birth of her son, had made a magnificent job of his upbringing, against all the odds which single mothers face. He had turned out well, that boy, as had many others like him. *Boys need a parent* is what Grace should have said.

Toby had a father, and yet here was Toby two-timing Cat. Had his father ever said anything to him about how one should behave towards women? It was an interesting question, and Isabel had no idea about whether fathers spoke to their sons about such things. Did fathers take their sons aside and say:

"Treat women with respect"? Or was that too old-fashioned? Perhaps she could ask Jamie about this, as he certainly knew how to treat women with respect, unlike Toby.

Isabel suspected that the way men behaved towards women depended on much more complex psychological factors. It was not a question of moral knowledge, she thought; it was more a matter of confidence in self and sexual integration. A man with a fragile ego, unsure of who he is, would treat a woman as a means of combating his insecurity. A man who knew who he was and who was sure of his sexuality would be sensitive to women's feelings. He would have nothing to prove.

Toby seemed confident, though; in fact, he oozed confidence. In his case, at least, it was something else—perhaps the absence of a moral imagination. Morality depended on an understanding of the feelings of others. If one had no moral imagination—and there were such people—then one simply would not be able to empathise with them. The pain, the suffering, the unhappiness of others would not seem real, because it would not be perceived. There was nothing new in this, of course; Hume had been talking about much the same thing when he discussed sympathy and the importance of being able to experience the emotions of others. Isabel wondered whether it would be possible to communicate Hume's insight to people today by talking about vibrations. Vibrations were a New Age concept. Perhaps Hume could be explained in terms of vibrations and fields of energy, and this would make him real to people who otherwise would have no inkling of what he meant. It was an interesting possibility, but like so many other possibilities, there was no time for it. There were so many books to write—so many ideas to develop—and she had time for none of it.

People thought, quite wrongly, that Isabel had time on her

hands. They looked at her situation, that of a woman of independent means, living in a large house, looked after by a full-time housekeeper, and with a part-time job as editor of some obscure journal that presumably had flexible deadlines. How could such a person be busy? they thought. Their own lives, in jobs which made more and more demands, were quite different, they imagined.

Of course, none of these reflections, relevant though they were to the moral issues which informed her life, addressed the quandary in which she now found herself. She had, by indulging in vulgar curiosity, discovered something about Toby of which Cat was presumably ignorant. The question before her now was that utterly trite one, which must have graced the columns of countless problem pages: *My best friend's boyfriend is cheating on her. I know this, but she does not. Should I tell her?*

It may have been a familiar problem, but the answer was far from clear. She had faced it before, a long time ago, and she was not sure whether she had made the right decision. In that case, the knowledge had not been of unfaithfulness, but of illness. A man with whom she had worked, and with whom over the years she had become reasonably friendly, had developed schizophrenia. He had been unable to continue working, but had responded well to treatment. He had then met a woman, to whom he proposed, and she had accepted. Isabel had decided that this woman was very keen to get married, but had never before been asked. She was unaware of his illness, though, and Isabel had debated whether or not to tell her. Eventually she had said nothing, and the woman had been dismayed when she subsequently found out what was wrong with her husband. She had borne it well, though, and they had moved to a house on the edge of Blairgowrie, where they led a quiet, protected life. She had never said that she regretted the marriage, but had Isabel told her, she could have made a more informed choice. She might have said no to the marriage, and been happier by herself, although that would have deprived the man of that measure of contentment and security which the marriage provided.

She often thought about this, and had decided that nonintervention was the right course of action in such a case. The problem was that one just did not know enough about what would happen afterwards, either if one did nothing or if one did something. The answer, then, was to keep one's distance from those situations in which one is not directly involved. But this was surely wrong. Cat was no stranger to her, and surely a close relative was entitled to warn? What if Toby were not Toby at all, but some impostor, a life-sentence prisoner released on licence, who even now pondered some further crime? It would be absurd to say that she could not warn in such a case. Indeed she would have more than a right to speak, she would have a duty to do so.

As she sat in the morning room, the unsullied crossword before her, her mug of coffee steaming in the slightly cooler air of the glassed-in room, she wondered how she would put the matter to Cat. One thing was certain: she could not tell her that she had been following Toby, as that would, quite rightly, provoke accusations of unwarranted interference in his, and Cat's, affairs. So she would have to start the whole disclosure on the basis of a lie, or at best a half-truth.

"I happened to be in Nelson Street and happened to see . . ."

What would Cat say? She would be shocked at the outset, as anyone would be on the news of a betrayal of this nature. And then perhaps she would move to anger, which would be directed against Toby, and not against the other girl, whoever she was. Isabel had read that women usually attack their partners on discovering infidelity, while men, in the same position, will direct their hostility against the other man, the intruder. For a moment she allowed herself to imagine the scene: Toby, unsuspecting, facing an angry Cat, his self-confident expression crumbling before the onslaught; blushing as the truth was outed. And then, she hoped, Cat would storm out, and that would be the end of Toby. A few weeks later, with her wounds still raw, but not so raw as to require privacy, Jamie could visit Cat in the delicatessen and suggest a meal together. He would be sympathetic, but Isabel would have to advise him to maintain some distance and not to be too quick to try to fill the emotional void. Then they would see. If Cat had any sense, she would realise that Jamie would never deceive her, and that men like Toby were best avoided. But there the fantasy ended; the likelihood was that Cat would make the same mistake again, and more than once, as people always did. Unsuitable men were replaced by unsuitable men; it seemed inevitable. People repeated their mistakes because their choice of partner was dictated by factors beyond their control. Isabel had imbibed sufficient Freud—and more to the point, Klein—to know that the emotional die was cast at a very early age. It all went back to childhood, and to the psychodynamics of one's relationship with one's parents. These things were not a matter of intellectual assessment and rational calculation; they sprang from events in the nursery. Not that everybody had a nursery, of course, but they had an equivalent—a *space,* perhaps.

CHAPTER ELEVEN

IT WAS THAT EVENING, after a day which she regarded as utterly wasted, that Isabel received a visit from Neil, the young man with whom she had had such an unrewarding conversation on her visit to Warrender Park Terrace. He arrived unannounced, although Isabel happened to be gazing out the window of her study when he walked up the path to the font door. She saw him look upwards, at the size of the house, and she thought she saw him hesitate slightly, but he went on to ring her bell and she made her way to the front door to let him in.

He was wearing a suit and tie, and she noticed his shoes, which were highly polished black Oxfords. Hen had said, quite irrelevantly, that he worked for a stuffy firm, and the outfit confirmed this.

"Miss Dalhousie?" he said superfluously as she opened the door. "I hope you remember me. You came round the other day . . ."

"Of course I do. Neil, isn't it?"

"Yes."

She ushered him into the hall and through the drawing-room door. He declined her offer of a drink, or tea, but she poured herself a small sherry and sat down opposite him.

"Hen said you were a lawyer," she began conversationally.

"Trainee lawyer," he corrected. "Yes. That's what I do."

"Like every second person in Edinburgh," said Isabel.

"Sometimes it seems like that. Yes."

There was a momentary silence. Isabel noticed that Neil's hands were clasped over his lap, and that his position, in general, was far from relaxed. He was tense and on edge, just as he had been when he had spoken to her last time. Perhaps that was how he was. Some people were naturally tense, coiled up like springs, suspicious of the world about them.

"I came to see you . . ." He trailed off.

"Yes," said Isabel brightly. "So I see."

Neil attempted a quick smile, but did not persist. "I came to see you about . . . about what we talked about the other day. I did not tell you the whole truth, I'm afraid. It's been preying on my mind."

Isabel watched him closely. The muscular tension in the face aged him, making lines about the corners of his mouth. The palms of his hands would be moist, she thought. She said nothing, but waited for him to continue.

"You asked me—you asked me quite specifically whether there was anything unusual in his life. Do you remember?"

Isabel nodded. She looked down at the sherry glass in her right hand and took a small sip. It was very dry; too dry, Toby had said when she had given him a glass. Too dry and it gets bitter, you know.

"And then I said that there was nothing," Neil went on. "Which was not true. There was."

"Now you want to tell me about it?"

Neil nodded. "I felt very bad about misleading you. I don't know why I did it. I suppose I just felt annoyed that you had come round to talk to us. I felt that it was none of your business."

Which it isn't, thought Isabel, but did not say it.

"You see," said Neil, "Mark said to me that there was something happening. He was scared."

Isabel felt her pulse race. Yes, she had been right. There had been something; Mark's death was not what it had seemed to be. It had a background.

Neil unclasped his hands. Now that he had started to speak, some of the tension appeared to dissipate, even if he still did not appear relaxed.

"You know that Mark worked for a firm of fund managers," he said. "McDowell's. They're quite a large firm these days. They handle a lot of big pension funds, and one or two smaller people. They're a well-known firm."

"I knew that," said Isabel.

"Well, in that job you see a lot of money moving. You have to watch things pretty closely."

"So I believe," said Isabel.

"And you have to be particularly careful about how you behave," Neil said. "There's something called insider trading. Do you know about that?"

Isabel explained that she had heard of the term, but was not sure exactly what it meant. Was it something to do with buying shares on the basis of inside information?

Neil nodded. "That's more or less what it is. You may get information in your job which allows you to predict the movement of share prices. If you know that a firm is going to be taken over, for example, that may send up the share price. If you buy in advance of the news getting out, then you make a profit. It's simple."

"I can imagine," said Isabel. "And I can imagine the temptation."

"Yes," agreed Neil. "It's very tempting. I've even been in a position myself to do it. I assisted in drafting an offer which I knew would have an effect on the value of the shares. It would have been simple for me to get somebody to buy some shares on my behalf. Dead simple. I could have made thousands."

"But you didn't?"

"You go to prison if you're caught," Neil said. "They take it very seriously. It's because you're getting an unfair advantage over the people who are selling the shares to you. You know something that they don't. It undermines the market principle."

"And you say that Mark had seen this happen?"

"Yes," said Neil. "He told me one evening, when we were in the pub together. He said that he had discovered insider trading going on in the firm. He said that he was completely sure of his facts, and he had the means of proving it. But then he said something else."

Isabel put down her sherry glass. It was obvious where this disclosure was going, and she felt uncomfortable.

"He said that he was worried that the people who were doing it knew that he had found out. He had been treated strangely, almost with suspicion, and he had been given a very strange little pep talk—a pep talk about confidentiality and duty to the firm— which he had interpreted as a veiled warning."

He looked up at Isabel, and she saw something in his eyes. What was it saying? Was it a plea for help? Was it the expression of some private agony, a sadness that he was unable to articulate?

"Was that all?" she asked. "Did he tell you who gave him this talk, this warning?"

Neil shook his head. "No, he didn't. He said that he couldn't say very much about it. But I could tell that he was frightened."

Isabel rose from her chair and crossed the room to close the curtains. As she did so, the movement of the material made a soft noise, like the breaking of a small wave on the beach. Neil watched her from where he was sitting. Then she returned to her chair.

"I don't know what you want me to do with this," she said. "Have you thought of going to the police?"

Her question seemed to make him tense once again. "I can't do that," he said. "They have already spoken to me several times. I told them nothing about this. I just told them what I told you the first time I spoke to you. If I went back now, it would look odd. I would effectively be saying that I had lied to them."

"And they may not like that," mused Isabel. "They could start thinking you had something to hide, couldn't they?"

Neil stared at her. Again there was that strange expression in his eyes. "I've got nothing to hide."

"Of course," said Isabel quickly, although she knew that this was not true; that he was concealing something. "It's just that once you don't tell the truth, then people begin to think that there may be a reason."

"There was no reason," said Neil, his voice now slightly raised. "I didn't talk about this because I knew very little about it. I thought that it had nothing to do with . . . with what happened. I didn't want to spend hours with the police. I just wanted everything to be over. I thought it might be simpler just to keep my mouth shut."

"Sometimes that is much simpler," said Isabel. "Sometimes it isn't." She looked at him, and he lowered his eyes. She felt pity for him now. He was a very ordinary young man, not particularly sensitive, not particularly aware. And yet he had lost a friend, somebody with whom he actually lived, and he must be feeling that much more than she, who had only witnessed the accident.

She looked at him. He seemed vulnerable, and there was an air to him that made her think of something else, another possibility. Perhaps there had been a dimension to his relationship with Mark that was not immediately obvious to her. It was even possible that he and Mark had been lovers; it was not all that unusual, she reflected, for people to be capable of sexual involvement with either sex, and although she had glimpsed him in Hen's room, that need not mean that there had not previously been different permutations in that flat.

"You miss him, don't you?" she said quietly, watching the effect on him of her words.

He looked away, as if studying one of the pictures on the wall. For a few moments he said nothing, and then he answered, "I miss him a great deal. I miss him every day. I think of him all the time. All the time."

He had answered her question, and answered her doubts.

"Don't try to forget him," she said. "People sometimes say that. They say that we should try to forget the people we lose. But we really shouldn't, you know."

He nodded and looked back at her briefly, before he looked away again, in misery, she thought.

"It was very good of you to come this evening," she said gently. "It's never easy to come and tell somebody that you were keeping something from them. Thank you, Neil."

She had not intended this to be a signal for him to leave, but that was how he interpreted it. He rose to his feet and put out a hand to shake hands with her. She stood up and took the proffered hand, noting that it was trembling.

AFTER NEIL HAD GONE she sat in the drawing room, her empty sherry glass at her side, mulling over what her visitor had said. The unexpected meeting had disturbed her in more ways than one. Neil was more upset than she had imagined by what had happened to Mark and was unable to resolve his feelings.

There was nothing that she could do about that, because he was clearly not prepared to speak about whatever it was that was troubling him. He would recover, of course, but time could provide the only solution for that. Much more disturbing had been the disclosures about insider trading at McDowell's. She felt that she could not ignore this, now that she had been made aware of it, and although whether or not the firm engaged in that particular form of dishonesty (or was it greed?) had nothing directly to do with her, it became her concern if this had some bearing on Mark's death. *A bearing on Mark's death:* What precisely did this mean? Did it mean that he had been murdered? This was the first time that she had allowed herself to spell out the possibility that clearly. But the question could not be evaded now.

Had Mark been sent to his death because he had threatened to disclose damaging information about somebody in the firm? It seemed outrageous even to pose the question. This was the Scottish financial community, with all its reputation for uprightness and integrity. These people played golf; they frequented the New Club; they were elders—some of them—of the Church of Scotland. She thought of Paul Hogg. He was typical of the sort of people who worked in such firms. He was utterly straightforward; conventional by his own admission, a person one met at the private shows at galleries and who liked Elizabeth Blackadder. These people did not engage in the sort of practises which had been associated with some of those Italian banks or even with the more freewheeling end of the City of London. And they did not commit murder.

But if for a moment one assumed that anybody, even the most outwardly upright, is capable of acting greedily and bending the rules of the financial community (it was not theft, after all, that one was talking about, but the mere misuse of information), might such a person not, if he were faced with exposure, resort to

desperate means to protect his reputation? In different, less cen-
sorious circles it would probably be less devastating to be exposed
as a cheat, simply because there were so many other cheats and
because almost everybody would be likely to have been engaged
in cheating at some point themselves. There were parts of southern Italy, parts of Naples, for example, she had read, where cheating was the norm and to be honest was to be deviant. But here, in
Edinburgh, the possibility of being sent to prison would be unthink-
able; how much more attractive, then, would it be to take steps to
avoid this, even if those steps involved removing a young man
who was getting too close to the truth?

She looked at the telephone. She knew that she had only to
call Jamie and he would come. He had said that before, on more
than one occasion—*You can give me a call anytime, anytime. I like
coming round here. I really do.*

She left her chair and crossed to the telephone table. Jamie
lived in Stockbridge, in Saxe-Coburg Street, in a flat he shared
with three others. She had been there once, when he and Cat
had been together, and he had cooked a meal for the two of them.
It was a rambling flat, with high ceilings and a stone-flag floor in
the hall and in the kitchen. Jamie was the owner, having been
bought the flat by his parents when he was a student, and the
flatmates were his tenants. As landlord he allowed himself two
rooms: a bedroom and a music room, where he gave his music lessons. Jamie, who had graduated with a degree in music, earned his
living from teaching bassoon. There was no shortage of pupils, and
he supplemented his earnings by playing in a chamber ensemble
and as an occasional bassoonist for Scottish Opera. It was, thought
Isabel, an ideal existence; and one into which Cat would fit so
comfortably. But Cat had not seen it that way, of course, and Isabel
feared that she never would.

Jamie was teaching when she called and promised to call her back in half an hour. While she waited for the call, she made herself a sandwich in the kitchen; she did not feel like eating a proper meal. Then, when that was finished, she returned to the drawing room and awaited his call.

Yes, he was free. His last pupil, a talented boy of fifteen whom he was preparing for an examination, had played brilliantly. Now, with the boy sent off home after the lesson, a walk across town to Isabel's house was just what he wanted. Yes, it would be good to have a drink with Isabel and perhaps some singing afterwards.

"I'm sorry," she said. "I don't feel in the mood. I want to talk to you."

He had picked up her anxiety and the plan to walk was dropped in favour of a quicker bus ride.

"Are you all right?"

"Yes," she said. "But I really need to discuss something with you. I'll tell you when you come."

The buses, so maligned by Grace, were on time. Within twenty minutes, Jamie was at the house and was sitting with Isabel in the kitchen, where she had started to prepare him an omelette. She had taken a bottle of wine from the cellar and had poured a glass for him and for herself. Then she started to explain about the visit to the flat and her meeting with Hen and Neil. He listened gravely, and when she began to recount the conversation she had had with Neil earlier that evening, his eyes were wide with concern.

"Isabel," he said as she stopped speaking. "You know what I'm going to say, don't you?"

"That I should keep out of things that don't concern me?"

"Yes, absolutely." He paused. "But I know from past experience that you never do. So I won't say it, perhaps."

"Good."

"Even if I think it."

"Fair enough."

Jamie grimaced. "So what do we do?"

"That's why I asked you to come round," said Isabel, refilling his glass of wine. "I had to talk the whole thing through with somebody."

She had been speaking while she prepared the omelette. Now it was ready and she slid it onto a plate that had been warming on the side of the stove.

"Chanterelle mushrooms," she said. "They transform an omelette."

Jamie looked down gratefully at the generous omelette and its surrounding of salad.

"You're always cooking for me," he said. "And I never cook for you. Never."

"You're a man," said Isabel in a matter-of-fact way. "The thought doesn't enter your head."

She realised, the moment she had spoken, that this was an unkind and inappropriate thing to say. She might have said it to Toby, and with justification, as she doubted whether he would ever cook for anybody, but it was not the right thing to say to Jamie.

"I'm sorry," she said. "That just came out. I didn't mean that."

Jamie had put his knife and fork down beside his plate. He was staring at the omelette. And he had started to cry.

CHAPTER TWELVE

OH MY GOODNESS, Jamie. I'm so sorry. That was a terrible thing to say. I had no idea that you would . . ."

Jamie shook his head vigorously. He was not crying loudly, but there were tears. "No," he said, wiping at his eyes with his handkerchief. "It's not that at all. It's not what you said. It's nothing to do with it."

Isabel sighed with relief. She had not offended him, then, but what could have provoked this rather extraordinary outburst of emotion on his part?

Jamie picked up his knife and fork and started to cut into his omelette, but put them down again.

"It's the salad," he said. "You've put in raw onion. My eyes are really sensitive to that. I can't go anywhere near raw onion."

Isabel let out a peal of laughter. "Thank God. I thought that those were real tears and that I'd said a dreadful, insensitive thing to you. I thought that it was my fault." She reached forward and took the plate away from the place in front of him. Then she scraped off the salad, and gave it back to him. "Just an omelette. As nature intended. Nothing else."

"That's perfect," he said. "I'm sorry about that. It's genetic, I think. My mother had exactly the same problem, and a cousin of hers too. We're allergic to raw onion."

"And I thought for a moment that it had something to do with Cat . . . and with the time you cooked dinner for the two of us in Saxe-Coburg Street."

Jamie, who had been smiling, now looked pensive. "I remember," he said.

Isabel had not intended to mention Cat, but now she had, and she knew what the next question would be. He always asked it, whenever she saw him.

"What is Cat up to?" he asked. "What is she doing?"

Isabel reached for her glass and poured herself some wine. She had not intended to drink anything more after her sherry with Neil, but there in the intimacy of the kitchen, with the yeasty smell of mushrooms assailing her nostrils, she decided otherwise; *akrasia,* weakness of the will, again. It would feel *safe* sitting there with Jamie, talking to him and sipping at a glass of wine. She knew that it would make her feel better.

"Cat," she said, "is doing what she always does. She's quite busy in the shop. She's getting on with life." She trailed off weakly. It was such a trite reply, but what more was there to say? To ask such a question, anyway, was the equivalent of asking "How are you?" on meeting a friend. One expects only one answer, an anodyne assurance that all is well, later qualified, perhaps, by some remark about the real situation, if the real situation is quite different. Stoicism first, and then the truth, might be the way in which this could be expressed.

"And that man she's seeing," said Jamie quietly. "Toby. What about him? Does she bring him round here?"

"The other day," said Isabel. "I saw him the other day. But not here."

Jamie reached for his glass. He was frowning, as if struggling to find precisely the right words. "Where, then?"

"In town," Isabel replied quickly. She hoped that this would be the end of this line of questioning, but it was not.

"Was he . . . was he with Cat? With her?"

"No," said Isabel. "He was by himself." She thought: That is, he was by himself to begin with.

Jamie stared at her. "What was he doing?"

Isabel smiled. "You seem very interested in him," she said. "And he's not really very interesting at all, I'm afraid." She hoped that this aside would reassure him as to whose side she was on, and that the conversation might move on. But it had the opposite effect. Jamie appeared to interpret it as paving the way for further discussion.

"What was he doing, then?"

"He was walking along the street. That's all. Walking along the street . . . in those crushed-strawberry corduroys that he likes to wear." The last part of her answer was unnecessary; it was sarcastic, and Isabel immediately regretted it. That was two unpleasant things she had said tonight, she thought. The first was that gratuitous remark about men not cooking; the second was an unworthy remark about Toby's trousers. It was easy, terribly easy, to become with time a middle-aged spinster with a sharp tongue. She would have to guard against this. So she added, "They're not too bad, crushed-strawberry corduroys. Presumably Cat likes them. She must . . ."

Again she stopped herself. She had been about to say that Cat must have found crushed-strawberry corduroys attractive, but that would have been tactless. It implied, did it not, that Jamie, and his trousers did not measure up. She allowed herself a furtive glance at Jamie's trousers. She had never noticed them before, largely because her interest in Jamie lay not in his trousers, but in his face, and his voice. In fact, it lay in the whole person; and that, surely, was the difference between Toby and Jamie. You could not like Toby as a person (unless you yourself were the wrong sort of person); you could only like him for his physique. Yes, she thought, that's all. Toby was a sex object in crushed-strawberry corduroys, that's all he was. And Jamie, by contrast, was . . . well, Jamie was just beautiful, with those high cheekbones of his and his skin and his voice which must surely melt the heart. And she wondered, too, what they were like as lovers. Toby would be all vigour while Jamie would be quiet, and gentle, and caressing, like a woman really. Which might be a problem, perhaps, but not one that she could realistically do very much about. For a few moments, a few completely impermissible moments, she thought: *I could teach him.* And then she stopped. Such thoughts were as unacceptable as imagining people being crushed by avalanches. Avalanches. The roar. The sudden confusion of crushed strawberry. The tidal wave of snow, and then the preternatural quiet.

"Did you speak to him?" asked Jamie.

Isabel returned from her thoughts. "Speak to whom?"

"To . . . Toby." It clearly involved some effort for him to bring himself to pronounce the name.

Isabel shook her head. "No," she said. "I just saw him." This, of course, was a half-truth. There was a distinction between lying and telling half-truths, but it was a very narrow one. Isabel had herself written a short article on the matter, following the publication of Sissela Bok's philosophical monograph *Lying*. She had argued for a broad interpretation, which imposed a duty to answer questions truthfully, and not to hide facts which could give a different complexion to a matter, but on subsequent thought she had revised her position. Although she still believed that one should be frank in answers to questions, this duty arose only where there was an obligation, based on a reasonable expectation, to make a full disclosure. There was no duty to reveal everything in response to a casual question by one who had no right to the information.

"You're blushing," said Jamie. "You're not telling me something."

So that, thought Isabel, was that. The whole edifice of philosophical debate on the fine nuances of truth telling is ultimately undermined by a simple biological process. *Tell a fib and you go red in the face.* It sounded so much less dignified than it did in the pages of Sissela Bok, but it was absolutely true. All the great issues were reducible to the simple facts of everyday human life and the trite metaphors, the axiomata, by which people lived. The international economic system and its underlying assumptions: *Finders keepers, losers weepers.* The uncertainty of life: *Step on a crack and the bears will get you* (which she had believed in so vividly as a child, walking up Morningside Road with Fersie McPherson, her nurse, carefully avoiding the cracks in the pavement).

"If I'm blushing," she said, "it's because I'm not telling you the whole truth. For which I apologise. I didn't tell you what I did because I feel embarrassed about it, and for . . ." She hesitated. There was another reason for not revealing what had happened, but now she had embarked on the road of disclosure; she would have to tell Jamie everything. He would sense it if she did not, and she did not want him to feel that she did not trust him. Did she trust him? Yes, she did. Of course she did. A young man like that, with his *en brosse* hair and his voice, could only be trustworthy. Jamies can be trusted; Tobys cannot.

Jamie watched her as she spoke. Now she continued: ". . . for the reason that there is something that I did not want you to know. Not because I don't trust you, which I do, but because I think that it has nothing to do with us. I saw something that we cannot do anything about. So I thought that there was no reason to tell you."

"What is it?" he asked. "You have to tell me now. You can't leave it at that."

Isabel nodded. He was right. She could not leave the matter like this. "When I saw Toby in town," she began, "he was walking down Dundas Street. I was on a bus and I saw him. I decided to follow him—please don't ask me why, because I don't know if I can give an adequate explanation for that. Sometimes one just does things—ridiculous things—that one can't explain. So I decided to follow him.

"He walked down Northumberland Street. Then, when we got to Nelson Street, he crossed the road and rang the bell on a ground-floor flat. There was a girl who came to the door. He embraced her, pretty passionately I think, and then the door closed, and that was that."

Jamie looked at her. For a moment he said nothing, then, very slowly, he lifted his glass and took a sip of his wine. Isabel noticed the fine hands and, for a moment, in his eyes, the reflected light from the wineglass.

"His sister," he said quietly. "He has a sister who lives in Nelson Street. I've actually met her. She's a friend of a friend."

Isabel sat quite still. She had not expected this. "Oh," she said. And then, "Oh."

CHAPTER THIRTEEN

Yes," SAID JAMIE. "Toby has a sister in Nelson Street. She works in the same property company as my friend does. They're both surveyors—not the sort who go out with theodolites, but valuers." He laughed. "And you thought that the result of your gumshoe activities was that you had discovered Toby being unfaithful. Ha! I wish you had, Isabel, but you haven't. That'll teach you to follow people."

Isabel had now recovered sufficient composure to laugh at herself. "I more or less hid behind a parked van," she said. "You should have seen me."

Jamie smiled. "It must have been exciting stuff. Pity about the result, but there we are."

"Well," said Isabel. "I enjoyed myself anyway. And it teaches me a lesson about having a nasty, suspicious mind."

"Which you don't have," said Jamie. "You are not suspicious. You are absolutely straight down the middle."

"You're very kind," said Isabel. "But I have bags of failings. Same as anybody else. Bags."

Jamie lifted up his glass again. "She's quite a nice girl, his sister," he said. "I met her at a party which Roderick—that's my surveyor friend—gave a few months ago. It was a rather different crowd of people from my own crowd, but it was good fun. And I thought that she was rather nice. Very attractive. Very tall, with blonde hair. A model type."

Isabel said nothing. Then she closed her eyes, and imagined herself for a moment on the corner of Nelson Street, half hidden by the van, seeing Toby at the door, and the door opening. She could picture it quite clearly, as she had always been able to recall visual details with accuracy. Now the picture was clear. The door opened and the girl appeared. She was not tall, for Toby had stooped to embrace her, and she did not have blonde hair. Her hair, quite unmistakeably, was dark. Black or brown. Not blonde.

She opened her eyes. "It was not his sister," she said. "It was somebody else."

Jamie was silent. Isabel imagined the conflict within him: displeasure, or even anger, at the fact that Cat was being deceived, and satisfaction that there was now a chance that Toby could be exposed. He would be thinking, too, it occurred to her, that he might be able to take Toby's place, which is what she herself had thought. But she at least knew that it would not be that simple; Jamie was unlikely to know that. He would be optimistic.

Isabel decided to take the initiative. "You can't tell her," she said. "If you went and told her, she would be angry with you. Even if she believes it—which she may not—she would feel like shooting the messenger. I guarantee that you would regret it."

"But she should know," protested Jamie. "It's . . . it's outrageous that he should be carrying on with somebody else. She should be told. We owe it to her."

"There are some things one has to find out oneself," said Isabel. "You have to let people make some mistakes themselves."

"Well, I for one don't accept that," Jamie retorted. "This is a simple case. He's a dog. We know it; she doesn't. We have to tell her."

"But the whole point is that if we do that, we're only going to anger her. Don't you see? Even if she went and found out that what we said was true, she would still be angry with us for telling her. I don't want her to . . . to write you off. But she will if you do that."

Jamie thought about what she had said. So she wanted him to get back with Cat. She had never actually said as much, but now it was in the open. And it was just as he had hoped it would be.

"Thanks," he said. "I see what you mean." He paused. "But why do you think he's two-timing her? If he likes this other girl—she's presumably his sister's flatmate—then why doesn't he just go off with her? Why use Cat like this?"

"Don't you see?" said Isabel.

"No, I don't. Maybe I just don't get it."

"Cat is wealthy," said Isabel. "Cat owns a business, and quite a bit else—a lot else actually, as you may or may not know. If you were somebody who was interested in money, and Toby is, I should think, then you may want to get your hands on some of it."

Jamie's astonishment was obvious. "He's after her money?"

Isabel nodded. "I've known quite a few cases like that. I've seen people marry for money and then think that they can behave as they like. They get the security of the money and carry on behind their wife's or husband's back. It's not all that unusual. Think of all those young women who marry wealthy older men. Do you think they behave like nuns?"

"I suppose not," said Jamie.

"Well, there you are. Of course, this is only one explanation. The other is that he simply wants to play the field. It's possible that he really likes Cat, but that he likes other women too. That's perfectly possible."

Isabel refilled Jamie's glass. They were getting through the bottle quite quickly, but it was turning into an emotional evening and the wine was helping. There was another bottle in the fridge if needed, and they could broach that later. As long as I keep control, thought Isabel. As long as I maintain enough of a level head so that I don't tell Jamie that if the truth be told, I'm half in love with him myself, and that there is nothing I would like more than to kiss that brow and run my fingers over that hair and hold him against me.

THE FOLLOWING MORNING Grace, who arrived early, said to herself: two glasses, an empty bottle. Crossing to the fridge, she saw the half-full corked bottle, and added, And a half. She opened the dishwasher and saw the omelette plate and the knife and fork, which told her that the visitor was Jamie: Isabel always cooked an omelette when he stayed for dinner. Grace was glad that Isabel had that young man in. She liked him, and she knew the background with Cat. She suspected, too, what Isabel was planning; that she would be plotting to get the two of them together again. She could forget that. People rarely went back that way. Once you were off somebody, then you tended to stay off them. That, at least, was Grace's experience. She had rarely found that she rehabilitated somebody once she had taken the decision to write them off.

She prepared the coffee. Isabel would be down soon, and she liked to have the coffee ready for her when she came into the kitchen. *The Scotsman* had arrived and Grace had brought it through from the front hall, where it was lying on the mosaic floor beneath the letter box. Now it was on the table, front page up, and Grace glanced at it while she ladled the coffee into the percolator. A resignation had been called for from a Glasgow politician suspected of fraud. (No surprise, thought Grace; none at all.) And there beneath it, a picture of that person of whom Isabel did not approve, the popinjay, as she called him. He had been crossing Princes Street and had collapsed, to be rushed off to the Infirmary. Grace read on: it had been a suspected heart attack, but no—and this was truly astonishing—he was found to have suffered a large split in his side, fortunately dealt with by quick and competent surgical stitching. He had made a full recovery, but then the diagnosis had been revealed: *he had burst with self-importance.*

Grace put down the coffee spoon. Surely not. Impossible. She picked up the newspaper to examine it further, and saw the date. The first of April. She smiled. *The Scotsman*'s little joke—how funny; but how apt.

CHAPTER FOURTEEN

IN SPITE OF THE FACT that he had drunk three glasses of wine and Isabel was towards the end of her second, Jamie had at first been doubtful about Isabel's proposition, but she had won him over, wheedling him, persuading him that they should at least give it a try.

To do what? To go to see Paul Hogg, of course, as the first step in finding out what it was that Mark Fraser had discovered, and about whom he had discovered it. Sitting at the kitchen table, the chanterelle omelette consumed, Jamie had listened intently as she explained to him about the conversation with Neil, and about how she felt that she could not ignore what he had revealed. She wanted to take the matter further, but she did not want to do it by herself. It would be safer, she said, with two, although the nature of the danger, if any, was not expanded upon.

At last Jamie had agreed. "If you insist," he said. "If you really insist, I'm prepared to go with you. But it's only because I don't want you charging off into this by yourself. It's not because I think it's a good idea."

As Isabel saw Jamie out of the house later that evening, they had agreed that she would telephone him at some point in the next few days, to discuss how they were to proceed with Paul Hogg. At least she had an acquaintanceship with him, which would enable them to seek him out. But exactly how this would be done, and on what pretext, remained to be worked out.

Barely had Jamie left the house than a thought occurred to Isabel. It almost sent her running after him to tell him about it, but she desisted. It was not all that late, and several neighbours walked their dogs along the street at that hour. She did not wish to be seen running after young men, in the street at least (though the metaphorical context would be as bad). That was not a situation in which anybody would wish to be seen, in much the same way as Dorothy Parker had pronounced that she would not wish to be caught, stuck at the hips, while climbing through anybody else's window. She smiled at the thought. What was so funny about this? It was difficult to explain, but it just was. Perhaps it was the fact that somebody who would never climb through a window nonetheless expressed a view on the *possibility* of climbing through a window. But why was that amusing? Perhaps there was no explanation, just as there was no rationale for the intense humour of the remark she had once heard at a lecture given by Domenica Legge, a great authority on Anglo-Norman history. Professor Legge had said: "We must remember that the nobles of the time did not blow their noses in quite the way in which we blow our own noses: *they had no handkerchiefs.*" This had been greeted with peals of laughter, and she still found it painfully amusing. But there was really nothing funny about it at all. It was a serious business, no doubt, having no handkerchiefs; mundane, certainly, but serious nonetheless. (What did the nobles do, then? The answer was, apparently, *straw.* How awful. How *scratchy.* And if the nobles were reduced to using straw, then what did those beneath them in the social order use? The answer was, of course, vivid: they blew their nose on their fingers, as many people still did. She had seen it herself once or twice, though not in Edinburgh, of course.)

It was not of handkerchiefs, or the lack of handkerchiefs, that she thought, but of Elizabeth Blackadder. Paul Hogg had bought the Blackadder which she had wanted. The exhibition at which he had bought it was a short one, and those who had bought paintings would by now have been allowed to remove them. This meant that anybody who wanted a further look at the painting would have to do so in Paul Hogg's flat in Great King Street. She could be just such a person. She could telephone Paul Hogg and ask to see the painting again, as she was thinking of asking Elizabeth Blackadder, who still had her studio in the Grange, to paint a similar picture for her. This was a perfectly reasonable thing to do. An artist might not wish to make a mere copy of an existing work, but might be quite willing to do something similar.

A lie, she thought, but only a lie at this stage of the plan's conception; lies can become truths. She had indeed planned to buy a Blackadder and there was no reason why she should not commission one. In fact, she would do exactly that, which meant that she could see Paul Hogg on these grounds with a perfectly good conscience. Not even Sissela Bok, author of *Lying,* could object. Then, having examined the Blackadder again, which he would be proudly displaying on his wall, she would delicately raise the possibility that Mark Fraser might have found out something *awkward* in the course of his work at McDowell's. Would Paul Hogg have any idea of what that might be? And if he did not, then she might be more specific and say to him that if he was attached to the young man—and he clearly had been fond of him, judging from his emotional reaction to what she had said in the Vincent Bar—then might he not be prepared to make some enquiries so as to prove or disprove the worrying hypothesis that all of this seemed to be pointing towards? It would have to be handled delicately, but it could be done. He might agree. And all the time, just to give her confidence, Jamie would be sitting beside her on Paul Hogg's chintzy sofa. *We* think, she could say; *we* wonder. That sounded much more reasonable than the same thing expressed in the singular.

She telephoned Jamie the next morning at the earliest decent hour; nine o'clock, in her view. Isabel observed an etiquette of the telephone: a call before eight in the morning was an emergency; between eight and nine it was an intrusion; thereafter calls could be made until ten in the evening, although anything after nine-thirty required an apology for the disturbance. After ten one was into emergency time again. On answering the telephone one should, if at all possible, give one's name, but only after saying good morning, good afternoon, or good evening. None of these conventions, she conceded, was observed to any great extent by others, and not, she noted, by Jamie himself, who answered her call that morning with an abrupt "Yes."

"You don't sound very welcoming," said Isabel disapprovingly. "And how do I know who you are? 'Yes' is not enough. And if you had been too busy to take the call, would you simply have said 'No'?"

"Isabel?" he said.

"Had you told me who you were, then I would have recipro-cated the courtesy. Your last question would then have been otiose."

Jamie laughed. "How long is this going to take?" he asked. "I have to get a train to Glasgow at ten. We're rehearsing for *Parsifal*."

"Poor you," said Isabel. "Poor singers. What an endurance test."

"Yes," Jamie agreed. "Wagner makes my head sore. But I really must get ready."

Isabel quickly explained her idea to him and then waited for his reaction.

"If you insist," Jamie said. "I suppose it sounds feasible enough. I'll come along if you insist. Really insist."

He could have been more accommodating, thought Isabel after she had rung off, but at least he had agreed. Now she would have to telephone Paul Hogg at McDowell's and ask him if and when it would be convenient to visit him. She was confident that he would welcome her suggestion. They had got on well together, and apart from the moment when she had inadvertently triggered in him a painful memory, the evening they had spent together had been a success. He had suggested, had he not, that she meet his fiancée, whose name she had forgotten but who could be referred to for the time being simply as "fiancée."

She telephoned at 10:45, a time when she believed there was the greatest chance that anybody who worked in an office would be having their morning coffee, and in fact he was, when she asked him.

"Yes. I'm sitting here with the *FT* on my desk. I should be reading it, but I'm not. I'm looking out the window and drinking my coffee."

"But I'm sure that you're about to take important decisions," she said. "And one of them will be whether you would allow me to look at your Blackadder again. I want to ask her to do one for me, and I thought that it might be helpful to look at yours again."

"Of course," he said. "Anybody can look at it. It's still in the exhibition. It has another week to run."

Isabel was momentarily taken by surprise. Of course she should have telephoned the gallery to find out whether the show was still on, and if it was, she should have waited until he had collected his painting.

"But it would be very nice to see you anyway," Paul Hogg went on helpfully. "I have another Blackadder you might like to see."

They made the arrangement. Isabel would come the following evening, at six, for drinks. Paul Hogg was perfectly happy for her to bring somebody with her too, a young man who was very interested in art and whom she would like him to meet. Of course that would be perfectly convenient, and nice too.

It was so easy, thought Isabel. It was so easy dealing with people who were well-mannered, as Paul Hogg was. They knew how to exchange those courtesies which made life go smoothly, which was what manners were all about. They were intended to avoid friction between people, and they did this by regulating the contours of an encounter. If each party knew what the other should do, then conflict would be unlikely. And this worked at every level, from the most minor transaction between two people to dealings between nations. International law, after all, was simply a system of manners writ large.

Jamie had good manners. Paul Hogg had good manners. Her mechanic, the proprietor of the small backstreet garage where she took her rarely used car for servicing, had perfect manners. Toby, by contrast, had bad manners; not on the surface, where he thought, quite wrongly, that it counted, but underneath, in his attitude to others. Good manners depended on paying moral attention to others; it required one to treat them with complete moral seriousness, to understand their feelings and their needs. Some people, the selfish, had no inclination to do this, and it always showed. They were impatient with those whom they thought did not count: the old, the inarticulate, the disadvantaged. The person with good manners, however, would always listen to such people and treat them with respect.

How utterly shortsighted we had been to listen to those who thought that manners were a bourgeois affectation, an irrelevance, which need no longer be valued. A moral disaster had ensued, because manners were the basic building block of civil society. They were the method of transmitting the message of moral consideration. In this way an entire generation had lost a vital piece of the moral jigsaw, and now we saw the results: a society in which nobody would help, nobody would feel for others; a society in which aggressive language and insensitivity were the norm.

She stopped herself. This was a train of thought which, though clearly correct, made her feel old; as old as Cicero declaiming, *O tempora! O mores!* And this fact, in itself, demonstrated the subtle, corrosive power of relativism. The relativists had succeeded in so getting under our moral skins that their attitudes had become internalised, and Isabel Dalhousie, with all her interest in moral philosophy and distaste for the relativist position, actually felt embarrassed to be thinking such thoughts.

She must stop this musing on moral imagination, she thought, and concentrate on things of more immediate importance, such as checking the morning's mail for the review and finding out why that poor boy Mark Fraser fell to his death from the gods. But she knew she would never abandon these broader issues; it was her lot. She may as well accept it. She was tuned in to a different station from most people and the tuning dial was broken.

She telephoned Jamie, forgetting that he would already have caught his train to Glasgow and would be, more or less at that moment, drawing into Queen Street Station. She waited for his answering machine to complete its speech, and then she left a message.

Jamie, yes I've phoned him, Paul Hogg. He was happy for us to call to see him tomorrow at six. I'll meet you half an hour before that, in the Vincent Bar. And Jamie, thanks for everything. I really appreciate your help on this. Thanks so much.

CHAPTER FIFTEEN

SHE WAS ANXIOUS in the pub, waiting for Jamie. It was a masculine place, at least at that hour, and she felt ill at ease. Women could go to pubs by themselves, of course, but she nonetheless felt out of place. The bartender, who served her a glass of bitter lemon with ice, smiled at her in a friendly way and commented on the fine evening. The clocks had just been put forward, and the sun was not setting now until after seven.

Isabel agreed, but could think of nothing useful to add, so she said: "It's spring, I suppose."

"I suppose," said the barman. "But you never know."

Isabel had returned to her table. *You never know.* Of course you never know. Anything could happen in this life. Here she was, the editor of the *Review of Applied Ethics,* about to go off in search of . . . of a murderer is what it amounted to. And in this task she was to be assisted, although somewhat reluctantly, by a beautiful young man with whom she was half in love but who was himself in love with her niece, who in turn appeared besotted with somebody else, who was having a simultaneous affair with his sister's flatmate. No, the barman certainly did not know, and if she told him he would scarcely believe it.

Jamie was ten minutes late. He had been practising, he said, and he had only looked at the clock just before five-thirty.

"But you're here," said Isabel. "And that's the important thing." She glanced at her watch. "We have about twenty minutes. I thought I might just go over with you how I plan to approach this."

Jamie listened, eyeing her from time to time over the edge of his beer glass. He remained uneasy about the whole project, but he had to agree that she was well rehearsed. She would raise the issue gently, particularly bearing in mind the apparent rawness of Paul Hogg's feelings on the matter. She would explain that she was not seeking to interfere, and the last thing that she was interested in was causing any embarrassment for McDowell's. But they owed it to Mark, and to Neil, who had brought the matter to her attention, to at least take the issue a little bit further. She herself, of course, was convinced that there was nothing in it, but at least they could lay the matter to rest with a good conscience if they had investigated it fully.

"Good script," Jamie commented after she had finished. "Covers it all."

"I can't see that he would be offended by any of that," said Isabel.

"No," said Jamie. "That's unless it's him."

"What's him?"

"Unless he did it himself. He might be the insider trader."

Isabel stared at her companion. "Why do you think that?"

"Well, why not? He's the person that Mark must have been working with most closely. He was the head of his section or whatever. If Mark knew anything, it must have been about the stuff that he was working on."

Isabel considered this. It was possible, she supposed, but she thought it unlikely. There had been no doubting the genuineness of the emotion he had shown on the occasion of their first meeting, when Mark's name had come up. He was devastated by what had happened; that was perfectly obvious. And if that were so, then he could not have been the person who arranged to dispose of Mark, which meant that he could not be the person fearing exposure.

"Do you see that?" she said to Jamie.

Jamie did, but he thought it wise to keep an open mind.

"We could be mistaken," he said. "Murderers feel guilt. They mourn their victims sometimes. Paul Hogg may be like that."

"He's not," said Isabel. "You haven't met him yet. He's not like that. It's somebody else we're looking for."

Jamie shrugged. "It might be. It might not. At least keep an open mind."

PAUL HOGG LIVED on the first floor of a Georgian town house in Great King Street. It was one of the most handsome streets in the New Town, and from his side, the south side, there was a view, from the top floors at least, of the Firth of Forth, a blue strip of sea just beyond Leith, and, beyond that, of the hills of Fife. The first floor had other reasons to commend it, though, even if the view was only of the other side of the street. In some streets at least, these flats were called the drawing-room flats, as they had been the main drawing rooms of the old, full houses. Their walls, therefore, were higher and their windows went from ceiling to floor, great expanses of glass which flooded the rooms with light.

They walked up the common stairway, a generous sweep of stone stairs, about which there lingered a slight smell of cat, and found the door with HOGG on a square brass plate. Isabel glanced at Jamie, who winked at her. His scepticism had been replaced by a growing interest in what they were doing, and it was she, now, who felt doubtful.

Paul Hogg answered the door quickly and took their coats. Isabel introduced Jamie, and the two shook hands.

"I've seen you somewhere," said Paul Hogg. "I don't know where."

"Edinburgh," said Jamie, and they laughed.

He led them through to the drawing room, which was a large, elegantly furnished room, dominated by an impressive white mantelpiece. Isabel noticed the invitations—at least four of them—propped up on the mantelpiece, and when Paul Hogg went out of the room to fetch their drinks, and they had not yet sat down, she sidled over and read them quickly.

Mr. and Mrs. Humphrey Holmes, At Home, Thursday 16th (Isabel had been invited too). Then, *George Maxtone requests the pleasure of the company of Ms. Minty Auchterlonie at a Reception at the Lothian Gallery, at 6 p.m., Tuesday, 18th May*; and *Minty: Peter and Jeremy, Drinks in the Garden (weather permitting, probably not), Friday, 21st May, 6:30 p.m.* And finally, *Paul and Minty: Please come to our wedding reception at Prestonfield House on Saturday, 15th May. Ceilidh, 8 p.m. Angus and Tatti. Dress: Evening/Highland.*

Isabel smiled, although Jamie was looking at her disapprovingly, as if she were reading something private. Jamie came over to join her and squinted briefly at the invitations. "You shouldn't read other people's things," he whispered. "It's rude."

"Pah!" hissed Isabel. "That's why these things are up here. To be read. I've seen invitations on mantelpieces *three years* out of date. Invitations to the garden party at Holyroodhouse, for instance. Years old, but still displayed."

She led him away from the mantelpiece to stand before a large watercolour of poppies in a garden. "That's her," she said. "Elizabeth Blackadder. Poppies. Garden walls with cats on them. But terribly well done in spite of the subject matter." And she thought: I have no pictures of poppies in my house; I have never been stuck at the hips going through somebody else's window.

This was where Paul Hogg, returning with two glasses in his hands, found them.

"There you are," he said cheerfully. "What you came to see."

"It's a very good one," said Isabel. "Poppies again. So important."

"Yes," said Paul. "I like poppies. It's such a pity that they fall to bits when you pick them."

"A clever defence mechanism," said Isabel, glancing at Jamie. "Roses should catch on to that. Thorns are obviously not enough. Perfect beauty should be left exactly as it is."

Jamie returned her look. "Oh," he said, and then was silent. Paul Hogg looked at him, and then looked at Isabel. Isabel, noticing this, thought: He's wondering what the relationship is. Toy boy, probably; or so he thinks. But even if that were the case, why should he be surprised? It was common enough these days.

Paul Hogg left the room briefly to fetch his own drink, and Isabel smiled at Jamie, raising a finger to her lip in a quick conspiratorial gesture.

"But I haven't said anything yet," said Jamie. "All I said was 'Oh.'"

"Quite enough," said Isabel. "An eloquent monosyllable."

Jamie shook his head. "I don't know why I agreed to come with you," he whispered. "You're half crazy."

"Thank you, Jamie," she said quietly. "But here's our host."

Paul Hogg returned and they raised their glasses to one another.

"I bought that painting at auction a couple of years ago," he said. "It was with my first bonus from the company. I bought it to celebrate."

"A good thing to do," said Isabel. "One reads about brokers, financial people, celebrating with those awful lunches that set them back ten thousand pounds for the wine. That doesn't happen in Edinburgh, I hope."

"Certainly not," said Paul Hogg. "New York and London maybe. Places like that."

Isabel turned towards the fireplace. A large gilt-framed picture was hung above it, and she had recognised it immediately.

"That's a fine Peploe," she said. "Marvellous."

"Yes," said Paul Hogg. "It's very nice. West coast of Mull, I think."

"Or Iona?" asked Isabel.

"Could be," said Paul Hogg vaguely. "Somewhere there."

Isabel took a few steps towards the painting and looked up at it. "That business with all those forgeries some years back," she said. "You weren't worried about that? Did you check?"

Paul Hogg looked surprised. "There were forgeries?"

"So it was said," said Isabel. "Peploes, Cadells. Quite a few. There was a trial. It caused some anxiety. I knew somebody who had one on his hands—a lovely painting, but it had been painted the week before, more or less. Very skilled—as these people often are."

Paul Hogg shrugged. "That's always a danger, I suppose."

Isabel looked up at the painting again. "When did Peploe paint this?" she asked.

Paul Hogg made a gesture of ignorance. "No idea. When he was over on Mull, perhaps."

Isabel watched him. It was an answer of staggering lameness, but at least it fitted with an impression that she was rapidly forming. Paul Hogg knew very little about art, and, moreover, was not particularly interested. How otherwise could one have a Peploe like that—and she was sure that it was genuine—how could one have a Peploe and not know the basic facts about it?

There were at least ten other pictures in the room, all of them interesting even if none was as dramatic as the Peploe. There was a Gillies landscape, for example, a very small McTaggart, and there, at the end of the room, a characteristic Bellamy. Whoever had collected these either knew a great deal about Scottish art or had stumbled upon a perfectly representative ready-made collection.

Isabel moved over to another picture. He had invited her to view his Blackadder and so it was quite acceptable to be nosy, about paintings at least.

"This is a Cowie, isn't it?" she asked.

Paul Hogg looked at the picture. "I think so."

It was not. It was a Crosbie, as anybody could have told. These paintings did not belong to Paul Hogg, which meant that they were the property of Minty Auchterlonie, who was, she presumed, his fiancée, and who had been named *separatim* on two of the invitations. And those two invitations, significantly, were both from gallery owners. George Maxtone owned the Lothian Gallery and was just the sort of person to whom one would go if one wanted to buy a painting by a major Scottish painter of the early twentieth century. Peter Thom and Jeremy Lambert ran a small gallery in a village outside Edinburgh but were also frequently commissioned by people who were looking for particular paintings. They had an uncanny knack of locating people who were prepared to sell paintings but who wished to do so discreetly. The two functions would probably be a mixture of friends and clients, or of people who were both.

"Minty—" Isabel began, meaning to ask Paul Hogg about his fiancée, but she was interrupted.

"My fiancée," he said. "Yes, she's coming any moment. She was working a bit late, though not late by her standards. Sometimes she's not back until eleven or twelve."

"Oh," said Isabel. "Let me guess. She's a . . . a surgeon, yes, that's what she is. She's a surgeon or a . . . a fireman?"

Paul Hogg laughed. "Very unlikely. She probably lights more fires than she puts out."

"What a nice thing to say about one's fiancée!" said Isabel. "How passionate! I hope that you'd say that about your fiancée, Jamie."

Paul Hogg shot a glance at Jamie, who scowled at Isabel, and then, as if reminded of duty, changed the scowl to a smile.

"Hah!" he said.

Isabel turned to Paul Hogg. "What does she do, then, that keeps her out so late at night?" She knew the answer to the question even as she asked it.

"Corporate finance," said Paul Hogg. Isabel detected a note of resignation, almost a sigh, and she concluded that there was tension here. Minty Auchterlonie, whom they were shortly to meet, would not be a clinging-vine fiancée. She would not be a comfortable homemaker. She would be tough, and hard. She was the one with the money, who was busy buying these expensive paintings. And what is more, Isabel was convinced that these paintings were not being acquired for the love of art; they were a strategy.

They were standing near one of the two large front windows, next to the Cowie that was a Crosbie. Paul looked out and tapped the glass gently. "That's her," he said, pointing out into the street. "That's Minty arriving now." There was pride in his voice.

Isabel and Jamie looked out the window. Below them, directly outside the entrance to the flat, a small, raffish sports car was being manoeuvred into a parking space. It was painted in British racing green and had a distinctive chrome front grille. But it was not a make which Isabel, who took a mild interest in cars, could recognise; Italian perhaps, an unusual Alfa Romeo, an older Spider? The only good car to come out of Italy, ever, in Isabel's opinion.

A few minutes later the door into the drawing room opened and Minty came in. Isabel noticed that Paul Hogg snapped to, like a soldier on the arrival of a senior officer. But he was smiling, and obviously delighted to see her. That always showed, she thought; people brightened when they were truly pleased to see somebody. It was unmistakeable.

She looked at Minty, whom Paul Hogg had crossed the room to embrace. She was a tall, rather angular woman in her late twenties; late enough twenties to require attention to makeup, which was heavily but skilfully applied. Attention had been paid to her clothes, too, which were clearly expensive and carefully structured. She kissed Paul Hogg perfunctorily on both cheeks, and then walked over towards them. She shook hands, her glance moving quickly from Isabel (*dismissed,* thought Isabel) to Jamie (*interested,* she noted). Isabel distrusted her immediately.

CHAPTER SIXTEEN

YOU ASKED HIM nothing about Mark," said Jamie heatedly as they closed the door at the bottom of the stair and stepped out into the evening street. "Not a single thing! What was the point of going there?"

Isabel linked her arm with Jamie's and led him towards the Dundas Street intersection. "Now," she said, "keep calm. It's only eight o'clock and we have plenty of time for dinner. It's on me tonight. There's a very good Italian restaurant just round the corner and we can talk there. I'll explain everything to you."

"But I just don't see the point," said Jamie. "We sat there talking to Paul Hogg and that ghastly fiancée of his and the subject, from start to finish, was art. And it was mostly you and that Minty person. Paul Hogg sat there looking up at the ceiling. He was bored. I could see it."

"She was bored too," said Isabel. "*I* could see that."

Jamie was silent, and Isabel gave his arm a squeeze. "Don't worry," she said. "I'll tell you over dinner. I would like a few moments to think just now."

They walked up Dundas Street, crossing Queen Street, and along towards Thistle Street, where Isabel said they would find the restaurant. The town was not busy, and there was no traffic in Thistle Street. So they walked a short distance in the road itself, their footsteps echoing against the walls on either side. Then, on the right, the discreet door of the restaurant.

It was not large—about eight tables in all, and there were only two other diners. Isabel recognised the couple and nodded. They smiled, and then looked down at the tablecloth, with discretion, of course, but they were interested.

"Well," said Jamie, as they sat down. "Tell me."

Isabel arranged her table napkin on her lap and picked up the menu. "You can take the credit," she began. "Or part of it."

"Me?"

"Yes, you. You said to me in the Vincent that I should be prepared to find out that Paul Hogg was the person we were after. That's what you said. And that made me think."

"So you decided that it was him," said Jamie.

"No," said Isabel. "It's her. Minty Auchterlonie."

"Hard-faced cow," muttered Jamie.

Isabel smiled. "You could say that. I might not use those exact words, but I wouldn't disagree with you."

"I disliked her the moment she came into the room," said Jamie.

"Which is odd, because I think that she liked you. In fact, I'm pretty sure that she . . . how shall I put it? She *noticed* you."

Her remark seemed to embarrass Jamie, who looked down at the menu which the waiter had placed before him. "I didn't see—" he began.

"Of course you didn't," said Isabel. "Only another woman would pick it up. But she took an interest in you. Not that it stopped her getting bored with both of us after a while."

"I don't know," said Jamie. "Anyway, she's a type that I just can't stand. I really can't."

Isabel looked thoughtful. "I wonder what it is that made us—both of us—take a bizz against her." The old Scots word "bizz," like so many Scots terms, could only be roughly translated. A bizz was a feeling of antipathy, but it had subtle nuances. A bizz was often irrational or unjustified.

"It's what she represents," Jamie offered. "It's a sort of mixture, isn't it, of ambition and ruthlessness and materialism and—"

"Yes," Isabel interrupted him. "Quite. It may be difficult to define, but I think we both know exactly what it is. And the interesting thing is that she had it and he didn't. Would you agree with that?"

Jamie nodded. "I quite liked him. I wouldn't choose him as a particularly close friend, but he seemed friendly enough."

"Exactly," said Isabel. "Unexceptionable, and unexceptional."

"And not somebody who would ruthlessly remove somebody who threatened to expose him."

Isabel shook her head. "Definitely not."

"Whereas she . . ."

"Lady Macbeth," Isabel said firmly. "There should be a syndrome named after her. Perhaps there is. Like the Othello syndrome."

"What's that?" asked Jamie.

Isabel took up a bread roll and broke it on her side plate. She would not use a knife on a roll, of course, although Jamie did. In Germany it once was considered inappropriate to use a knife on a potato, a curious custom which she had never understood. An enquiry she had made of a German friend had received a strange explanation, which she could only assume had not been serious. "A nineteenth-century custom," he had explained. "Perhaps the emperor had a face like a potato and it was considered disrespectful." She had laughed, but when she later saw a portrait of the emperor, she thought it might just be true. He did look like a potato, just as Quintin Hogg, Lord Hailsham, had looked slightly porcine. She imagined him at breakfast, being served bacon, and laying down his knife and fork and sighing, regretfully, "I just can't . . ."

"The Othello syndrome is pathological jealousy," said Isabel, reaching for the glass of gassy mineral water which the attentive waiter had now poured her. "It afflicts men, usually, and it makes them believe that their wife or partner is being unfaithful to them. They become obsessed with the thought, and nothing, nothing can persuade them otherwise. They may eventually end up being violent."

Jamie, she noticed, was listening very carefully to her as she spoke, and the thought occurred to her: *He sees something there.* Was he jealous of Cat? Of course he was. But then Cat was having an affair with somebody else, in his view at least.

"Don't worry," she said reassuringly. "You're not the sort to be pathologically jealous."

"Of course not," he said, too hurriedly, she thought. Then he added, "Where can one read about it? Have you read something about it?"

"There's a book in my library," said Isabel. "It's called *Unusual Psychiatric Syndromes* and it has some wonderful ones in it. For example, cargo cults. That's where whole groups of people believe that somebody is going to come and drop supplies to them. Cargo. Manna. The same thing. There have been remarkable cases in the South Seas. Islands where people believed that eventually the Americans would come and drop boxes of food, if only they waited long enough."

"And others?"

"The syndrome where you imagine that you recognise people.

You think you know them, but you don't. It's neurological. That couple over there, for example, I'm sure I know them, but I probably don't. Maybe I've got it." She laughed.

"Paul Hogg's got that too," said Jamie. "He said he'd seen me. It was the first thing he said."

"But he probably had. People notice you."

"I don't think they do. Why would they?"

Isabel looked at him. How charming it was that he did not know. And perhaps it was best that he should not. That might spoil him. So she said nothing, but smiled. Misguided Cat!

"So what has Lady Macbeth got to do with it?" asked Jamie.

Isabel leaned forward in her chair.

"Murderess," she whispered. "A cunning, manipulative murderess."

Jamie sat quite still. The light, bantering tone of the conversation had come to an abrupt end. He felt cold. "Her?"

Isabel did not smile. Her tone was serious. "I realised pretty quickly that the paintings in that room were not his, but hers. The invitations from the galleries were for her. He knew nothing about the paintings. She was the one who was buying all those expensive daubs."

"So? She may have money."

"Yes, she has money, all right. But don't you see, if you have large amounts of money which you may not want to leave lying about the place in bank accounts, then buying pictures is a very good way of investing. You can pay cash, if you like, and then you have an appreciating, very portable asset. As long as you know what you're doing, which she does."

"But I don't see what this has got to do with Mark Fraser. Paul Hogg is the one who worked with him, not Minty."

"Minty Auchterlonie is a hard-faced cow—as you so perceptively call her—who works in corporate finance in a merchant bank. Paul Hogg comes home from work and she says: 'What are you doing at the office today, Paul?' Paul says this and that, and tells her, because she's in the same line as he is. Some of this information is pretty sensitive, but pillow talk, you know, has to be frank if it's to be at all interesting, and she picks it all up. She goes off and buys the shares in her name—or possibly using some sort of front—and lo and behold the large profit is made, all on the basis of inside information. She takes the profit and puts it into pictures, which leave less of a trail. Or alternatively, she has an arrangement with an art dealer. He gets the information from her and makes the purchase. There's no way of linking him to her. He pays her in paintings, taking his cut, one assumes, and the paintings are simply not officially sold, so there's no record in his books of a taxable profit being made."

Jamie sat openmouthed. "You worked all this out this evening? On the way up here?"

Isabel laughed. "It's nothing elaborate. Once I realised it was not him, and once we had actually met her, then it all fell into place. Of course it's only a hypothesis, but I think it might be true."

It may have been clear thus far to Jamie, but it was not clear to him why Minty should have tried to get rid of Mark. Isabel now explained this. Minty was ambitious. Marriage to Paul Hogg, who was clearly going somewhere in McDowell's, would suit her well. He was a pleasant, compliant man, and she probably felt lucky to have him as her fiancé. Stronger, more dominating men would have found Minty too difficult to take, too much competition. So Paul Hogg suited her very well. But if it came out that Paul Hogg had passed on information to her—even if innocently—then that would cost him his job. He would not have been the insider trader, but she would. And if it came out that she had done this, then not only would she lose her own job, but she would be unemployable in corporate finance. It would be the end of her world, and if such an outcome could be averted only by arranging for something tragic to happen, then so be it. People like Minty Auchterlonie had no particular conscience. They had no idea of a life beyond this one, of any assessment, and without that, the only thing that stood between her and murder was an internal sense of right and wrong. And in that respect, Isabel said, one did not have to look particularly closely to realise that Minty Auchterlonie was deficient.

"Our friend Minty," said Isabel at length, "has a personality disorder. Most people would not recognise it, but it's very definitely there."

"This Lady Macbeth syndrome?" asked Jamie.

"Maybe that too," said Isabel, "if it exists. I was thinking of something much more common. Psychopathy, or sociopathy—call it what you will. She's sociopathic. She will have no moral compunction in doing whatever is in her interests. It's as simple as that."

"Including pushing people over the gods at the Usher Hall?"

"Yes," said Isabel. "Absolutely."

Jamie thought for a moment. Isabel's explanation seemed plausible, and he was prepared go along with it, but did she have any idea of what they might do next? What she had suggested was surmise, no more. Presumably there would need to be some form of proof if anything more were to be done. And they had no proof, none at all; all that they had was a theory as to motive. "So," he said. "What now?"

Isabel smiled. "I have no idea."

Jamie could not conceal his irritation at her insouciance. "I don't see how we can leave it at that. We've gone so far. We can't just leave the matter there."

The tone of Isabel's response was placatory. "I wasn't suggesting that we leave anything anywhere. And it doesn't matter that I have no idea what to do, right at the moment. A period of doing nothing is exactly what's needed."

Seeing Jamie taken aback by this, Isabel went on to explain. "I think she knows," she said. "I think that she knows why we were there."

"She said something?"

"Yes. When I was talking to her—you were chatting to Paul Hogg at the time—she said to me that she had heard from her fiancé that I was interested in—those were her exact words, 'interested in'—Mark Fraser. She waited for me to say something, but I just nodded. She came back to the subject a little later and asked me whether I had known him well. Again I dodged her question. It made her uneasy, I could see it. And I'm not surprised."

"So do you think she knows that we suspect her?"

Isabel took a sip of wine. From the kitchen came wafting a smell of garlic and olive oil. "Smell that," she said. "Delicious. Does she think we know? Maybe. But whatever she may think, I'm pretty sure that we are going to hear from her at some stage. She will want to know more about what we're up to. She'll come to us. Let's just give her a few days to do that."

Jamie looked unconvinced. "These sociopaths," he said. "What do they feel like? Inside?"

Isabel smiled. "Unmoved," she said. "They feel unmoved. Look at a cat when it does something wrong. It looks quite unmoved. Cats are sociopaths, you see. It's their natural state."

"And is it their fault? Are they to blame?"

"Cats are not to blame for being cats," said Isabel, "and therefore they cannot be blamed for doing the things that cats do, such as eating garden birds or playing with their prey. Cats can't help any of that."

"And what about people like that? Can they help it?" asked Jamie.

"It's very problematic whether they are to be blamed for their actions," said Isabel. "There's an interesting literature on it. They might argue that their acts are the result of their psychopathology. They act the way they do because of their personality being what it is, but then they never *chose* to have a personality disorder. So how can they be responsible for that which they did not choose?"

Jamie looked towards the kitchen. He saw a chef dip a finger into a bowl and then lick it thoughtfully. A sociopathic chef would be a nightmare. "It's the sort of thing that you might discuss with your friends," he said. "The Sunday Philosophy Club. You could discuss the moral responsibility of people like that."

Isabel smiled ruefully. "If I could get the club together," she said. "Yes, if I could get the club to meet."

"Sunday's not an easy day," said Jamie.

"No," Isabel agreed. "That's what Cat says too." She paused. She did not like to mention Cat too much in Jamie's presence because he always looked wistful, almost lost, when she did so.

CHAPTER SEVENTEEN

WHAT I NEED, thought Isabel, is a few days free of intrigue. I need to get back to editing the review, to doing the crosswords without interruption, to going for the occasional walk into Bruntsfield to have an inconsequential chat with Cat. I do not need to spend my time conspiring with Jamie in pubs and restaurants and brushing up against scheming corporate financiers with expensive tastes in art.

She had not slept well the previous night. She had said goodbye to Jamie after their meal at the restaurant and had not arrived back at the house until well after eleven. Once in bed, with the light switched out, and the moonlight throwing into her room the shadow of the tree outside her window, she had lain awake, thinking of the impasse which she feared they had reached. Even if the next move was down to Minty Auchterlonie, there were difficult decisions to be made. And then there was the whole business of Cat and Toby. She wished that it had never occurred to her to follow him, as the knowledge that she had acquired weighed heavily upon her conscience. She had decided that for the time being she would do nothing about it, but she knew that this was only shelving a problem which she would have to confront at some time or other. She was not sure how she would be able to deal with Toby when next she saw him. Would she be able to maintain her normal attitude, which, even if not friendly at heart, was at least as polite as circumstances demanded?

She slept, but only fitfully, with the result that she was still sound asleep when Grace arrived the next morning. If she was not downstairs, Grace inevitably came up to check on her, bearing a reviving cup of tea. She woke up to Grace's knock.

"A bad night?" Grace asked solicitously as she placed the cup of tea on Isabel's bedside table.

Isabel sat up in bed, rubbing her eyes. "I don't think I went to sleep until two," she said.

"Worries?" asked Grace, looking down at her.

"Yes," said Isabel. "Worries and doubts. This and that."

"I know the feeling," said Grace. "It happens to me too. I start worrying about the world. I wonder where it's all going to end."

"Not with a bang but a whimper," said Isabel vaguely. "That's what T. S. Eliot said, and everybody always quotes him on it. But it's really a very silly thing to say, and I'm sure that he regretted it."

"Silly man," said Grace. "Your friend Mr. Auden would never have said that, would he?"

"Certainly not," said Isabel, twisting round in bed to reach for the teacup. "Although he did say some silly things when he was young." She took a sip of tea, which always seemed to have an immediate effect on her clarity of mind. "And then he said some silly things when he was old. In between, though, he was usually very acute."

"Cute?"

"Acute." Isabel started to get out of bed, feeling with her toes for the slippers on the bedside rug. "If he wrote something which was wrong, which was meretricious, he would go back to it and change it, if he could. Some of his poems he denounced altogether. 'September 1st, 1939' was an example."

She drew the curtains. It was a bright spring day, with the first signs of heat in the sun. "He said that poem was dishonest, although I think it's got some wonderful lines. Then, in *Letters from Iceland,* he wrote something which had absolutely no meaning, but which sounded magnificent. *And the ports have names for the sea.* It's a marvellous line, isn't it? But it doesn't mean anything, does it, Grace?"

"No," said Grace. "I don't see how ports can have names for the sea. I don't see it."

Isabel rubbed her eyes again. "Grace, I want to have a simple day. Do you think that you can help me?"

"Of course."

"Could you answer the phone? Tell anybody that I'm working, which I intend to be. Tell them that I'll be able to phone them back tomorrow."

"Everybody?"

"Except Cat. And Jamie. I'll speak to them, although I hope that they don't phone today. Everybody else will have to wait."

Grace approved. She liked to be in control of the house, and being asked to turn people away was a most welcome instruction.

"It's about time you did this," she said. "You're at everybody's beck and call. It's ridiculous. You deserve a bit of time to yourself."

Isabel smiled. Grace was her greatest ally. Whatever disagreements they might have, in the final analysis she knew that Grace had her interests firmly at heart. This was loyalty of a sort which was rare in an age of self-indulgence. It was an old-fashioned virtue of the type which her philosophical colleagues extolled but could never themselves match. And Grace, in spite of her tendency to disapprove of certain people, had many other virtues. She believed in a God who would ultimately do justice to those to whom injustice had been done; she believed in work, and the importance of never being late or missing a day through "so-called illness," and she believed in never ignoring a request for help from anybody, no matter their condition, no matter the fault that lay behind their plight. This was true generosity of spirit, concealed behind a sometimes slightly brusque exterior.

"You're wonderful, Grace," Isabel said. "Where would any of us be without you?"

SHE WORKED THE ENTIRE morning. The post had brought a further bundle of submissions for the review and she entered the details of each of these in the book which she kept for the purpose. She suspected that several would not survive the first stage of screening; although one of these, "Gambling: An Ethical Analysis," revealed, at first glance, some possibilities. What ethical problems did gambling occasion? Isabel thought that there was a straightforward utilitarian argument to this, at the very least. If you had six children, as gamblers so often seemed to do (another sort of gambling? she wondered) then one had a duty to steward one's resources well, for the children's sakes. But if one was well-off, with no dependents, then was there anything intrinsically wrong in placing, if not one's last sou, then one's surplus sous, on a bet? Isabel thought for a moment. Kantians would be in no doubt about the answer to that, but that was the problem with Kantian morality: it was so utterly predictable, and left no room for subtlety; rather like Kant himself, she thought. In a purely philosophical sense, it must be very demanding to be German. Far better to be French (irresponsible and playful) or Greek (grave, but with a light touch). Of course, her own heritage, she thought, was enviable: Scottish commonsense philosophy on one side and American pragmatism on the other. That was a perfect combination. There had, of course, been those years at Cambridge, and that meant Wittgensteinism and a dose of linguistic philosophy, but that never did anybody any harm, as long as one remembered to reject it as one matured. *And, I may as well admit it, I am mature,* she thought, as she looked out the window of her study, into the garden, with its luxuriant shrubs and the first blossoms of white coming out on the magnolia.

She selected one of the more promising articles to read that morning. If it was worthwhile, she could then send it out for peer review that afternoon, and that would give her the sense of accomplishment that she needed. The title had caught her attention, largely because of the topicality of genetics—which formed the background to the problem—and because of the problem itself, which was, once again, truth telling. She was surrounded, she felt, by issues of truth telling. There had been that article on truth telling in sexual relationships, which had so entertained her and which had already been commented upon favourably by one of the journal's referees. Then there had been the Toby problem, which had brought the dilemma into the very centre of her own moral life. The world, it seemed, was based on lies and half-truths of one sort or another, and one of the tasks of morality was to help us negotiate our way round these. Yes, there were so many lies: and yet the sheer power of truth was in no sense dimmed. Had Aleksandr Solzhenitsyn not said, in his Nobel address, "One word of truth will conquer the whole world." Was this wishful thinking on the part of one who had lived in an entanglement of Orwellian state-sponsored lies, or was it a justifiable faith in the ability of truth to shine through the darkness? It had to be the latter; if it was the former, then life would be too bleak to continue. In that respect, Camus was right: the ultimate philosophical question was suicide. If there was no truth, then there would be no meaning, and our life was Sisyphean. And if life were Sisyphean, then what point in continuing with it? She reflected for a moment on the list of bleak adjectives. Orwellian, Sisyphean, Kafkaesque. Were there others? It was a great honour to a philosopher, or a writer, to become an adjective. She had seen "Hemingwayesque," which might be applied to a life of fishing and bullfighting, but there was no adjective, so far, for the world of failure and rundown loci chosen by Graham Greene as the setting for his moral dramas. "Greene-like"? she wondered. Far too ugly. "Greeneish," perhaps. Of course, "Greeneland" existed.

And here was truth telling again, this time in a paper from a philosopher in the National University of Singapore, a Dr. Chao. "Doubts About Father" was the title, and the subtitle was "Paternalism and Truthfulness in Genetics." Isabel moved from her desk to the chair near the window—the chair in which she liked to read her papers. As she did so, the telephone in the hall rang. After three rings it was answered. She waited; no call came from Grace. So she turned her attention to "Doubts About Father."

The paper, which was clearly written, began with a story. Clinical geneticists, Dr. Chao said, were often confronted with misattributed paternity, and these cases posed difficult issues of how, if at all, these mistakes should be revealed. Here is a case, he wrote, which involved just such an issue.

Mr. and Mrs. B. had given birth to a child with a genetic illness. Although the child could be expected to live, the condition was sufficiently serious to raise the issue of whether Mrs. B. should be tested during future pregnancies. Some fetuses would be affected, while others would not be. The only way to tell was prenatal screening.

So far, so good, thought Isabel. Of course, there were broader issues about screening, including major ones of eugenics, but Dr. Chao did not seem concerned with those, which was quite right: this was about truth telling and paternalism. Dr. Chao continued: Mr. and Mrs. B. had to have a genetic test to confirm their carrier status. In order for this particular condition to manifest itself, both parents of the affected child would have to be carriers of the relevant gene. When the doctor received the test results, however, these showed that while Mrs. B. was a carrier, Mr. B. was not. The child who had been born with the condition, then, *must have been by another man.* Mrs. B. (Mrs. Bovary perhaps, thought Isabel), who was not described, *had a lover.*

One solution was to tell Mrs. B. in private and then to leave it up to her to decide whether she would confess to her husband. At first blush this solution seemed attractive, as it would mean that one could avoid being responsible for possibly breaking up the marriage. The objection to this, though, was that if Mr. B. were not told, then he would go through life thinking that he was carrier of a gene which he did not, in fact, possess. Was he entitled to have this knowledge conveyed to him by the doctor, with whom he had a professional relationship? The doctor clearly owed him a duty, but what were the limits of this?

Isabel turned the last page of the article. There were the references, all set out in the correct form, but there was no conclusion. Dr. Chao did not know how to resolve the issue that he had raised. That was reasonable enough: it was quite legitimate to ask questions which one could not answer, or which one did not want to answer. But, on the whole, Isabel preferred papers which took a position.

It occurred to Isabel to ask Grace for her view on this. It was time for morning coffee, anyway, and she had an excuse to go through to the kitchen. There she found Grace, unloading the dishwasher.

"I am going to tell you a rather tricky story," said Isabel. "Then I'm going to ask you to give me your reaction. Don't bother about reasons, just tell me what you would do."

She related the story of Mr. and Mrs. B. Grace continued to unload plates as she listened, but abandoned her work when the story came to an end.

"I would write Mr. B. a letter," she said firmly. "I would tell him not to trust his wife."

"I see," said Isabel.

"But I wouldn't sign my own name," Grace added. "I would write anonymously."

Isabel could not conceal her surprise. "Anonymously? Why?"

"I don't know," said Grace. "You said that I should not bother with reasons. I should just tell you what I would do. And that's it."

Isabel was silent. She was used to hearing Grace express unusual views, but this curious preference for an anonymous letter astounded her. She was about to press Grace further, but her housekeeper changed the subject.

"Cat phoned," she said. "She did not want to disturb you, but she would like to pop in for tea this afternoon. I said that we would let her know."

"That's fine," said Isabel. "I would like to see her."

Truth telling. Paternalism. She was no further forward, she felt, but suddenly she decided. She would ask Grace her views.

"Here's another one, Grace," she said. "Imagine that you found out that Toby was seeing another girl and not telling Cat about it. What would you do?"

Grace frowned. "Difficult," she said. "I don't think I'd tell Cat."

Isabel relaxed. At least they thought the same way on that issue.

"But then," Grace went on, "I think I'd probably go to Toby and tell him that unless he gave Cat up, I'd tell the other girl. That way I'd get rid of him, because I wouldn't want somebody like that to marry Cat. That's what I'd do."

Isabel nodded. "I see. And you'd have no hesitation in doing that?"

"None," said Grace. "None at all." Then she added, "Not that this would ever happen, would it?"

Isabel hesitated; here was another occasion on which a lie could slip out. And the moment's hesitation was enough.

"Oh my God!" said Grace. "Poor Cat! Poor girl! I never liked that boy, you know, never. I didn't like to say it, but now you know. Those strawberry jeans of his, you know the ones he wears? I knew what they meant, right from the beginning. See? I knew."

CHAPTER EIGHTEEN

CAT ARRIVED FOR TEA at three-thirty, having left Eddie in charge of the shop. She was let into the house by Grace, who looked at her strangely, or so Cat thought; but then Grace was strange, she always had been, and Cat had always known that. Grace had theories and convictions about virtually everything, and one never knew what was going on in her head. How Isabel put up with those conversations in the kitchen, Cat had no idea. Perhaps she ignored most of it.

Isabel was in her summerhouse, correcting proofs. The summerhouse was a small octagonal building, constructed of wood and painted dark green. It stood at the back, against the high stone wall that enclosed the garden; in his illness her father had spent whole days in it, looking out over the lawn, thinking and reading, although it was hard for him to turn the pages and he would wait for Isabel to do that. For some years after his death she had been unable to go into it, such were the memories, but gradually she had taken to working in it, even in winter, when it could be heated by a Norwegian wood-burning stove which stood in one corner. It was largely undecorated, save for three framed photographs which had been hung on the back wall. Her father, in the uniform of the Cameronians, in Sicily, under a harsh sun, standing in front of a requisitioned villa; all that bravery and sacrifice, so long ago, for a cause that was utterly, utterly right. Her mother—sainted American mother; once awkwardly referred to by Grace as her sanitized American mother—sitting with her father in a café in Venice. And herself as a child with her parents, on a picnic, she thought. Foxed at the edges, the photographs needed restoration, but at present they were undisturbed.

It was a warm day for spring—more of a summer's day, really—and she had opened the double glass doors of the summerhouse. Now she saw Cat approaching her across the lawn, a small brown bag in her hand. It would be something from the delicatessen; Cat never came empty-handed, and would give Isabel a small jar of truffle pâté or olives picked at random from the shelves of her shop.

"Belgian chocolate mice," said Cat, laying the packet on the table.

"Cats bring mice as an offering," remarked Isabel, laying the proofs to one side. "My aunt—your great-aunt—had a cat which caught mice and put them on her bed. So thoughtful."

Cat sat down on the wicker chair next to Isabel's. "Grace tells me that you're in seclusion," she said. "Not to be disturbed except by me."

That was tactful of Grace, thought Isabel. It was not helpful to mention Jamie too often.

"Life has been getting rather complicated," said Isabel. "I wanted a day or two to get on with some work and decomplicate. I'm sure you know how it feels."

"Yes," said Cat. "Curl-up-and-get-away-from-it-all days. I have them too."

"Grace will bring us tea and we can have a chat," said Isabel. "I've done enough work for the day."

Cat smiled. "And I'm going to throw in the towel too," she said. "Eddie can look after things until closing time. I'm going to go home and get changed. Then I . . . we're going out."

"Good," said Isabel. We. Toby, of course.

"We're going to celebrate," said Cat, looking sideways at Isabel. "Dinner, then a club."

Isabel caught her breath. She had not expected it, but she had dreaded it nonetheless. And now the moment had arrived. "A celebration?"

Cat nodded. She did not look at Isabel as she spoke, but was staring out over the lawn. Her tone was cautious. "Toby and I are engaged," she said. "Yesterday evening. We'll put it in the papers next week. I wanted you to be the first to know." She paused. "I think that he's told his parents now, but apart from them, nobody else knows. Only you."

Isabel turned to her niece and reached to take her hand. "Darling, well done. Congratulations." She had mustered a supreme effort, like a singer straining for a high note, but her attempt proved inadequate. Her voice sounded flat and unenthusiastic.

Cat looked at her. "Do you mean that?"

"I only want you to be happy," said Isabel. "If this is what makes you happy, then of course I mean that."

Cat weighed these words for a moment. "The congratulations of a philosopher," she said. "Can't you say something personal?" She did not give Isabel time to respond, although Isabel had no answer ready and would have had to battle to find one. "You don't like him, do you? You're simply not prepared to give him a chance— even for my sake."

Isabel lowered her eyes. She could not lie about this. "I haven't warmed to him. I admit it. But I promise you: I'll make every effort, even if it's hard."

Cat seized on her words. Her voice was raised now, the indignation coming through. "Even if it's hard? Why should it be so hard? Why do you have to say that?"

Isabel was not in control of her emotions. This news was devastating, and she forgot her intention not to mention what she had seen. Now it came out. "I don't think that he's faithful to you," she said. "I've seen him with somebody else. That's why. That's why."

She stopped, horrified by what she had said. She had not meant to say it—she knew it was wrong—and yet it had come out, as if spoken by somebody else. Immediately she felt miserable, thinking: *So are wrongs committed, just like that, without thinking.* The doing of wrong was not a hard thing, preceded by careful thought; it was a casual thing, done so easily. That was Hannah Arendt's insight, was it not? The pure banality of evil. Only good is heroic.

Cat was quite still. Then she shrugged off the hand which Isabel had lightly placed upon her shoulder. "Let me get this straight," she said. "You say that you've seen him with another woman. Is that what you say?"

Isabel nodded. She could not recant now, and that left honesty as the only option. "Yes. I'm sorry. I hadn't meant to tell you, because I really don't think that it's my business to interfere in your affairs. But I did see him. I saw him embracing another girl. He was going to see her. It was in the doorway to her flat. I was . . . I was passing by. I saw it happen."

"Where was this?" she asked quietly. "Where exactly did you see this?"

"Nelson Street," said Isabel.

Cat was silent for a moment. Then she began to laugh, and the tension drained from her. "His sister, Fiona, lives there, you know. Poor Isabel! Of course you had it all mixed up. He often goes to see Fiona. Of course he gives her a kiss. They're very fond of one another. And it's a touchy-feely family."

No, thought Isabel. They're not a touchy-feely family; not at least according to my understanding of the term.

"Actually, it was his sister's flatmate," said Isabel. "It wasn't his sister."

"Lizzie?"

"I have no idea what her name is," said Isabel.

Cat snorted. "It's nonsense," she said firmly. "You've misinterpreted a peck on the cheek. And now you're not even prepared to accept that you're wrong. It would be different if you acknowledged that, but you aren't. You hate him so much."

Isabel fought back. "I do not hate him. You have no right to say that." But she knew that Cat did, for even as she spoke, the image of an avalanche came into her mind, and she felt ashamed.

Cat now rose to her feet. "I'm very sorry about this. I understand why you might have wanted to tell me what you told me, but I think that you're being totally unfair. I love Toby. We're going to get married. That's all there is to it." She stepped out of the summerhouse.

Isabel rose from her chair, scattering the proofs as she did so. "Cat, please. You know how fond I am of you. You know that. Please . . ." She trailed off. Cat had started to run across the lawn, back to the house. Grace was at the kitchen door, a tray in her hand. She moved to one side to let Cat past, and the tray fell to the ground.

THE REST OF THE DAY was ruined. After Cat's departure, Isabel spent an hour or so discussing the situation with Grace, who did her best to be reassuring.

"She may be like that for the time being," she said. "She may have closed her mind to the possibility right now. But she will think about it and the possibility will work away in her mind. She'll start to think maybe, just maybe, it's true. And then the scales will begin to fall from her eyes."

Isabel thought the situation bleak, but she had to acknowledge that there was something in what Grace had said. "In the meantime she's not going to forgive me, though."

"Probably not," said Grace, in a matter-of-fact way. "Although it might help if you wrote to her and told her how sorry you were. She'll get round to forgiving you in due course, but it will be easier if you've left the door open."

Isabel did as Grace suggested, and wrote a brief letter to Cat. She apologised for the distress she had caused her and hoped that Cat would forgive her. But even as she wrote, *Please forgive me,* she realised that only a few weeks before she herself had said to Cat, *There's such a thing as premature forgiveness,* because a lot of nonsense was talked about forgiveness by those who simply did not grasp (or had never heard of) the point that Professor Strawson had made in *Freedom and Resentment* about reactive attitudes and how important these were—Peter Strawson, whose name, Isabel noted, could be rendered anagrammatically, and unfairly, as *a pen strews rot.* We needed resentment, he said, as it was resentment which identified and underlined the wrong. Without these reactive attitudes, we ran the risk of diminishing our sense of right and wrong, because we could end up thinking it just doesn't matter. So we should not forgive prematurely, which is presumably what Pope John Paul II had in mind when he waited for all those years before he went to visit his attacker in his cell. Isabel wondered what the pope had said to the gunman. "I forgive you"? Or had he said something very different, something not at all forgiving? She smiled at the thought; popes were human, after all, and behaved like human beings, which meant that they must look in the mirror from time to time and ask themselves: Is this really me in this slightly absurd outfit, waiting to go out onto the balcony and wave to all these people, with their flags, and their hopes, and their tears?

A HYPOTHESIS DEVELOPED in a restaurant, after several glasses of Italian wine, and in the company of an attractive young man, was one thing; a hypothesis that could stand the cold light of day was another. Isabel was well aware of the fact that all she had in the case of Minty Auchterlonie was a conjecture. If it was true that there were irregularities in McDowell's, and if it was true that Mark Fraser had stumbled upon them, then it did not necessarily mean that Paul Hogg was implicated. Isabel's idea about how he could be implicated was feasible, she supposed, but no more than that. McDowell's was a large firm, she understood, and there was no reason why Paul Hogg should be the one to whom Mark's discovery related.

Isabel realised that if she wished to develop a firmer foundation for her hypothesis, indeed if she wished to make it remotely credible, then she would need to find out more about McDowell's, and that would not be easy. She would need to talk to people in the financial world; they would know even if they did not work in McDowell's itself. The Edinburgh financial community had all the characteristics of a village, as did the legal community, and there would be gossip. But she would need more than that: she would need to discover how one might be able to find out whether somebody had traded improperly on private information. Would this involve monitoring share transactions? How on earth would one go about that, trying to glean information about who bought what in all the millions of transactions that take place on the stock exchanges every year? And of course people would be careful to cover their tracks through the use of nominees and offshore agents. If there were very few prosecutions for insider trading—and indeed hardly any convictions—this was for good reason. One simply could not prove it. And if that was the case, then anything that Minty did with the information she gathered from her fiancé would be impossible to track down. Minty could act with impunity, unless—and this was a major qualification— unless the somebody from within, somebody like Mark Fraser, could link her transactions with information which he knew Paul Hogg would have possessed. But Mark, of course, was dead. Which meant that she would have to go and see her friend Peter Stevenson, financier, discreet philanthropist, and chairman of the Really Terrible Orchestra.

CHAPTER NINETEEN

WEST GRANGE HOUSE was a large square house, built in the late eighteenth century and painted white. It stood in large grounds in the Grange, a well-set suburb that rubbed shoulders with Morningside and Bruntsfield, an easy walk from Isabel's house and an easier one from Cat's delicatessen. Peter Stevenson had wanted the house for as long as he could remember and had leapt at the chance to buy it when it unexpectedly came on the market.

Peter had been a successful merchant banker and had decided in his mid-forties to pursue an independent career as a company doctor. Firms in financial trouble could call on him to attempt a rescue, or firms with bickering boards could invite him in to mediate their squabbles. In his quiet way he had brought peace to troubled business lives, persuading people to sit down and examine their issues one by one.

"Everything has a solution," he observed to Isabel in answer to a question she put to him about his work as he showed her into his morning room. "Everything. All you have to do is to strip the problem down and then start from there. All one has to do is to make a list and be reasonable."

"Which people often aren't," said Isabel.

Peter smiled. "You can work round that. Most people can become reasonable even if they aren't in the beginning."

"Except for some," Isabel had persisted. "The profoundly unreasonable. And there are quite a few of those, quick and dead. Idi Amin and Pol Pot, to name two."

Peter reflected on her turn of phrase. Who still spoke of the quick and the dead? Most people had lost that understanding of "quick" and would look blank if they heard it. How typical of Isabel to keep a word alive, like a gardener tending to a feeble plant. Good for Isabel.

"The irretrievably unreasonable tend not to run businesses," he said, "even if they try to run countries. Politicians are different from businessmen or company people. Politics attracts quite the wrong sort of person."

Isabel agreed. "Absolutely. All those overgrown egos. It's why they go into politics in the first place. They want to dominate others. They enjoy power and its trappings. Few of them go into politics because they want to improve the world. Some might, I suppose, but not many."

Peter thought for a moment. "Well, there are the Gandhis and the Mandelas, I suppose, and President Carter."

"President Carter?"

Peter nodded. "A good man. Far too gentle for politics. I think that he found himself in the White House by mistake. And he was far too honest. He made those embarrassingly honest remarks about his private temptations, and the press had a field day. And every single one of those who took him to task would have harboured exactly the same sort of thoughts themselves. Who hasn't?"

"I know all about fantasies," said Isabel. "I know what he meant . . ." She paused. Peter looked at her quizzically, and she continued quickly, "Not that sort of fantasy. I have thoughts about avalanches . . ."

Peter smiled and gestured to a chair. "Well, *chacun à son rêve.*"

Isabel sat back in her chair and looked out over the lawn. The garden was larger than her own, and more open. Perhaps if she cut down a tree she would get more light, but she knew that she could never do that; she would have to go before the trees went. Oak trees were sobering in that respect; every time you looked at them they reminded you that they were likely to be around well after you had gone.

She looked at Peter. He was a bit like an oak tree, she thought; not to look at, of course—in that respect he was more of a wisteria, perhaps—but he was a person whom one could trust. Moreover, he was discreet, and one could talk to him without fear of what one said being broadcast. So if she asked him about McDowell's, as she now did, nobody else would know she was interested.

He pondered her question for a moment. "I know quite a few of the people there," he said. "They're pretty sound, as far as I know." He paused. "But I do know of somebody who might talk to you about them. I think he's just left after some sort of spat. He might be prepared to talk."

Isabel answered quickly. This was exactly what she had wanted; Peter knew everybody and could put you in touch with anyone. "That's exactly what I would like," she said, adding, "Thank you."

"But you have to be careful," Peter continued. "First, I don't know him myself, so I can't vouch for him. And then you have to bear in mind that he might have some sort of grudge against them. You never know. But if you want to see him, he sometimes comes to our concerts because he has a sister who plays in the orchestra.

So you need to come to our concert tomorrow night. I'll make sure you get the chance to talk to him at the party afterwards."

Isabel laughed. "Your orchestra? The Really Terrible Orchestra?"

"The very same," said Peter. "I'm surprised you haven't been to one of our concerts before. I'm sure I invited you."

"You did," said Isabel, "but I was away at the time. I was sorry to miss it. I gather that it was . . ."

"Terrible," said Peter. "Yes, we're no good at all, but we have fun. And most of the audience comes to laugh, anyway, so it doesn't matter how badly we play."

"As long as you do your best?"

"Exactly. And our best, well, I'm afraid it's not very good. But there we are."

Isabel looked out over the lawn. It interested her that those who had done one thing very well in their lives would often try to master something else, and fail. Peter had been a very successful financier; now he was a very marginal clarinettist; success undoubtedly made failure easier to bear, or did it? Perhaps one became accustomed to doing things well and then felt frustrated when one did other things less well. But Isabel knew that Peter was not driven in this way; he was happy to play the clarinet *modestly*, as he put it.

ISABEL CLOSED HER EYES, and listened. The players, seated in the auditorium of St. George's School for Girls, which patiently hosted the Really Terrible Orchestra, were tackling a score beyond their capabilities; Purcell had not intended this, and would probably not have recognised his composition. It was slightly familiar to Isabel—or passages of it were—but it seemed to her that different sections of the orchestra were playing quite different pieces, and in different times. The strings were particularly ragged, and sounded several tones flat, while the trombones, which should have been in six-eight time, like the rest of the orchestra, seemed to be playing in common time. She opened her eyes and looked at the trombonists, who were concentrating on their music with worried frowns; had they looked at the conductor they would have been set right, but the task of reading the notes was all they could manage. Isabel exchanged smiles with the person in the seat beside her; the audience was enjoying itself, as it always did at a Really Terrible Orchestra concert.

The Purcell came to an end, to the evident relief of the orchestra, with many of the members lowering their instruments and taking a deep breath, as runners do at the end of a race. There was muted laughter amongst the audience, and the rustle of paper as they consulted the programme. Mozart lay ahead, and, curiously, "Yellow Submarine." There was no Stockhausen, Isabel noticed with relief, remembering, for a moment, and with sadness, that evening at the Usher Hall, which was why she was here, after all, listening to the Really Terrible Orchestra labouring its way through its programme before its bemused but loyal audience.

There was rapturous applause at the end of the concert, and the conductor, in his gold braid waistcoat, took several bows. Then audience and players went through to the atrium for the wine and sandwiches that the orchestra provided its listeners in return for attendance at the concert.

"It's the least we can do," explained the conductor in his concluding remarks. "You have been so tolerant."

Isabel knew a number of the players and many of those in the audience, and she soon found herself in a group of friends hovering over a large plate of smoked salmon sandwiches.

"I thought they were improving," said one, "but I'm not so sure after this evening. The Mozart . . ."

"So that's what it was."

"It's therapy," said another. "Look how happy they were. These are people who could never otherwise play in an orchestra. This is group therapy. It's great."

A tall oboist turned to Isabel. "You could join," he said. "You play the flute, don't you? You could join."

"I might," said Isabel. "I'm thinking about it." But she was thinking about Johnny Sanderson, who must be the man at Peter Stevenson's side, being led in her direction by her host, and looking at her through the crowd.

"I wanted you two to meet," said Peter, effecting the introduction. "We might be able to persuade Isabel to join us, Johnny. She's much better than us but we could do with another flautist."

"You could do with everything," said Johnny. "Music lessons, to start with . . ."

Isabel laughed. "They weren't too bad. I liked 'Yellow Submarine.'"

"Their party piece," said Johnny, reaching for a slice of brown bread and smoked salmon.

They spoke about the orchestra for a few minutes before Isabel changed the subject. He had worked with McDowell's, she had heard; had he enjoyed being there? He had. But then he thought for a moment and looked at her sideways, in mock suspicion. "Was that why you wanted to meet me?" He paused. "Or rather why Peter wanted us to meet?"

Isabel met his gaze. There was no point in dissembling here, she thought; she could tell that Johnny Sanderson was astute.

"Yes," she said simply. "I'm interested in finding out about them."

He nodded. "There's not much to find out," he said. "It's a pretty typical setup. They're rather dull, in fact, most of them. I was on social terms with a few of them, I suppose, but for the most part I found them somewhat . . . tedious. Sorry. That sounds a bit arrogant, but that's what they were. Number people. Mathematics."

"Paul Hogg?"

Johnny shrugged. "Decent enough. A bit earnest for my taste, but good at his job. He's typical of the type that used to work there. Some of the new appointments are a bit different. Paul's old-style Edinburgh finance. Straight down the middle."

Isabel passed him the plate of smoked salmon, and he helped himself to a further slice. She lifted her glass and sipped at the wine, which was of a far better quality than the wine which was normally served at such events. That was Peter's doing, she thought.

Something he had said had interested her. If Paul Hogg was typical of the type that used to work at McDowell's, and if he was straight down the middle, as Johnny had put it, then what were the new people like? "So McDowell's is changing?" she said.

"Of course," said Johnny. "Just like the rest of the world. Everything. Banks, finance houses, brokers—everybody. There's a new spirit of toughness. Corners are cut. It's the same everywhere, isn't it?"

"I suppose so," said Isabel. He was right, of course; the old moral certainties were disappearing everywhere and were being replaced by self-interest and ruthlessness.

Johnny swallowed his brown bread and salmon and licked at the tip of a finger. "Paul Hogg," he mused. "Paul Hogg. Mmm. I thought that he was a bit of a mummy's boy, frankly, and then he went and produced this eighty-four-horsepower bitch of a fiancée, Minty something or other. Auchtermuchty. Auchendinny."

"Auchterlonie," prompted Isabel.

"Not a cousin of yours, I hope," said Johnny. "I hope I haven't trodden on any toes."

Isabel smiled. "What you said about her was roughly my own estimation, but perhaps a bit more charitable."

"I see that we understand each other. She's as hard as nails. She works for that setup in North Charlotte Street, Ecosse Bank. She's an absolute tart, if you ask me. She runs round with a couple of young men from Paul's office. I've seen her when Paul has been out of town. I saw her down in London once, in a bar in the City when they thought that nobody else from Edinburgh was around. Well, I was there and I saw her. Hanging all over a rising star from Aberdeen who got his knees under the table at McDowell's because he's good at juggling figures and taking risks that paid off. Ian Cameron, he's called. Plays rugby for some team or other. Physical type, but clever nonetheless."

"Hanging all over him?"

Johnny gestured. "Like this. All over him. Nonplatonic body language."

"But she's engaged to Paul Hogg."

"Exactly."

"And Paul, does he know about this?"

Johnny shook his head. "Paul's an innocent. He's an innocent who's taken up with a woman who's probably a bit too ambitious for him. It happens."

Isabel took another sip at her wine. "But what does she see in Paul? Why would she bother?"

"Respectability," said Johnny firmly. "He's good cover if you want to get on in the Edinburgh financial world. His father was a founding partner of Scottish Montreal and the Gullane Fund. If you were nobody, so to speak, and you wanted to become somebody, no better choice than poor Paul. Perfect. All the right connections. Dull Fettesian dinners. Corporate seats at the Festival Theatre, with opera supper. Perfect!"

"And in the meantime she gets on with her own career?"

"Absolutely. She's interested in money, I would say, and probably not much else. Well, I correct myself. Men friends. A bit of rough like Ian Cameron."

Isabel was silent. Faithlessness, it seemed, was nothing unusual; the discovery of Toby's conduct had surprised her, but now that she had heard this story about Minty, perhaps this was exactly what she should expect. Perhaps one should be surprised by constancy, which is what the sociobiologists were hinting at anyway. Men had a strong urge to have as many partners as possible in order to ensure the survival of their genes, we were told. But women? Perhaps they were subconsciously attracted to the men who were subconsciously ensuring the maximum chance of gene perpetuation, which meant that Minty and Ian were perfect partners.

Isabel felt confused, but not so confused as not to be able to ask her next question in such a way as to make it sound innocent. "And I suppose Ian and Minty can engage in pillow talk about deals and money and things like that. Can't you picture it?"

"No," said Johnny. "Because if they did it would be insider trading and I would personally take the very greatest pleasure in catching them at it and nailing their ears to the New Club door."

Isabel imagined the picture. It was almost as good as imagining Toby caught in his avalanche. But she stopped herself, and said, instead, "I think that is exactly what has been happening."

Johnny stood quite still, his glass halfway to his lips, but halted. He stared at Isabel. "Are you serious?"

She nodded. "I can't tell you exactly why I think this, but I can assure you that I have good reason to believe it. Could you help me to prove it? Could you help me to track the deals? Could you do it?"

Johnny put down his glass. "Yes. I could. Or I could try. I've got no time for financial dishonesty. It's ruining the market. It undermines all of us—really badly. These people are a pest."

"Good," said Isabel. "I'm glad."

"But whatever you do, you must keep this quiet," added Johnny. "If you're wrong, then we would be in serious trouble. You can't make defamatory allegations about these things. They'd sue us. I'd look stupid. Do you understand?"

Isabel did.

CHAPTER TWENTY

ON THE EVENING of that unpleasant afternoon when Isabel had voiced her fears in the face of Cat's good news, Cat and Toby had gone to the restaurant earlier than they had intended, as a table had not been available later on. A meeting of the Franco-British Legal Association had been held by the Faculty of Advocates and many of the members had booked tables for dinner afterwards. It would be a good place to talk about the jurisprudence of the Conseil d'Etat, and other matters, of course.

Cat had left Isabel's house in tears. Grace had tried to talk to her as she entered the kitchen, but she had not been prepared to listen. At that stage her emotions were entirely ones of anger. Isabel could not have made her feelings about Toby plainer; right from the beginning she had kept him at a distance, viewing him, she thought, with such distaste that she would not be surprised if he had picked up on it himself, even if he had never said anything about it. She understood, of course, that there were differences of outlook between them, but surely that was no reason for Isabel to be so dismissive. Toby was not an intellectual in the way Isabel was, but what difference did that make? They had enough common ground to meet somewhere; it was not as if he was a complete ignoramus, as she had pointed out to Isabel on more than one occasion.

And yet Isabel had remained distant, all the time comparing him adversely with Jamie. That was what irritated her more than anything else. Relationships between people could not be the basis of comparison by others. Cat knew what she wanted from a relationship, which was a bit of fun, and passion too. Toby was passionate. He wanted her with an urgency that excited her. Jamie had not done that. He talked too much and was always trying to please her. Where were his own feelings? Did none of that actually matter to him? Perhaps Isabel did not understand that. How could she? She had been disastrously married a long, long time ago, and since then, as far as she knew, there had been no lovers. So she really was in no position to understand, far less to comment on, something of which she had little inkling.

By the time she reached the delicatessen, her immediate anger had abated. She had even considered retracing her steps and making an attempt at a reconciliation with Isabel, but if she was to meet Toby at six, as she had planned, she would have to get back to her flat quite soon. The shop was only moderately busy, and Eddie seemed to be coping well. He had been more cheerful over the past few days, which she found encouraging, but she did not want to count on him too much. More time would be needed, she felt—years, perhaps.

She spoke briefly to Eddie and then made her way back to her flat. She was still preoccupied with her conversation with Isabel, but was now making a determined effort to put it out of her mind. Tonight was to be their private celebration for the engagement, and she did not want it ruined any more than it had been. Isabel was simply wrong.

Toby was prompt, bounding up the stairs to her door and presenting her with a large spray of carnations. In his other hand he was carrying a bottle of champagne, wrapped in tissue paper, but chilled. They went into the kitchen, where Cat prepared a vase for the flowers and Toby busied himself with opening the champagne. It had been shaken by his running up the stairs and the cork exploded with a loud report and the foam cascaded over the side of the bottle. Toby made a joke about this which made Cat blush.

They toasted each other before moving through to the sitting room. Then, shortly before their taxi arrived, they moved through to the bedroom and embraced. Toby said that he loved the smell in her bedroom; he disorganised her dress, and she had to struggle to keep her composure. Never before have I felt so intensely, she thought; never.

Over dinner they talked about mundane matters, about the wording of the announcement in *The Scotsman,* and about the reaction of Toby's parents when he told them the news.

"The old man seemed mighty relieved," he said. "He said, 'About bloody time,' or something like that. Then I told him that I'd need a raise in pay, and that took the smile off his face."

"And your mother?" she asked.

"She went on about what a nice girl you are," he said. "She was pretty relieved too. I think she's always been worried about my taking up with some awful scrubber. Not that she's got any grounds to believe that."

"Of course not," joked Cat.

Toby smiled at her. "I'm glad that you said yes." He took her hand. "I would have been pretty upset if you'd said no."

"What would you have done?" asked Cat. "Found another woman?"

The question hung in the air for a moment. She had not thought about it, but now, quite suddenly, she felt something in his hand, as if he had been given a small electric shock; a slight jolt. She looked at him, and for a second or two she saw a shadow pass, a change in the light in his eyes. It was almost imperceptible, but she saw it.

She let go of his hand, and momentarily flustered, she brushed at the crumbs of bread around her plate.

"Why would I do that?" said Toby. He smiled. "Not me."

Cat felt her heart beating wildly within her as Isabel's warning, suppressed until now, came back to her.

"Of course not," she said lightly. "Of course not." But the image came to her of Toby and that other girl, Fiona's flatmate; and he was naked, and standing by a window, looking out, as Toby did when he got out of bed; and she, the other girl, was watching him, and she closed her eyes to rid herself of this thought, of this dreadful image, but it would not leave her.

"What are we going to do?" Cat asked suddenly.

"When? Do when?"

She tried to smile. "What are we going to do now? Should we go back to the flat? Or shall we go and see somebody? I feel sociable."

"If anybody's at home," said Toby. "What about Richard and Emma? They're always there. We could take them a bottle of champagne and tell them the good news."

Cat thought quickly. Distrust, like a rapidly creeping strain, egged her on. "No. I don't want to go all the way down to Leith. What about Fiona? She's your sister, after all. We should celebrate with her. Let's go down to Nelson Street."

She watched him. His lips parted slightly as she began, as if he was on the point of interrupting her, but he let her finish.

"I don't think so," he said. "We can see her tomorrow at my parents' place. We don't need to go there now."

"No," she said, "we must go down to Fiona's. We must. I really want to."

He did not protest further, but she could tell that he was uneasy, and he was silent in the taxi, looking out the window as they drove down the Mound and then over the ridge of George Street. She did not say anything, other than to ask the taxi to stop outside a late-night wine shop. Toby got out silently, bought a bottle of champagne, and then came back into the taxi. He made a remark about the man in the shop and then said something inconsequential about their planned visit to his parents the following day. Cat nodded, but did not take in what he was saying.

They stopped outside the flat in Nelson Street. Toby paid off the taxi while Cat waited on the steps. There were lights inside; Fiona was in. Waiting for Toby, she rang the bell, glancing at him as she did so. He was fiddling with the paper in which the bottle of champagne had been twist-wrapped.

"You'll tear it," she said.

"What?"

"You'll tear the paper."

The door opened. It was not Fiona, but another woman. She looked at Cat blankly, and then saw Toby.

"Fiona . . . ," began Cat.

"Not in," said the other woman. She moved forward towards Toby, who seemed for a moment to back away, but she reached out and took his wrist. "Who's your friend?" she said. "Toby? Who—"

"Fiancée," said Cat. "I'm Cat."

CHAPTER TWENTY-ONE

ISABEL HAD POSTED her letter of apology to Cat the day before the Really Terrible Orchestra concert and Cat had responded a couple of days later. The reply came on a card bearing Raeburn's picture of the Reverend Robert Walker skating on the ice at Duddingston Loch, a picture as powerful and immediately recognisable, in its local way, as *The Birth of Venus*. Great art, she felt, had a calming effect on the viewer; it made one stop in awe, which is exactly what Damien Hirst and Andy Warhol did not do. You did not stop in awe. They stopped you in your tracks, perhaps, but that was not the same thing; awe was something quite different.

She turned the eighteenth-century clergyman on his back and read Cat's message: *Of course, you're forgiven. You always are. Anyway, something has happened, and it has proved that you were right. There, I thought that would be so difficult to say, and I suppose it was. My pen almost ground to a halt. But anyway come and have coffee in the shop and I can let you try this new cheese that's just come in. It's Portuguese and it tastes of olives. Cat.*

Isabel felt grateful for her niece's good nature, even if an aspect of that same nature was a lack of judgement when it came

to men. There were many young women who would not so readily have forgiven the intrusion; and of course there were fewer
still who would have admitted that an aunt was right in such a
matter. Of course, this was welcome news, and Isabel looked forward to finding out how Toby had been exposed; perhaps Cat had
followed him, as she herself had, and had been led to a conclusion by that most convincing of evidence—the evidence of one's
own eyes.

She walked into Bruntsfield, savouring the warmth which
was beginning to creep into the sun. There was building work in
Merchiston Crescent—a new house was being crammed into a
small corner plot, and there was a bag of cement on the muddy
pavement. Then, a few steps later, she saw gulls, circling above
roofs, looking for a place to nest. The gulls were considered pests
in the neighbourhood—large, mewing birds that swooped down
on those who came too close to their nesting places—but we
humans built too, and left cement and stones and litter, and were
as aggressively territorial. The review was planning an environ-
mental ethics issue the following year and Isabel had been solic-
iting papers. Perhaps somebody would write about the ethics of
litter. Not that there was much to say about that: litter was
unquestionably bad and surely nobody would make a case in its
favour. And yet why was it wrong to drop litter? Was it purely an
aesthetic objection, based on the notion that the superficial pol-
lution of the environment was unattractive? Or was the aesthetic
impact linked to some notion of the distress which others felt in
the face of litter? If that was the case, then we might even have a
duty to look attractive to others, in order to minimise their distress. There were interesting implications to that.

And one of these implications presented itself to Isabel a
mere fifty paces later, outside the post office, from which emerged

a young man in his mid-twenties—Jamie's age, perhaps—with several sharp metal spikes inserted into his lower lip and chin. The sharp metal points jutted out jauntily, like tiny sharpened phalluses, which made Isabel reflect on how uncomfortable it must have been to kiss a man like that. Beards were one thing—and there were women who complained vigorously about the reaction of their skins to contact with bearded men—but how much more unpleasant it would be to feel these metal spikes up against one's lips and cheeks. Cold, perhaps; sharp, certainly; but then, who would wish to kiss this young man, with his scowl and his discouraging look? Isabel asked herself the question and answered it immediately: of course numerous girls would wish to kiss him, and probably did; girls who had rings in their belly buttons and their noses, and who wore studded collars. Spikes and rings were complementary; after all. All this young man would have to do was look for the corresponding plumage.

As she crossed the road to Cat's delicatessen, Isabel saw the spiky young man dart across the road ahead of her and suddenly stumble at the edge of the pavement. He tripped and fell, landing on a knee on the concrete paving stone. Isabel, a few steps behind him, hastened to his side and reached out to him, helping him to his feet. He stood up, and looked down at the ripped knee of his discoloured denim jeans. Then he looked up at her and smiled.

"Thank you." His voice was soft, with a hint of Belfast in it.

"It's so easy to stumble," said Isabel. "Are you all right?"

"I think so. I've torn my jeans, that's all. Still, you pay for ripped jeans these days. I got mine free."

Isabel smiled, and suddenly the words came out of her, unbidden, unanticipated. "Why have you got those spikes in your face?"

He did not look annoyed. "My face? These piercings?" He fingered at the spike which projected from his lower lip. "It's my jewellery, I suppose."

"Your jewellery?" Isabel stared at him, noticing the tiny golden ring which he had inserted into an eyebrow.

"Yes," said the young man. "You wear jewellery. I wear jewellery. I like it. And it shows that I don't care."

"Don't care about what?"

"About what people think. It shows that I have my own style. This is me. I'm not in anybody's uniform."

Isabel smiled at him. She appreciated his directness, and she liked his voice with its definite cadences. "Good for you," she said. "Uniforms are not a good idea." She paused. The sun was glinting off one of the spikes, casting a tiny, bobbing reflection onto his upper lip. "Unless, of course, you have donned another uniform in your eagerness to avoid uniforms. That's a possibility, isn't it?"

The young man tossed his head backwards. "Okay," he said, laughing. "I'm the same as everybody else with piercings. So?"

ISABEL LOOKED AT HIM. This was a strange conversation, and she would have liked to prolong it. But she reminded herself that she had to see Cat and that she could not spend the morning standing there with that young man discussing facial piercing. So they said good-bye to each other, and she made her way into the delicatessen, where Eddie, standing beside a shelf on which he was stacking Portuguese sardines, glanced at her and then looked back, with some intensity, at the sardines.

She found Cat in her office, finishing off a telephone call. Her niece replaced the receiver and looked at her. Isabel noticed, with relief, that there seemed to be no resentment in her expression. The card she received had reflected what Cat really felt. Good.

"You got my card?"

"Yes, I did. And I'm still very sorry that I upset you. I take no pleasure in hearing about it." She knew, as she said this, that it was not true, and faltered at the last words.

Cat smiled. "Maybe. Maybe not. But let's not talk about it if you don't mind."

They drank a cup of coffee together and then Isabel returned home. There was work to do—a new crop of articles had arrived for the review—but she found that she could not settle to it. She wondered when she would hear from Johnny Sanderson, if he would call back at all.

HE DID TELEPHONE Isabel, as he had said he would, a few days after the Really Terrible Orchestra concert. He could meet her, he said, at the Scotch Malt Whisky Society rooms in Leith that Friday evening at six. There was a whisky nosing, and she could sample the whisky—if she had the stomach for it. He had information for her, which he could pass on at the event itself. There would be opportunities to talk.

Isabel knew very little about whisky, and rarely drank it. But she knew that it had much the same apparatus of sampling as did wine, even if the language was very different. Whisky nosers, as they called themselves, eschewed what they saw as the pretentiousness of wine vocabulary. While oenophiles resorted to recondite adjectives, whisky nosers spoke the language of everyday life, detecting hints of *stale seaweed,* or even *diesel fuel.* Isabel saw the merit in this. The Island malts, which she could barely bring herself to sample—in spite of her father's enthusiasm for them—reminded her of antiseptic and the smell of the school swimming pool; and as for taste, "diesel fuel" seemed to express it perfectly. Not that she would utter these views in the rooms of the Scotch Malt Whisky Society, or even confess them to Johnny Sanderson, who was said by some to have whisky in his veins, on the strength of four generations of Highland distillers in his pedigree, starting, he proudly pointed out, with a humble crofter who ran an illegal still at the back of his sheep fank. Purveyors of alcohol were well known to found dynasties, of course: that was the case, she thought, with a politician whom Isabel's grandfather had known slightly before the Second World War. Isabel's grandfather, a principled man, had seen through him and had rebuffed an enticing offer for their company. Thereafter he had merely shuddered when the politician's name was mentioned, an eloquent enough comment—more expressive, indeed, than mere words.

Isabel was amused by the idea that gestures should accompany verbal references. She was intrigued to see devout Catholics cross themselves at the mention of the BVM—and she liked the acronym BVM itself, which made Mary sound so reassuringly modern and competent, like a CEO or an ICBM, or even a BMW. And in places like Sicily, there were people who spat to the side when the names of their enemies were uttered, or as was sometimes the case in Greece, when Turkey or even a Turk was spoken of. She recalled the Greek uncle of a friend of hers, who was protected by his family from all mention of Turkey, lest he have a heart attack. Or the proprietor of a Greek island hotel at which she had once stayed, who refused to acknowledge that the distant coast of Turkey could just be made out from the terrace of the hotel; he simply denied that land could be seen, and did not see it. So might one wish Turkey out of existence, if one were so inclined. All of this was to be avoided, of course, and Isabel knew it. She had never spat at the mention of a name, or even rolled her eyes upwards—well, that perhaps she had done once or twice, when the name of a well-known figure in the arts cropped up. But that, she felt, was fully justified, unlike the views of Greeks on Turks, and of Turks, one imagined, on Greeks.

Johnny Sanderson was already there when she arrived, and he led her to a quiet seat in the corner of the room.

"One question right at the beginning," he said. "Do you like it, or hate it? If you hate it, I'll get you a glass of wine instead."

"I like some whiskies," said Isabel. "Some."

"Such as?"

"Speysides. Soft whiskies. Whiskies that don't bite."

Johnny nodded. "Reasonable enough," he said. "Macallan. A lovely fifteen-year-old Speyside. It would offend nobody."

Isabel sat back while Johnny went to order the whiskies from the bar. She liked this temple to whisky, with its high ceilings and its airiness. And she liked the people, too: direct and open-faced people who believed in fellowship and good humour. They were people, she imagined, who did not disapprove of their fellow man, unlike those who patrolled mores today; these people were tolerant, just as gourmets, by and large, tended to have tolerant, expansive outlooks. It was the obsessive dieters who were unhappy and anxious.

A paper had been submitted to the review which suggested that there was a duty to be thin. "Fat Is a Moral Issue" had been the title which the author had chosen; Isabel thought it an intriguing title. But the argument was poor; entirely predictable and entirely depressing. In a world of need, it was wrong to be anything other than thin. Until everybody was in a position to consume a surfeit of calories, then nobody should carry extra weight. The fat were therefore not entitled to be what they were. *Fairness of distribution* demanded otherwise.

She had read the paper with increasing irritation, but then, at the end, when she had tossed it aside and gone into the kitchen for a slice of cake, she had paused at the very plate on which the cake rested, and stopped, and thought. The author of "Fat Is a Moral Issue" may have been pious in her tone, but she was right: the claims of the needy for food were moral claims of a particular sort. One could not ignore them—one could not walk away from them, even if those who made them on behalf of the hungry sounded like killjoys. And that, perhaps, was the problem: it was the *tone* with which the author had made her point—her *accusing* tone—that had irritated Isabel; it was the moral condescension in it that made her feel that she was being accused of self-indulgence and greed. But the fundamental truth contained in her paper could not be shrugged off: we cannot ignore the pleas of the hungry. And if that meant that we needed to examine the overconsumption which deprived others of food, then that had to be done. And with that thought, she had looked at the cake and then put it back in its tin in the cupboard.

Johnny raised his glass to her. "This is lovely stuff," he said. "Fifteen quiet years in its cask. Fifteen years ago I was, let me think, thirty, and we had just had our first child and I thought that I was awfully clever and was going to make a million by forty."

"And did you?"

"No. I never made a million. But I reached my fortieth birthday anyway, which is a greater privilege in a way."

"Quite," said Isabel. "Some would give a million for a single year, let alone forty."

Johnny looked into his whisky glass. "Greed," he said. "Greed takes so many forms. Polite or naked. But it's always the same at heart. Our friend Minty, for example . . ."

"You found out something?"

Johnny looked behind him. A group of people had gathered round a table at the other end of the room. The table was set out with rows of glasses and cut-glass jugs of water.

"Charlie's about to begin," he said. "He's sniffing the air."

Isabel glanced in the direction of the whisky noser, a well-built man in a comfortable tweed suit and sporting a large moustache. She watched as he poured a glass of whisky and held it up against the light.

"I know him," she said.

"Everybody does," said Johnny. "Charlie Maclean. He can smell whisky from fifty yards. Amazing nose."

Isabel looked down at her modest malt and took a small sip of the liquid. "Tell me what you found out about Minty."

Johnny shook his head. "Nothing. All I said was that she was greedy, which she undoubtedly is. What I did find out was rather more interesting than that. I found out about what her young friend Ian Cameron has been doing. I knew some of it already, of course, but I gathered quite a bit more from my friends among the discontented in McDowell's."

Isabel said nothing, waiting for him to continue. At the other end of the room, Charlie Maclean was pointing out some quality in the whisky to his attentive audience, one or two of whom were nodding eagerly.

"But first, you should have a bit of background," Johnny said. "Firms like McDowell's are not all that old. They've only recently celebrated their twentieth birthday, I think. And they didn't start with vast resources either—fifty thousand or so would have been all that the original two partners would have brought in. Nowadays, fifty thousand would be small change for them."

Isabel watched Johnny as he spoke. He was looking at his whisky glass, turning it gently to drive a thin meniscus of liquid up the sides, exactly as Charlie Maclean was now doing for his audience at the other end of the room.

"We grew very quickly," Johnny went on. "We took in pension funds and invested them carefully in solid stocks. The market, of course, was doing well and everything looked very good. By the end of the eighties we were managing more than two billion, and even if our fee was slipping slightly below the half percent we had been taking for our services, you can still imagine what that meant in terms of profit.

"We took on lots of bright people. We watched what was happening in the Far East and in developing countries. We moved in and out fairly successfully, but of course we had our fingers burned with Internet stocks, as just about everybody did. That was probably the first time we had a fright. I was there then and I remember how the atmosphere changed. I remember Gordon McDowell at one meeting looking as if he'd just seen a ghost. Quite white.

"But it didn't bring us down—it just meant that we had to be quicker on our feet. And we also had to work a bit harder to keep our clients, who were very nervous about what was happening to their funds in general and were beginning to wonder whether they would be safer in the City of London. After all, the reason why one went to Edinburgh in the first place was to get solidity and reliability. If Edinburgh started to look shaky, one might as well throw in one's lot with the riskier side of things in London.

"It's about this time that we looked around for some new people. We picked up this Cameron character and a few others like him. He started watching new stocks, which seemed to be about the only place where one could make a decent bit of money. But of course these new issues were subscribed to by the large people in London and New York, and Edinburgh usually wouldn't get much of a look-in. This was pretty sickening when you saw them go up in value by two or three hundred percent within a few months of issue. And all this profit went to those who were in a cosy relationship with the issuing houses in London and who were given a good allocation.

"Cameron started to get his hands on to some of these issues. He also started to take charge of one or two other things, moving funds slowly out of stocks that were not going to do so well. He's very good at that, our friend Cameron. Quite a few stocks were quietly disposed of a month or so ahead of a profit warning. Nothing very obvious, but it was happening. I didn't know about that until I spoke to my friends who had been working with him—I was in a different department. But they told me of two big sales that had taken place in the last six months, both of them before a profit warning."

Isabel had been listening intently. This was the flesh that her skeletal theory needed. "And would there be any concrete evidence of insider knowledge in these two cases? Anything one could put one's finger on?"

Johnny smiled. "The very question. But I'm afraid that you won't like the answer. The fact of the matter is that both of these sales were of stocks in companies in which Minty Auchterlonie's bank was involved as adviser. So she might well have had inside knowledge which she passed on to him. But then, on the other hand, she might not. And there is, in my view, no way in which we could possibly prove it. In each case, I gather, there's a minute of the meeting at which Cameron raised the possibility of selling the stocks. In both cases he came up with a perfectly cogent reason for doing so."

"And yet the real reason may well have been what Minty said to him?"

"Yes."

"And there's no chance of proving that money changed hands between Cameron and Minty?"

Johnny looked surprised. "I don't think that money would necessarily change hands—unless he was sharing his bonus with her. No, I think it more likely that they were doing this for mixed motives. She was involved with him sexually and wanted to keep him. That's perfectly possible. People give their lovers things because they're their lovers. That's an old story."

"Or?" prompted Isabel.

"Or Minty was genuinely concerned about Paul Hogg's department getting into the mire and wanted to give it a boost because Paul Hogg was part of her overall plan to penetrate the heart of the Edinburgh establishment. It was not in her interests as the future Mrs. Paul Hogg to have hitched her star to a has-been."

Isabel mulled over what she had been told. "So what you're telling me, then, is that there may well have been insider trading, but that we're never going to be able to prove it? Is that it?"

Johnny nodded. "I'm sorry," he said. "That's about it. You could try to take a closer look at Minty's financial situation and see if there are any unexplained windfalls, but I don't see how you'll get that information. She'll bank at Adam & Company, I suspect, and they are very discreet and you'd never get round any of their staff—they're very correct. So what do you do?"

"Shrug the whole thing off?"

Johnny sighed. "I suspect that's all we can do. I don't like it, but I don't think that we'll be able to do anything more."

Isabel lifted her glass and took a sip of her whisky. She had not wanted to mention her real suspicions to Johnny, but she felt grateful to him for the enquiries that he had made and she wanted to confide in somebody other than Jamie. If Johnny thought that her theory about what had happened in the Usher Hall was far-fetched, then perhaps she should abandon it.

She put her glass down on the table. "Would you mind if I tell you something?" she asked.

Johnny gestured airily. "Anything you wish. I know how to be discreet."

"A little while ago," said Isabel, "a young man fell to his death from the gods in the Usher Hall. You probably read about it."

Johnny thought for a moment before he replied. "I think I remember something like that. Horrible."

"Yes," Isabel went on. "It was very distressing. I happened to be there at the time—not that that's relevant—but what is interesting is that he worked at McDowell's. He would have gone there after you had left, but he was in Paul Hogg's department."

Johnny had raised his glass to his lips and was watching Isabel over the rim. "I see."

He's not interested, thought Isabel. "I became involved," she went on. "I happened to be told by somebody who knew him well that he had discovered something very awkward for somebody in the firm." She paused. Johnny was looking away, watching Charlie Maclean.

"And so he was pushed over that balcony," she said quietly. "Pushed."

Johnny turned round to face her. She could not make out his

expression; he was interested now but the interest was tinged with incredulity, she thought.

"Very unlikely," he said after a while. "People don't do that sort of thing. They just don't."

Isabel sighed. "I believe that they might," she said. "And that's why I wanted to find out about Minty and this insider trading. It could all add up."

Johnny shook his head. "No," he said. "I think that you should let go of it. I really don't think this is going to get you anywhere."

"I'll think about it. But I'm very grateful to you, anyway."

Johnny acknowledged her thanks with a lowering of his eyes. "And if you want to get in touch with me, here's my mobile number. Give me a call anytime. I'm up and about until midnight every day."

He handed her a card on which a number had been scrawled, and Isabel tucked it into her bag.

"Let's go and hear what Charlie Maclean has to say," said Johnny, rising to his feet.

"Wet straw," said Charlie at the other end of the room, putting his nose into the mouth of the glass. "Smell this dram, everyone. Wet straw, which means a Borders distillery in my book. Wet straw."

CHAPTER TWENTY-TWO

O F COURSE JOHNNY was right, Isabel thought—and she had decided accordingly by the following morning. That was the end of it; she would never be able to prove insider trading by Minty Auchterlonie, and even if she did, it would still be necessary to link this with Mark's death. Johnny knew these people much better than she did, and he had been incredulous of her theory. She should accept that, and let the whole matter rest.

She had reached this conclusion sometime during the night of the whisky tasting, when she had woken up, stared at the shadows on the ceiling for a few minutes, and finally made her decision. Sleep followed shortly afterwards, and the next morning—a brilliant morning on the cusp of spring and summer—she felt an extraordinary freedom, as one does at the end of an examination, when the pen and pencil are put away and nothing more remains to be done. Her time was her own now; she could devote herself to the review and to the pile of books that was stacked invitingly in her study; she could treat herself to morning coffee in Jenners, and watch the well-heeled Edinburgh ladies engage in their gossip, a world which she might so easily have slipped into and which she had avoided by a deliberate act of self-determining choice—thank heavens. And yet, was she any happier than they were, these women with their *safe* husbands and their children who were set to become like their parents and perpetuate this whole, self-confident world of haut-bourgeois Edinburgh? Probably not; they were happy in their way (*I must not be condescending,* she thought), and she was happy in hers. And Grace in hers and Jamie in his, and Minty Auchterlonie . . . She stopped herself, and thought. Minty Auchterlonie's state of mind is simply no concern of mine. No, she would not go to Jenners that morning, but she would walk into Bruntsfield and buy something that smelled nice from Mellis's cheese shop and then drink a cup of coffee in Cat's delicatessen. Then, that evening, there was a lecture she could attend at the Royal Museum of Scotland. Professor Lance Butler of the University of Pau, a lecturer whom she had heard before and who was consistently entertaining, would speak on Beckett, as he always did. That was excitement enough for one day.

And of course there were the crosswords. Downstairs now, she retrieved the newspapers from the mat on the hall and glanced at the headlines. NEW CONCERN FOR COD STOCKS, she read on the front page of *The Scotsman,* and saw the picture of idle fishing boats tied up at Peterhead; further gloom for Scotland and for a way of life that had produced such a strong culture. Fishermen had composed their songs; but what culture would a generation of computer operators leave behind them? She answered her own question: more than one might imagine—an electronic culture of e-mail tales and computer-generated images, fleeting and derivative, but a culture nonetheless.

She turned to the crossword, recognising several clues immediately. *The falls, artist is confusingly preceded again* (7), which required no more than a moment's thought: Niagara. Such a cliché in the crossword world, and this irritated Isabel, who liked novelty, however weak, in clues. And then, to pile Pelion (6) upon Ossa (4), there was *Writers I shortly have, thoughtful* (7). Isabel was pensive, which solved that one, until she tripped up over *An unending Greek god leads to an exclamation, Mother!* (6). This could only be zeugma—Zeu(s) g (gee!) ma—a word with which she was unfamiliar, and it sent her to Fowler's *Modern English Usage,* which confirmed her suspicion. She liked Fowler (*avian hunter of words,* she thought) for his opinions, which were clear and directive. Zeugmata, he explained, were a bad thing and incorrect—unlike syllepses, with which they were commonly confused. So *Miss Bolo went home in a flood of tears and a sedan chair* was sylleptical, requiring a single word to be understood in a different sense, while *See Pan with flocks, with fruits Pomona crowned* was a zeugma and called for the insertion of another quite different verb, *surrounded,* which was not there.

By the time that Grace arrived, Isabel had finished her breakfast and had dealt with the morning mail. Grace, who was late, arrived in a state of anxiety and a taxi; a sylleptical arrival, Isabel noted. Grace was strict about punctuality and hated to be even a few minutes late, hence the costly taxi and the anxiety.

"The battery of my alarm clock," she explained as she came into the kitchen, where Isabel was sitting. "You never think of changing them, and then they die on you."

Isabel had already prepared the coffee and she poured her housekeeper a cup, while Grace tidied her hair in front of the small mirror that she had hung on the wall beside the pantry door.

"I was at my meeting last night," Grace said, as she took her first sip of coffee. "There were more people there than usual. And a very good medium—a woman from Inverness—who was quite remarkable. She got right to the heart of things. It was quite uncanny."

Grace went on the first Wednesday of each month to a spiritualist meeting in a street off Queensferry Place. Once or twice she had invited Isabel to accompany her but Isabel, who feared that she might laugh, had declined the invitation and Grace had not persevered. Isabel did not approve of mediums, who she felt were, for the most part, charlatans. It seemed to her that many of the people who went to such meetings (although not Grace) had lost somebody and were desperate for contact beyond the grave. And rather than help them to let go, these mediums encouraged them to think that the dead could be contacted. In Isabel's view it was cruel and exploitative.

"This woman from Inverness," Grace went on, "she's called Annie McAllum. You can tell that she's a medium just by looking at her. She has that Gaelic colouring—you know, the dark hair and the translucent skin. And green eyes too. You can tell that she has the gift. You can tell."

"But I thought that anybody could be a medium," said Isabel. "You don't have to be one of those fey Highlanders to do it."

"Oh, I know that," said Grace. "We had a woman from Birmingham once. Even from a place like that. The gift can be received by anyone."

Isabel suppressed a smile. "And what did this Annie McAllum have to say?"

Grace looked out the window. "It's almost summer," she said.

Isabel stared at her in astonishment. "That's what she said? Now, that's really something. You have to have the gift to work that out."

Grace laughed. "Oh no. I was just looking out at the magnolia. I said that it's almost summer. She said lots of things."

"Such as?"

"Well," said Grace, "there's a woman called Lady Strath-martin who comes to the meetings. She's well into her seventies now and she's been coming to the meetings for years apparently, since well before I joined. She lost her husband, you see, quite a long time ago—he was a judge—and she likes to contact him on the other side."

Isabel said nothing, and Grace continued. "She lives in Ainslie Place, on the north side, and the Italian consul, a woman, lives below her. They go to a lot of things together, but she's never brought the consul to our meetings until last night. And so she was sitting there, in the circle, and Annie McAllum suddenly turned to her and said: *I can see Rome. Yes, I can see Rome.* I caught my breath at that. That was amazing. And then she said: *Yes, I think that you're in touch with Rome.*"

There was a silence as Grace looked expectantly at Isabel and Isabel stared mutely at Grace. Eventually Isabel spoke. "Well," she said cautiously, "perhaps that's not all that surprising. She is, after all, the Italian consul, and you would normally expect the Italian consul to be in touch with Rome, wouldn't you?"

Grace shook her head, not in denial of the proposition that Italian consuls were in touch with Rome, but with the air of one who was expected to explain something very simple which simply had not been grasped. "But she wasn't to know that she was the Italian consul," she said. "How would somebody from Inverness know that this woman was the Italian consul? How would she have known?"

"What was she wearing?" asked Isabel.

"A white gown," said Grace. "It's really a white sheet, made up into a gown."

"The Italian consul? A white gown?"

"No," said Grace, again with a patient look. "The mediums often put on a gown like that. It helps them make contact. No, the Italian consul was wearing a very smart dress, if I remember correctly. A smart dress and smart Italian shoes."

"There you are," said Isabel.

"I don't see how that makes any difference," said Grace.

HAD GRACE HAD the gift, then she might have said: *Expect a telephone call from a man who lives in Great King Street,* which is what happened that morning at eleven. Isabel was in her study by then, having postponed the walk into Bruntsfield until noon, and was engrossed in a manuscript on the ethics of memory. She set aside her manuscript reluctantly and answered the call. She had not expected Paul Hogg to telephone her, nor had she anticipated the invitation to drinks early that evening—a totally impromptu party, he pointed out, with no notice at all.

"Minty's keen that you should come," he said. "You and your friend, that young man. She really hopes that you'll be able to make it."

Isabel thought quickly. She was no longer interested in Minty; she had taken the decision to abandon the whole issue of insider trading and Mark's death, and she was not sure whether she should now accept an invitation which appeared to lead her directly back into engagement with the very people she had decided were no concern of hers. And yet there was an awful fascination in the prospect of seeing Minty up close, as one viewed a specimen. She was an awful woman—there was no doubt about that—but there could be a curious attraction in the awful, as there was in a potentially lethal snake. One liked to look at it, to stare into its eyes. So she accepted, adding that she was not sure whether Jamie would be free, but she would ask him. Paul Hogg sounded pleased, and they agreed on a time. There would only be one or two other people there, he said, and the party would be over in good time for her to make her way up to the museum and Professor Butler's lecture.

She returned to the article on the ethics of memory, abandoning the thought of the walk to Bruntsfield. The author of the paper was concerned with the extent to which the forgetting of personal information about others represented a culpable failure to commit the information to memory. "There is a duty to at least attempt to remember," he wrote, "that which is important to others. If we are in a relationship of friendship or dependence, then you should at least bother about my name. You may fail to remember it, and that may be a matter beyond your control—a nonculpable weakness on your part—but if you made no effort to commit it to memory in the first place, then you have failed to give me something which is my due, recognition on your part of an important aspect of my identity." Now this was certainly right: our names are important to us, they express our essence. We are protective of our names and resent their mishandling: Charles may not *like* being called Chuck, and Margaret may not approve of Maggie. To Chuck or Maggie a Charles or a Margaret in the face of their discomfort is to wrong them in a particularly personal way; it is to effect a unilateral change in what they really are.

Isabel paused in this line of thought and asked herself: What is the name of the author of this paper I am reading? She realised that she did not know, and had not bothered with it when she had taken the manuscript from the envelope. Had she failed in a duty to him? Would he have expected her to have his name in her mind while she read his work? He probably would.

She thought about this for a few minutes, and then rose to

her feet. She could not concentrate, and she certainly owed the author her undivided attention. Instead she was thinking of what lay ahead: a drinks party in Paul Hogg's flat that had clearly been engineered by Minty Auchterlonie. Minty had been flushed out, that at least was clear; but it was not clear to Isabel what she should now do. Her instinct was to abide by her decision to disengage. I need to forget all this, she thought; I need to forget, in an act of deliberate forgetting (if such a thing is really possible). The act of a mature moral agent, an act of recognition of the moral limits of duty to others . . . but what, she wondered, would Minty Auchterlonie be wearing? Now she laughed at herself. I am a philosopher, Isabel thought, but I am also a woman, and women, as even men know, are interested in what others wear. That is not something of which women should be ashamed; it is men who have the gap in their vision, rather as if they did not notice the plumage of the birds or the shape of the clouds in the sky, or the red of the fox on the wall as he sneaked past Isabel's window. Brother Fox.

CHAPTER TWENTY-THREE

SHE MET JAMIE at the end of Great King Street, having seen him walking up the hill, across the slippery cobbles of Howe Street.

"I'm very glad that you could make it," she said. "I'm not sure that I could face these people on my own."

Jamie raised an eyebrow. "This is rather like going into the lion's den, isn't it?"

"Lioness," corrected Isabel. "A bit, maybe. But then I don't think that we shall pursue anything. I've decided that I'm not going to get any further into all this."

Jamie was surprised. "You're dropping it?"

"Yes," said Isabel. "I had a long chat with somebody called Johnny Sanderson last night. He worked with these people and knows them well. He says that we won't be able to prove anything and he also poured cold water on the idea that Minty had anything to do with Mark's death. I thought long and hard about it. He rather brought me to my senses, I suppose."

"You never cease to astonish me," said Jamie. "But I must say that I'm rather relieved. I've never approved of your messing about in other people's affairs. You're becoming more sensible by the hour."

Isabel tapped him on the wrist. "I could still surprise you," she said. "But anyway, I accepted this evening out of a sense of horrible fascination. That woman is a bit like a snake, I've decided. And I want to see her up close again."

Jamie made a face. "She makes me uneasy," he said. "It's you who called her sociopathic. And I'll have to be careful that she doesn't push me out the window."

"Of course, you know that she likes you," said Isabel casually.

"I don't want to know that. And I don't know how you've worked that out."

"All you have to do is watch people," said Isabel, as they arrived at the front door and she reached forward to the bell marked HOGG. "People give themselves away every five seconds. Watch the movement of eyes. It says absolutely everything you need to know." Jamie was silent as they climbed the stairs, and still looked pensive as the door on the landing was opened by Paul Hogg. Isabel wondered whether she should have said what she had said to Jamie; in general, and this was quite against the conventional wisdom, men did not like to hear that women found them attractive, unless they were prepared to reciprocate the feeling. In other cases, it was an irritation—burdensome knowledge that made men uneasy. That was why men ran away from women who pursued them, as Jamie would steer clear of Minty now that he knew; not that she would regret Jamie's keeping well away from Minty. That would be an appalling thought, she suddenly reflected: Jamie being ensnared by Minty, who would add him to her list of conquests, a truly appalling prospect that Isabel could not bear to contemplate. And why? Because I feel protective of him, she conceded, and I cannot bear for anybody else to have him. Not even Cat? Did she really want him to go back to Cat, or was it only because she knew that this would never happen that she was able to entertain the thought of it?

There was no time to resolve these thoughts. Paul Hogg greeted them warmly and led them into the drawing room; the same drawing room with its misattributed Crosbie and its vibrant Peploe. There were two other guests there already, and as they were introduced to them Isabel realised that she had met them before. He was a lawyer, an advocate with political ambitions, and she wrote a column for a newspaper. Isabel read the column from time to time, but found it tedious. She was not interested in the mundane details of journalists' lives, which seemed to be the stuff of this woman's writing, and she wondered whether her conversation would be in the same mould. She looked at the woman, who smiled encouragingly at her, and Isabel immediately relented, thinking that perhaps she should make the effort. The lawyer smiled too and shook hands warmly with Jamie. The journalist looked at Jamie, and then glanced back briefly at Isabel, who noticed this quick movement of the eyes and knew immediately that this woman thought that she and Jamie were a couple *in that sense* and that she was now revising her opinion of Isabel. Which she was indeed doing, for the woman now cast her eyes down, at Isabel's figure—so obvious, thought Isabel, but it was curiously satisfying to be thought to have a much younger boyfriend, particularly one who looked like Jamie. The other woman would be immediately jealous because her man, who sat up all night working in the Advocates Library, would be worn out and not much fun, and always talked of politics, which is what politicians inevitably did. So there was the journalist thinking: This Isabel woman has a sexy young boyfriend—just look at him—which is what I would really want, if the truth be told, if one were totally honest . . . But then Isabel thought: Is it right to allow people to entertain the wrong impression about something significant, or should one correct a misapprehension in another? There were moments when being the editor of the *Review of Applied Ethics* was burdensome: it seemed so difficult to be off-duty; difficult to forget, in fact, as Professor . . . Professor . . . might have observed.

Minty now made her entry. She had been in the kitchen, and came into the drawing room holding a silver tray of canapés. She put the tray down on a table, moved over to the lawyer, and kissed him on both cheeks. *Rob, I've voted for you twice since we last met. Twice!* And then on to the journalist. *Kirsty, so good of you to come at no notice whatsoever.* Then to Isabel: *Isabel!* That was all, but there was a change in the light in her eyes, subtle, but observable. *And it's Jamie, isn't it?* The body language changed now; she stood closer to Jamie as she greeted him, and Isabel noticed, to her satisfaction, that Jamie moved back slightly, as a magnet will do when confronted with the wrong end of another magnet.

Paul had been on the other side of the room preparing drinks, and now he returned. They took their glasses and turned to one another. It was an easy conversation—surprisingly easy, thought Isabel. Paul asked Rob about a current political campaign and he replied with amusing details of a constituency fight. The names of the protagonists were well known: a towering ego and a notorious womaniser engaged in dispute over a minor office. Then Minty mentioned another political name which brought forth a snort from Rob and a knowing shaking of the head from Kirsty. Jamie said nothing; he knew no politicians.

A little later, when Jamie was talking to Kirsty—about something that had happened in the Scottish Opera orchestra, Isabel noted—Isabel found herself standing next to Minty, who took her arm gently and steered her over towards the fireplace. There were even more invitations on the mantelpiece than last time, Isabel noticed, although she could not read them now (except for one, which was in large print, presumably to allow for easy reading by one's guests).

"I'm very pleased that you could come," said Minty, her voice lowered. Isabel realised that this was not a conversation to be overheard, and when she replied she spoke in similarly hushed tones.

"I sensed that you wanted to talk to me."

Minty's gaze moved slightly to one side. "There is something, actually," she said. "I gather that you are interested in McDowell's. I've heard that you've been speaking to Johnny Sanderson."

Isabel had not expected this. Had somebody reported to Minty that she had been in a huddle with Johnny at the whisky tasting?

"Yes, I've spoken to him. I know him slightly."

"And he's been talking to people at McDowell's. He used to work there, of course."

Isabel nodded. "I know that."

Minty took a sip of wine. "Then do you mind my asking: What is your interest in the firm? You see, first you asked Paul about it, and then you start talking to Johnny Sanderson, and so on, and this makes me wonder why you're suddenly so interested. You're not in a financial job, are you? So what explains the interest in our affairs?"

"Your affairs? I didn't realise you worked for McDowell's."

Minty bared her teeth in a tolerant smile. "Paul's affairs are closely linked with mine. I am, after all, his fiancée."

Isabel thought for a moment. On the other side of the room, Jamie looked in her direction and they exchanged glances. She was uncertain what to do. She could hardly deny the interest, so why not tell the truth?

"I was interested," she began. "I was interested, but not any longer." She paused. Minty was watching her, listening intently. "I'm no longer involved. But I was. You see, I saw a young man fall to his death a little while ago. I was the last person he saw on this earth and I felt that I had to enquire about what had happened. He worked for McDowell's, as you know. He knew something untoward was happening there. I wondered whether there was a link. That's all."

Isabel watched the effect of her words on Minty. If she was a murderess, then this was as good as a direct accusation. But Minty did not blanch; she stood quite still; there was no shock, no panic, and when she spoke her voice was quite even. "So you thought that this young man had been disposed of? Is that what you thought?"

Isabel nodded. "It was a possibility I felt that I had to look into. But I've done so and I realise that there's no proof of anything untoward."

"And who might have done it, may I ask?"

Isabel felt her heart beating loud within her. She wanted to say: *You.* It would have been a simple, a delicious moment, but she said instead: "Somebody who feared exposure, obviously."

Minty put her glass down and raised a hand to her temple, which she massaged gently, as if to aid thought. "You evidently have a rich imagination. I doubt very much if anything like that happened," she said. "And anyway, you should know better than to listen to anything Johnny Sanderson had to say. You know he was asked to leave McDowell's?"

"I knew that he had left. I didn't know in what circumstances."

Minty now became animated. "Well, maybe you should have

asked. He didn't see eye to eye with people there because he was unable to adjust to new circumstances. Things had changed. But it was not just that, it was because he was suspected of insider deals, which means, in case you don't know, that he used confidential information to play the market. How do you think he lives as he does today?"

Isabel said nothing; she had no idea how Johnny Sanderson lived.

"He has a place up in Perthshire," Minty went on, "and a whole house in Heriot Row. Then there's a house in Portugal, and so on. Major assets all over the place."

"But you never know where people get their money from," said Isabel. "Inheritance, for a start. It might be inherited wealth."

"Johnny Sanderson's father was a drunk. His business went into receivership twice. Not a notoriously good provider."

Minty picked up her glass again. "Don't listen to anything he tells you," she said. "He hates McDowell's and anything to do with them. Take my advice and keep away from him."

The look which Minty now gave Isabel was a warning, and Isabel had no difficulty in interpreting it as a warning to stay away from Johnny. And with that she left Isabel and returned to Paul's side. Isabel stood where she was for a moment, looking at a picture beside the mantelpiece. It was time to leave the party, she thought, as her hostess had clearly indicated that such welcome as she had been accorded had now expired. Besides, it was time to walk up the Mound to the museum and to the lecture on Beckett.

CHAPTER TWENTY-FOUR

THE LECTURE AT THE MUSEUM was well attended and Professor Butler was on form. Beckett survived the professor's reassessment, much to Isabel's relief, and afterwards, at the reception, she was able to talk to several old friends who had also attended. Both of these things—Beckett's survival and the meeting with old friends—contributed to a raising of her spirits. The conversation with Minty had been unpleasant, although she was very much aware that it could have been worse. She had not expected Minty to launch into an attack on Johnny Sanderson, but then she had not expected the other woman to know that she and Johnny had met. Perhaps she should not have been surprised by this; it was hard to do anything in Edinburgh without its getting around; look at Minty's own affair with Ian Cameron. Presumably she would not have imagined that others knew all about that.

Isabel wondered what Minty might take from their meeting. She would be confident, perhaps, that Isabel was no longer a danger to her; Isabel had very explicitly said that she was no longer taking an interest in the internal affairs of McDowell's. And even if she were involved in Mark's death, which Isabel—on the basis of Minty's reactions to her comments about this—was now firmly convinced could not be the case, then she would be bound to conclude that Isabel had uncovered nothing about how it had happened. She doubted, then, if she would hear any more from Minty Auchterlonie, or from the unfortunate Paul Hogg. She would miss them, in a curious way; they were contacts with a different world.

She stayed at the reception until it started to break up. She spoke briefly to Professor Butler himself. "My dear, I'm so glad that you enjoyed what I had to say. I have no doubt that I shall say more on the subject one day, but I shan't inflict that on you. No, I shall not." She appreciated his urbanity, so increasingly rare in modern academic circles, where narrow specialists, devoid of any broad culture, had elbowed out those with any sense of courtesy. So many academic philosophers were like that, she thought. They spoke to nobody but themselves, because the civilities of broader discourse eluded them and because their experience of the wider world was so limited. Not all of them, of course. She had a mental list of the exceptions, but it seemed to be shrinking.

It was shortly after ten that she walked up Chambers Street and took her place in the small queue at the bus stop on George IV Bridge. There were taxis about, prowling down the street with their yellow signs lit, but she had decided in favour of a bus. The bus would drop her in Bruntsfield, more or less directly outside Cat's delicatessen, and she would enjoy the ten-minute walk along Merchiston Crescent and down her own road.

The bus arrived, and as she noticed from the timetable displayed in the bus shelter, it was exactly on time; she would have to mention this to Grace, but perhaps not, as it might provoke a tirade against the transport authorities. It's all very well running on time at night, when there's nobody about. What we want are buses that run on time *during the day,* when you need them.

Isabel stepped into the bus, bought her ticket, and made her way to a seat at the back. There were few other passengers: a man in an overcoat, his head sunk against his chest; a couple with arms around each other, impervious to their surroundings; and a teenage boy with a black scarf wound round his neck, Zorro-style. Isabel smiled to herself: a microcosm of our condition, she thought. Loneliness and despair; love and its self-absorption; and sixteen, which was a state all its own.

The boy alighted from the bus at the same time as Isabel, but went off in the opposite direction. She crossed the road and began the walk along Merchiston Crescent, past East Castle Road and West Castle Road. The occasional car went past, and a cyclist with a flashing red light attached to his back, but otherwise she was alone.

She reached the point where her road, a quiet, leafy avenue, ran off to the right. A cat ran past her and leapt onto a garden wall before disappearing; a light shone out from a house on the corner, and a door slammed. She followed the pavement down towards her house, past the large wooden gates of the house on the corner and the carefully tended garden of a neighbour. And then, under the boughs of the tree that grew on the corner of her property, she stopped. Further down the road, about fifty yards or so, two cars were parked. One she recognised as belonging to the son of one set of neighbours; the other, a sleek Jaguar, had been left with its parking lights on. She walked down, peered into the car, which she noticed was locked, and then looked up at the house outside which it was parked. The house was in darkness, which suggested that the owner of the car was not being entertained there. Well, there was not much she could do to alert him. The battery might last out a few hours, but beyond that he would need help in starting.

Isabel walked back up the road towards her house. Outside the gate she paused; she was not sure why. She looked into the shadows under the tree, and saw movement. It was the striped cat from next door, who liked to lurk under her trees. She would like to have warned him of Brother Fox, who might take a cat if he were feeling peckish, but she did not have the words, so she willed a warning instead.

She opened her gate and began to walk down the path to her front door, in shadows, protected from the streetlight by the spruce and by a small stand of birches at the entrance to her driveway. And it was then that she felt the hand of fear upon her; an irrational fear, but a cold one. Had she talked that evening to a woman who might, calmly and calculatingly, have planned the demise of another? And had this woman uttered a warning?

She fished her key out of her pocket and prepared to insert it into the door; but then tested the door first, pushing gently against it. It did not budge, which meant that it was locked. She fitted the key into the lock, turned it, and heard the bolts slide within. Then, opening the door carefully, she stepped into her outer hall and fumbled for the light switch.

Isabel had an alarm, but she had grown careless in setting it, using it only when she went away for the night. If she had set it she would have been more confident; as it was, she could not be sure whether or not anybody had been in the house. But of course nobody would have been in the house; it was ridiculous to imagine it. Just because she had had that frank conversation with Minty Auchterlonie did not mean that Minty was watching her. She made a conscious effort to put the thought to one side, as one should do with all fears. Living by oneself it was important not to feel afraid, as every noise made by the house at night—every squeak or groan which a Victorian house made—would be a cause for alarm. But she was feeling fear, and she could not suppress it. It was fear which made her go into the kitchen and turn on all the lights, and then move from room to room on the ground floor and light them. There was nothing to see, of course, and by the time she went upstairs, she was prepared to turn these lights out again. But going into her study to check her answering machine, she saw the small red light winking at her, which meant that there were messages. She hesitated for a moment, and then decided to listen to the messages. There was only one.

Isabel, it's Minty Auchterlonie here. I wonder if we could meet up to have another talk. I hope that you didn't think I was rude this evening. I'll give you my number. Call me to arrange coffee or lunch or whatever. Thank you.

Isabel was surprised, but reassured by the message, and she noted the number on a piece of paper and slipped it into her pocket. Then she left the study, turning out the light behind her. She was no longer afraid; slightly uneasy, perhaps, and still puzzled as to why Minty should wish to speak to her again.

She went into her bedroom, which was at the front of the house. It was a large room, with an unusual bay window and window seat off to one side. She had left the curtains pulled to, and the room was in complete darkness. She turned on the bedside lamp, a small reading light that made a tiny pool of light in the large, shadowy room. Isabel did not bother with the main light; she would lie on her bed, she thought, reading for fifteen minutes or so, before she prepared for bed. Her mind was active, and it was too early to turn in.

Isabel slipped off her shoes, picked up a book from her dressing table, and lay down on her bed. She was reading an account of a trip to Ecuador, an amusing story of misunderstandings and dangers. She was enjoying it, but her mind kept returning to her conversation with Johnny Sanderson. He had been so helpful and reassuring, and he had told her that she could telephone him at any time. *Anytime before midnight.* It was clear to her that Minty had tried to put her off any further enquiries by suggesting that it was Johnny who was the insider trader. That was clearly outrageous, and she would not mention it to him. Or should she? If he knew that, then would his view of the situation differ? It is possible that he might revise his view if he knew that Minty was actively trying to discourage Isabel. She could phone Johnny now and talk to him about it; otherwise she would lie there and not get to sleep thinking of it.

Isabel reached over and picked up the telephone beside her bed. Johnny's card was protruding from the pages of her pocket address book. She took the card out and looked at it in the dim light of the bedside lamp. Then she picked up the telephone receiver and keyed in the number.

There was a moment's delay. Then she heard it: a distinctive, high-pitched ringing tone, coming from somewhere just outside her bedroom.

CHAPTER TWENTY-FIVE

ISABEL FELT PARALYSED, lying in the bed, the telephone receiver in her hand. Because the large room was in semidarkness, with only her small bedside lamp illuminated, there were shadows—from cupboards, curtains, the small dressing room off to the side. When she recovered her power to move, it might have been to lunge for the light switch, but it was not. She half leapt, half tumbled from her bed, the telephone falling to the floor behind her, and in one or two bounds she reached the door. Then, holding the thick wooden banister to steady herself, she half threw herself down the stairs. She could have fallen, but did not; nor did she slip when she raced across the downstairs hallway and clutched at the door that separated the inner and outer halls. It yielded, and she flung it back upon its hinges, shattering the stained-glass panel which it contained. With the sound of falling glass, she screamed involuntarily, and a hand was laid upon her arm.

"Isabel?"

She spun round. She had a light on in the kitchen, and it shone through to the hall, making it possible for her to see that it was Johnny Sanderson standing in the hall beside her.

"Isabel. Have I frightened you? I'm terribly sorry."

Isabel stared at him. The hand was tight about her arm, almost painful.

"What are you doing here?" Her voice sounded cracked, and she cleared her throat without thinking.

"Calm down," said Johnny. "I'm terribly sorry if I gave you a fright. I had come to see you and I found the door open. I was a little bit concerned, as the house was in darkness. So I came in and checked that everything was all right. Then I went out into the garden, just to look round. I thought that there might have been an intruder."

Isabel thought quickly. What Johnny said was just possibly true. If one found a house with an open door, and with no sign of the owner about, then it might well be that one would look about the place to check that all was in order. But what had his mobile phone been doing upstairs?

"Your telephone," said Isabel, moving over to the light switch to turn it on. "I dialled it and it rang."

Johnny looked at her curiously. "But it's in my pocket," he said. "Look." He reached into the pocket of the jacket he was wearing, and then stopped. "Or at least it was there."

Isabel took a deep breath. "You must have dropped it."

"So it seems," said Johnny. He smiled. "That must have given you a dreadful fright."

"It did."

"Well, yes, I suppose it would. Again, I'm sorry."

Isabel pulled herself away from Johnny's grip, which was dropped. She looked down at the broken stained glass; it had portrayed the harbour at Kirkcudbright, the hull of the fishing boat tiny shards now. As she looked down, the thought came to her, a thought which overthrew all her assumptions: *Minty was right.*

Minty was not the person they should have been investigating; it was Johnny. By coincidence they had gone right to the person who was behind whatever it was that Mark had uncovered.

It was a realisation that was sudden and complete. She did not have to reconsider it, as she stood there in her hall, confronted by Johnny Sanderson. Good was bad; light was dark; it was as simple as that. A road followed in faith was the road that led nowhere, because it stopped, suddenly and without warning, at a sign which said, unambiguously, *Wrong way*. And the human mind, jolted out of its assumptions, could either refuse the new reality or switch tracks. Minty might be ambitious, hard, scheming, and promiscuous (all rolled into one elegant package), but she did not push young men over balconies. Johnny Sanderson might be a cultivated, sympathetic member of the Edinburgh establishment, but he was greedy, and money could seduce anybody. And then, when everything was threatened by the possibility of exposure, it would be such an easy step to remove the threat.

She looked at Johnny. "Why did you come to see me?"

"There was something I wanted to talk about."

"And what was that?"

Johnny smiled. "I really don't think that we should talk much now. After this . . . after this disturbance."

Isabel stared at him, struck by the sheer effrontery of the response.

"A disturbance which you created," she said.

Johnny sighed, as if confronted with a pedantic objection. "I merely intended to discuss the matter we were discussing the other day. That's all."

Isabel said nothing, and after a few moments Johnny continued: "But we'll do that some other time. I'm sorry that I gave you that fright." He turned and looked back up the stairs. "Would you

mind if I recovered my phone? You say that it's up in your bedroom? Would you mind?"

AFTER JOHNNY HAD GONE, Isabel went into the kitchen and
fetched a dustpan and broom. She carefully picked up the larger
pieces of broken glass and wrapped them in newspaper, and then
she swept up the smaller fragments and carried them back into
the kitchen in the dustpan. Then she sat down at the kitchen
telephone and dialled Jamie's number.

It took Jamie some time to answer and Isabel knew that she
had woken him up.

"I'm very sorry," she said. "I had to speak to you."

Jamie's voice was thick with sleep. "I don't mind."

"Could you come round to the house? Right now."

"Right now?"

"Yes. I'll explain when you come. Please. And would you mind
staying here overnight? Just tonight."

He sounded as if he was fully woken up now. "It'll take me
half an hour. Will that be all right?"

ISABEL HEARD HIS TAXI arrive and went to the front door to
greet him. He was wearing a green windcheater and was carrying
a small black overnight bag.

"You're an angel. You really are."

He shook his head, as if in disbelief. "I can't imagine what
you want to talk about. But still, that's what friends are for."

Isabel led him into the kitchen, where she had prepared tea.
She motioned to a chair and poured him a cup.

"You're not going to believe this," she began. "I've had an eventful evening."

She told him of what had happened and his eyes widened as she spoke. But it was clear to her that he did not doubt her for a moment.

"But you can't believe him. Nobody would wander into somebody else's house like that just because the door was open . . . if it was open in the first place."

"Which I doubt," said Isabel.

"Then what on earth was he doing? What did he have in mind? Doing you in?"

Isabel shrugged her shoulders. "I suspect that he might wonder about my intentions. If he's the one we should have been suspecting all along, then he might be worried that I had some proof. Some documents linking him with insider deals."

"This is what this is?"

"I assume so. Unless he was planning something else, which is rather unlikely, at this stage."

"So what do we do now?"

Isabel looked at the floor. "I have no idea. Or not now. I think I should just go to bed and we can talk about it tomorrow." She paused. "Are you sure that you don't mind staying? It's just that I can't face being in the house by myself tonight."

"Of course I don't mind," said Jamie. "I wouldn't leave you by yourself. Not after all that."

"Grace keeps one of the spare rooms made up," she said. "It's at the back. It's nice and quiet. You can have that."

She took him upstairs and showed him the room. Then she said good night, leaving him standing just inside his room. He smiled, and blew her a kiss.

"I'm just along here," he said. "If there's any attempt by Johnny to disturb your sleep, you just give me a shout."

"I think that's the last we'll see of him tonight," said Isabel. She felt safer now, but there was still the thought that unless she did something, the issue of Johnny Sanderson was unresolved. Jamie was there tonight, but he would not be there the following night, nor the night after that.

CHAPTER TWENTY-SIX

IF GRACE FELT any surprise at finding Jamie in the house the next morning, she concealed it well. He was by himself in the kitchen when she came in, and for a few moments he seemed at a loss as to what to say. Grace, who had picked up the mail from the floor of the hall, broke the silence.

"Four more articles this morning," she said. "Applied ethics. No shortage of applied ethics."

Jamie looked at the pile of mail. "Did you notice the door?"

"I did."

"There was an intruder."

Grace stood quite still. "I thought so. That alarm. I've been telling her for years, years, to use it. She never does. She never listens." She drew breath. "Well, I didn't actually think anything. I didn't know what to think. I thought that maybe you two had had a party last night."

Jamie grinned. "No. I came when she called me. I stayed over—in one of the spare rooms."

Grace listened gravely as Jamie explained what had happened. As he came to the end of the explanation, Isabel came into the kitchen, and the three of them sat down at the table and entered into discussion.

"This has gone far enough," said Jamie. "You're out of your depth now and you are going to have to hand the whole thing over."

Isabel looked blank. "To?"

"The police."

"But what exactly are we going to hand over to them?" asked Isabel. "We have no proof of anything. All we have is a suspicion that Johnny Sanderson is mixed up in insider trading and that this may have had something to do with Mark Fraser's death."

"What puzzles me, though," said Jamie, "is the fact that McDowell's must have had their own suspicions about him. You say that Minty explained that this is why he was asked to leave. So if they knew, then why should he be worried about your finding anything out?"

Isabel thought about this. There would be a reason. "Perhaps they wanted the whole thing hushed up. This would suit Johnny Sanderson, of course, and he would not want anybody from the outside—that is, you and me—finding out about it and making a fuss. The Edinburgh establishment has been known to close ranks before this. We should not be unduly surprised."

"But we have last night," said Jamie. "At least we have something more concrete on him."

Isabel shook her head. "Last night proves nothing," she said. "He has his story about why he came in. He'll stick to that and the police would probably just accept that. They won't want to get involved in some private spat."

"But we could point out the link with the allegations of insider trading," said Jamie. "We could tell them about what Neil told you and about the paintings. There's enough here to give rise to a reasonable suspicion."

Isabel was doubtful. "I don't think there is. The police can't demand that you explain where you get your money from. They don't work that way."

"And Neil?" Jamie persisted. "What about the information that Mark Fraser was frightened of something?"

"He has already declined to go to the police about that," said Isabel. "He would probably deny that he'd ever spoken to me. If he changed his story, then the police could accuse him of misleading them. He's not going to say anything, if you ask me."

Jamie turned to Grace, wondering whether she would support him in his suggestion. "What do you think?" he asked. "Do you agree with me?"

"No," she said. "No, I don't."

Jamie looked at Isabel, who raised an eyebrow. There was an idea forming in her mind. "Set a thief to catch a thief," she said. "As you say, we're out of our depth here. We can't prove anything about these financial goings-on. We certainly can't prove anything about a link between all that and Mark Fraser's death. In fact, it looks as if that probably isn't the issue—there simply isn't any link. So what we need to do is get the message to Johnny Sanderson that we're no longer involved in any way. That should keep him from me."

"Do you really think he might . . . might try to harm you?" Jamie asked.

"I felt pretty frightened last night," said Isabel. "He could. But then it's occurred to me that we could get Minty to tell him that she's fully aware of his visit here. If she gets the message to him that she knows that he's been leaning on me, then he would presumably not try anything further. If I came to any harm, he would have at least one archenemy who would point the finger at him."

Jamie sounded doubtful. "So we should talk to Minty?"

Isabel nodded. "Frankly, I can't face it. I wondered if you . . ."

Grace rose to her feet. "No," she said. "I'll do this. You tell me where this Minty woman is to be found and I'll go and have a word with her. Then, just in case there's any doubt, I'll go and have a word with this Sanderson person. I'll leave him in no doubt that he's not to come round here again."

Isabel glanced at Jamie, who nodded. "Grace can be very firm," he said, adding quickly, "Of course, I mean that in the nicest possible way."

Isabel smiled. "Of course," she said. She was silent for a few moments, and then went on. "You know, I feel that I'm showing an appalling lack of moral courage. I've looked into a very unpleasant world and have simply drawn back in fright. I'm throwing in every towel in sight."

"What more can you do?" said Jamie crossly. "You've already interfered. Now you can't do anything more. You're fully entitled to look after yourself. Be reasonable for once."

"I'm walking away from it all," said Isabel quietly. "I'm walking away because somebody has given me a bad fright. It's exactly what they want me to do."

Jamie's frustration was now palpable. "All right, then," he said. "Tell us what you can do instead. Tell us where we go from here. You can't, can you? That's because there's nothing else for you to do."

"Exactly," said Grace. And then she went on, "Jamie here is right. You're wrong. You're not a moral coward. You're the least cowardly person I know. The least."

"I agree," said Jamie. "You're brave, Isabel. And we love you for it. You're brave and good and you don't even know it."

ISABEL WENT THROUGH to her study to deal with the mail, leaving Jamie and Grace in the kitchen. After a few minutes,

Jamie looked at his watch. "I have a pupil at eleven," he said. "But I could come back this evening."

Grace thought this a good idea, and accepted on Isabel's behalf. "Just for a few more days," she said. "If you don't mind . . ."

"I don't," said Jamie. "I wouldn't leave her by herself in the middle of all this."

As he left the house, Grace followed him out onto the path, catching him by the arm. Glancing behind her towards the house, she lowered her voice as she spoke to him.

"You're wonderful, you know. You really are. Most young men wouldn't bother. But you do."

He was embarrassed. "I don't mind. I really don't."

"Yes, well, maybe. But here's another thing. Cat's got rid of that fellow with the red breeks. She wrote to Isabel about it."

Jamie said nothing, but blinked once or twice.

Grace tightened the pressure on his forearm. "Isabel told her," she whispered. "She told her about how Toby is carrying on with another girl."

"She told her that?"

"Yes, and she was mighty upset. She ran out, sobbing her eyes out. I tried to speak to her, but she wouldn't listen to me."

Jamie began to laugh, but checked himself quickly. "I'm sorry. I'm not laughing at Cat's being upset. I was just so pleased that now maybe she knows what he's like. I . . . ."

Grace nodded. "If she had any sense she'd get back to you."

"Thank you. I'd like that, but I don't know if it's going to happen."

Grace looked into his eyes. "May I say something really personal? Would you mind?"

"Of course I wouldn't. Fire away." He had been instantly buoyed by the news which Grace had imparted and now he was ready for anything.

"Your trousers," whispered Grace. "They're very dull. You've got a great body . . . sorry to be so direct, you know, I wouldn't normally talk like this to a man. And your face is tremendous. Tremendous. But you have to . . . you have to be a bit more sexy. That girl is, well, she's *interested* in that sort of thing."

Jamie stared at her. Nobody had spoken to him like that before. She undoubtedly meant it well, but what exactly was wrong with his trousers? He looked down at his legs, at his trousers, and then he looked at Grace.

She was shaking her head; not in disapproval, but in sorrow, as at missed opportunities, potential unfulfilled.

JAMIE RETURNED SHORTLY before seven that evening, bringing with him an overnight case. The glaziers had been that afternoon and the stained-glass panel in the inner hall door had now been replaced with a large sheet of plain glass. Isabel was in her study when he arrived and she asked him to wait for a few minutes in the drawing room while she finished off a letter she was drafting. She seemed to be in good spirits when she let him in, he thought, but when she came through, her expression was more sombre.

"I had two calls from Minty," she said. "Do you want to hear about them?"

"Of course I do. I was thinking about it all day."

"Minty was really angry when Grace told her about last night. She said that she and Paul would go round immediately to have a word with Johnny Sanderson, which they did, apparently. And then she called back and said that I need not worry anymore about him, that he had been well and truly warned off. Apparently they have something else on him that they could threaten him with, and he backed down. So that's it."

"And Mark Fraser? Was anything said about Mark's death?"

"No," said Isabel. "Nothing. But if you ask me, I would say that there's still a chance that Mark Fraser was pushed over the balcony by Johnny Sanderson, or by somebody acting on his behalf. But we shall never be able to prove it, and I assume that Johnny Sanderson knows it. So that's the end of that. Everything has been tidied away. The financial community has tucked its dirty washing out of sight. A young man's death has been tucked away too. And it's business as usual, all round."

Jamie looked at the floor. "We're not very brilliant investigators, are we?"

Isabel smiled. "No," she said. "We're a couple of rather helpless amateurs. A bassoonist and a philosopher." She paused. "But there is something to be cheerful about, I suppose, in the midst of all this moral failure."

Jamie was curious. "And what would that be?"

Isabel rose to her feet. "I think we might just allow ourselves a glass of sherry on that one," she said. "It would be indecent to open the champagne." She moved over to the drinks cabinet and extracted two glasses.

"What precisely are we celebrating?" asked Jamie.

"Cat is no longer engaged," said Isabel. "For a very brief period she was in grave danger of marriage to Toby. But she came round this afternoon and we had a good cry on each other's shoulders. Toby is history, as you people so vividly put it."

Jamie knew that she was right, one should not celebrate the end of a relationship with champagne. But one could go out to dinner, which is what he proposed, and what she accepted.

CHAPTER TWENTY-SEVEN

Isabel did not like to leave things unfinished. She had engaged in the whole issue of Mark Fraser's fall on the basis that she had become involved, whether she liked it or not. This moral involvement was almost over, except for one thing. She decided now to see Neil, and tell him the outcome of her enquiries. He was the one who had effectively asked her to act, and she felt that she should explain to him how matters had turned out. The knowledge that there was no connection between Mark's apparent disquiet and the fall could help him, if he was feeling unhappy about his having done nothing himself.

But there was something more that drew her to seek out Neil. Ever since her first meeting with him, on that awkward evening when she had seen him darting across the hall, she had felt puzzled by him. The circumstances of their meeting, of course, had not been easy; she had disturbed him in bed with Hen, and that was embarrassing, but it was more than that. At that first meeting, he had been suspicious of her and his answers to her questions had been unforthcoming. Of course, she was not entitled to expect a warm welcome—he could easily, and understandably, have resented anybody coming to ask about Mark—but it went beyond that.

She decided to see him the following day. She tried to telephone him to arrange to go round to the flat, but there was no reply from the flat number and he was unavailable at his office. So she decided to risk an unannounced visit again.

As she walked up the stairs she reflected on what had happened in the interval between her last visit and this. Only a few weeks had passed, but in that time it seemed that she had been put through a comprehensive and thoroughly efficient emotional wringer. Now here she was, back exactly where she had started. She rang the bell, and as last time, Hen let her in. This time, her welcome was warmer and she was immediately offered a glass of wine, which she accepted.

"I've actually come to see Neil," she said. "I wanted to talk to him again. I hope he won't mind."

"I'm sure he won't," said Hen. "He's not back yet, but I don't think he'll be long."

Isabel found herself recalling the previous visit, when Hen had lied to her about Neil's absence and she had seen him dash naked across the hallway. She wanted to smile, but did not.

"I'm moving out," said Hen, conversationally. "Flitting. I've found a job in London and I'm going down there. Challenges. Opportunities. You know."

"Of course," said Isabel. "You must be very excited."

"I'll miss this place, though," said Hen. "And I'm sure I'll come back to Scotland. People always do."

"I did," said Isabel. "I was in Cambridge for some years, and America, and then I came back. Now I suppose I'm here for good."

"Well, give me a few years first," said Hen. "Then we'll see."

Isabel wondered about Neil. Would he stay, or was she going to take him with her? Somehow she thought that she would not. She asked.

"Neil's staying here," said Hen. "He has his job."

"And the flat? He'll keep it on?"

"I think so." Hen paused. "I think he's a bit upset about it, actually, but he'll get over things. Mark's death was very hard for him. Hard for all of us. But Neil has taken it very badly."

"They were close?"

Hen nodded. "Yes, they got on. Most of the time. I think I told you that before."

"Of course," said Isabel. "Of course you did."

Hen reached for the wine bottle which she had placed on the table and from which she now topped up her glass. "You know," she said, "I still find myself thinking about that evening. That evening when Mark fell. I can't help it. It gets me at odd times of the day. I think of him sitting there, in his last hour or so, his last hour ever. I think of him sitting there listening to the McCunn. I know that music. My mother used to play it at home. I think of him sitting there and listening."

"I'm so sorry," said Isabel. "I can imagine how hard it must be for you." The McCunn. *Land of the Mountain and the Flood.* Such a romantic piece. And then the thought occurred to her, and for a moment her heart stood still.

"You knew what they played that night?" she asked. Her voice was small, and Hen looked at her in surprise.

"Yes, I did. I forget what the rest was, but I noticed the McCunn."

"Noticed?"

"On the programme," said Hen, looking quizzically at Isabel. "I saw it on the programme. So what?"

"But where did you get the programme? Did somebody give it to you?"

Again Hen looked at Isabel as if she was asking pointless questions. "I think I found it here, in the flat. In fact, I could probably lay my hands on it right now. Do you want to see it?"

Isabel nodded, and Hen rose to her feet and riffled through a pile of papers on a shelf. "Here we are. That's the programme. Look, there's the McCunn and the other stuff is listed here."

Isabel took the programme. Her hands were shaking.

"Whose programme is it?" she asked.

"I don't know," said Hen. "Neil's maybe. Everything in the flat is either his or mine or . . . Mark's."

"It must be Neil's," said Isabel quietly. "Mark didn't come back from the concert, did he?"

"I don't see why the programme is so important," said Hen. She gave the impression now of being slightly irritated, and Isabel took the opportunity to excuse herself.

"I'll go downstairs and wait for Neil," she said. "I don't want to hold you up."

"I was going to have a bath," said Hen.

"Well, you go ahead and do that," said Isabel quickly. "Does he walk back from work?"

"Yes," said Hen, getting to her feet. "He comes up from Toll-cross. Over the golf links there."

"I'll meet him," said Isabel. "It's a gorgeous evening and I'd like the walk."

*　*　*

SHE WENT OUTSIDE, trying to keep calm, trying to control her breathing. Soapy Soutar, the boy downstairs, was dragging his reluctant dog to a patch of grass at the edge of the road. She walked past him, stopping to say something.

"That's a nice dog."

Soapy Soutar looked up at her. "He disnae like me. And he eats his heid off."

"Dogs are always hungry," said Isabel. "That's what they're like."

"Aye, well this one has a hollow stomach, my mum says. Eats and disnae want to go for walks."

"I'm sure he likes you, though."

"No, he disnae."

The conversation came to a natural end, and she looked down over the links. There were two people making their separate ways up the diagonal path, and one of them, a tall figure in a lightweight khaki raincoat, looked as if he might be Neil. She began to walk forward.

It was Neil. For a moment or two it seemed as if he did not recognise her, but then he smiled and greeted her politely.

"I came to see you," she said. "Hen said that you would be on your way home, so I thought I'd meet you out here. It's such a wonderful evening."

"Yes, it's grand, isn't it?" He looked at her, waiting for her to say something else. He was uneasy, she thought, but then he would be.

She took a deep breath. "Why did you come to me?" she asked. "Why did you come to talk about Mark's worries?"

He answered quickly, almost before she had finished her question. "Because I had not told you the whole truth."

"And you still haven't."

He stared at her, and she saw his knuckle tighten about the

handle of his briefcase. "You still haven't told me that you were there. You were there in the Usher Hall, weren't you?"

She held his gaze, watching the passage of emotions. There was anger to begin with, but that soon passed, and was replaced by fear.

"I know you were there," she said. "And now I have proof of it." This was only true to an extent, but she felt that it would be enough, at least for the purpose of this meeting.

He opened his mouth to speak. "I—"

"And did you have anything to do with his death, Neil? Did you? Were there just the two of you left up there after everybody else had gone downstairs? That's true, isn't it?"

He could no longer hold her gaze. "I was there. I was."

"I see," said Isabel. "And what happened?"

"We had an argument," he said. " I started it. I was jealous of him and Hen, you see. I couldn't take it. We had an argument and I gave him a shove, sideways, to make my point. I had no intention of it being anything more than that. Just a shove, hardly anything. That's all I did. But he overbalanced."

"Are you telling me the truth now, Neil?" Isabel studied his eyes as he looked up to reply, and she had her answer. But then there was the question of why he was jealous of Mark and Hen. But did that matter? She thought not; because love and jealousy may have many different wellsprings, but are as urgent and as strong whatever their source.

"I am telling the truth," he said slowly. "But I couldn't tell anybody that, could I? They would have accused me of pushing him over the edge and I would have had no witnesses to say that it was anything but that. If I had, I would have been prosecuted. It's culpable homicide, you know, if you assault somebody and they die, even if you had no intention of killing them and it's only a shove. But it was an accident; it really was. I had no intention, none at all . . ." He paused. "And I was too scared to tell anybody about it. I was just scared. I imagined what it would be like if nobody believed me."

A man walked by, stepping onto the grass to avoid them, wondering (Isabel imagined) what they were doing, standing in earnest conversation under the evening sky. Settling a life, she thought; laying the dead to rest; allowing time and self-forgiveness to start.

"I believe you," said Isabel.

Philosophers in their studies, Isabel reflected, grapple with problems of this sort. Forgiveness is a popular subject for them, as is punishment. We need to punish, not because it makes us feel any better—ultimately it does not—but because it establishes the moral balance: it makes a declaration about wrongdoing; it maintains our sense of a just world. But in a just world one punishes only those who mean wrong, who act from an ill will. This young man, whom she now understood, had never meant ill. He had never intended to harm Mark—anything but—and there was no reason, no conceivable justification, for holding him responsible for the awful consequences of what was no more than a gesture of irritation. If the criminal law of Scotland stipulated differently, then the law of Scotland was simply morally indefensible, and that was all there was to it.

Neil was confused, Isabel thought. Ultimately it was all about sex, and not knowing what he wanted, and being immature. If he were punished now, for something that he had never meant to happen, what point would be served by that? One more life would be marred, and the world, in this case, would not be a more just place for it.

"Yes, I believe you," said Isabel. She paused. The decision was really quite simple, and she did not need to be a moral philosopher to take it. "And that's the end of the matter. It was an accident. You're sorry about it. We can leave it at that."

She looked at him, and saw that he was in tears. So she reached out and took his hand, which she held until they were ready to walk back up the path.

ABOUT THE AUTHOR

Alexander McCall Smith is the author of the international phenomenon The No. 1 Ladies' Detective Agency series. This novel is the first of a new series, The Sunday Philosophy Club. He spent his childhood in Zimbabwe and has worked in Botswana and Swaziland. He lives in Scotland, where he is a professor of medical law at Edinburgh University.